'I need a wife.'

'Why me? With all my debts, I can only be an encumbrance to you.'

'Because you are the only one who interests me. The only one I want—debts and all,' Christopher smiled. 'I want to make you smile, to laugh, and I want you to savour all I have to offer.'

Clarissa looked at him, at the serious expression in his eyes, and thought how unfortunate it was that she did not love him.

Dear Reader

Welcome back to both Sheila Bishop and Helen Dickson! FAIR GAME is an interesting exploration of how lives can be seriously ruffled, and obvious to all, in a small seaside community, while MASTER OF TAMASEE takes us from London to Charleston in America, where we see the early beginnings of the move against the slave trade which led later to the American Civil War. The love stories twined into these themes should delight you. Enjoy!

The Editor

Helen Dickson was born and still lives in South Yorkshire with her husband and two sons on a busy arable farm where she combines writing with keeping a chaotic farmhouse. An incurable romantic, she writes for pleasure, owing much of her inspiration to the beauty of the countryside. She enjoys reading and music; history has always captivated her, and she likes travel and visiting ancient buildings.

Recent title by the same author:

HONOUR BOUND

MASTER OF TAMASEE

Helen Dickson

*First published in Great Britain 1992
by Mills & Boon Limited*

© Helen Dickson 1992

*Australian copyright 1992
Philippine copyright 1992
This edition 1992*

ISBN 0 263 77889 4

*Masquerade is a trademark published by
Mills & Boon Limited, Eton House,
18–24 Paradise Road, Richmond, Surrey, TW9 1SR.*

*Set in 10 on 11 pt Linotron Times
04-9210-78740*

*Typeset in Great Britain by Centracet, Cambridge
Made and printed in Great Britain*

CHAPTER ONE

THE Milton carriage was only one of a glittering array that rattled and streamed through the Portland stone gateway of Holland House, and Clarissa, seated beside Betsy, her companion, and across from her father, Harry Milton, was trying hard not to think about the long night ahead. How she hated these frequent dinner parties which they were invited to attend while in London. She sighed, wishing she were back at Ashton Park in Kent with her brother, Richard.

Amid the shouting of coachmen and the jingle of harness the carriage came to a halt, waiting for the ones in front to discharge their occupants at the foot of the steps of Holland House. Slowly their carriage edged its way along, and Clarissa leaned her head against the soft upholstery, thinking with longing of the quiet solitude and leafy green meadows of home. She closed her eyes and, as so often of late, the image of Edward's handsome, laughing face flashed before her. They would have been married now had he not been killed, along with her brother, Simon, at the battle of Albuera in Spain with Wellington's army in May, seven months earlier.

She would never forget the day when the tragic news had come to them at Ashton Park and all the pain that had come with it. The only pain she had ever experienced in her twenty-one years had been when her mother had died two years ago after a long illness. Then, that had been terrible, but it had not been like the pain and desolation she had felt over the deaths of her betrothed and older brother. Never had she believed she could feel such pain, such anguish that went deep—deeper than anything she had ever known. She had continued to carry on but, determined never again to feel for any man the way she had for Edward, that no man could ever take his place, she had hardened her heart, built an emotional wall around herself, resolved that no man would ever breach it.

Followed by Betsy, she stepped out of the carriage and, escorted by her father, climbed the steps to the splendour and opulence of Holland House, ablaze with lights shining from every window. From somewhere inside the musicians began to play, their music filling the rooms, dipping and rising, sweet and sublime, which at any other time she would have found soothing. But not tonight. The strains of the violins matched her nerves, which were as taut as their strings. As she entered the glittering world of fashionable London society where chandeliers blazed and baskets full of flowers scented the air with a lovely delicious fragrance, she thought, wistfully, how different it would be if Edward were here to share it with her.

They were greeted by Lady Holland, brimming over with her usual exuberance. She was one of the most popular hostesses at this time—in fact, probably one of the most favoured in London society—giving the most elaborate and brilliant parties, surpassed only by those given by the Prince Regent at Carlton House. Invitations were only sent out to those with a particular social standing.

Clarissa liked Lady Holland. She had been a good friend of her father's for many years and was a clever, astute woman with an amazing wit. If somewhat domineering and bossy, she was no fool, and her guests could always be assured of some high-level, interesting conversation covering a wide range of topics at her crowded dinner table. Over the years Holland House had become the social centre of many Whig politicians and literary men.

'Why, Clarissa,' said Lady Holland, taking her gloved hand in her own and squeezing it with genuine affection. 'How lovely you look. I'm so glad you were able to come,' and to her father, poking his portly frame good-humouredly with her folded fan, 'You must be proud of your daughter, Harry. Clarissa does you credit. Now—off you go, my dear, while I talk to your father,' she said, giving Clarissa a knowing smile. 'Letty Davenport was looking for you earlier. She's just dying to tell you about her visit to Brighton. We'll have a chat later on.'

Clarissa smiled gratefully, knowing Lady Holland was well aware of her father's over-indulgence where both alcohol and gambling were concerned and would be sure to keep a watchful eye on him while he was under her roof. She turned and went in search of Letty, moving through richly furnished and carpeted rooms, swarming with nobility and gentry alike. Anyone who could lay claim to wealth and position was here. This was supposed to be an even grander affair than usual, given in honour of the Prince Regent, but Clarissa didn't particularly care. All she was concerned about was getting through it and making sure her father didn't drink too much or gamble away any more of his wealth at Faro or Whist.

Betsy paused to talk to an acquaintance and Clarissa moved on alone, searching for Letty. As she made her way down the long gallery she did not notice the man standing apart from the rest, leaning casually against an over-large statue with a calm but bored expression on his darkly handsome face. But then he saw Clarissa, and for the first time since arriving in London from America two days ago he became alert, amazed at having found so soon what he had crossed the Atlantic for.

He watched her move with a serene grace along the gallery, her figure swaying slightly as she walked, and he stared, suddenly transfixed. She was quite tall and breathtakingly beautiful in a slim, high-waisted dress of shimmering lavender silk, beneath which he could discern all her alluring curves and imagine all the hidden delights of her slender body.

The effect was stunning. She aroused envy in almost every woman present and admiration in the eyes of the men, although none could have said whether it was given to the proud beauty of her face, with her thick pale gold hair coiled expertly about her head, or to the exquisite perfection of her body—or to the lustre of the Milton pearls resting on the creamy swell of her breasts.

Christopher watched her smile and offer words of greeting to people she passed, but her smile was as if pinned to her face and her actions mechanical—a façade. She appeared remote and detached, totally uninterested in everything that was going on around her, which aroused all his curiosity.

Sensing his gaze, Clarissa paused and turned, seeing the stranger immediately and fixing him with a cool, indifferent stare. He was dressed in black with a white cravat and silk stockings. There was no fuss to his dress and yet there was no denying that he had exquisite style. Only once had she seen a man so soberly dressed and that was George Brummell, the good friend of the Prince Regent and also the dictator of men's fashion.

This man possessed a commanding presence and was tall, taller than any man present, and built with all the virility of an ancient Greek athlete, with long limbs and powerful, broad shoulders. His features were dark and handsome, his hair thick and black, taken back from a pronounced peak. His presence formed a stark contrast to all the other gentlemen present who seemed to fade into insignificance beside him. There was an air of complete assurance about him and he seemed curiously out of place among all this gentility, the fine dandies and frills and flounces of Lady Holland's party. He seemed to belong to another world, one where the wind and sun had turned his skin the colour of bronze, one that was wild and exciting and far removed from Holland House.

There was a cool recklessness about his swarthy face, and his stare was bold—as bold as that of someone appraising a horse, she thought indignantly, dragging her eyes from his and turning away immediately, feeling insulted by his look, considering it the height of bad manners for a gentleman—if he could be called that—to stare quite so openly at a lady, and in public too. But for the first time since Edward's death there was a delicate flush mantling her cheeks. It had been a long time since a man had aroused any kind of emotion in her.

Christopher whistled softly under his breath as she turned away. My God, he thought, what a glorious creature she is, and before she had disappeared at the end of the hundred-foot-long gallery he had already made up his mind to make her acquaintance before the night was over.

Clarissa soon found Letty, her real name being Letitia Davenport. They had become firm friends some years ago when they had both attended Lady Margaret's Academy for Young Ladies here in London. Letty had been the one good thing about coming up to London. She was small with an abundance of glossy auburn hair, which her hairdresser had arranged into fashionable Grecian curls. Lively green eyes danced in her small, elfin face with a smattering

of pale gold freckles over her nose. She was generous
and warm-hearted and had been a great comfort when
Edward was killed, but she was also vivacious and a
terrible flirt, constantly surrounded by a lively circle of
friends—especially masculine friends, whom she not
only encouraged but also seemed to thrive on their
attention. Clarissa was glad of her company tonight
and that they were placed near each other at dinner
along with Betsy.

Betsy was a distant cousin of Clarissa's who, after
the death of her parents, had found herself quite
destitute. On hearing of her sad plight and wanting to
help, Clarissa's mother had suggested that she come
and live with them to be Clarissa's companion. Suitably
grateful, Betsy had readily accepted. She was eight
years older than Clarissa and had been with her for five
years now, having become more like an older sister
than a companion.

While they were waiting for the first course Clarissa
glanced up the table, loaded with long-stemmed crystal
glasses and gold and silver plate and wine. Her father
was seated next to the opulent Lady Melbourne, the
two already engaged in lively conversation. Clarissa's
heart sank despairingly, for his wig was already askew
and his over-bloated face flushed crimson from drinking too much wine. She tore her eyes away from them,
praying he wouldn't drink much more, but she knew
this was futile. He would be well and truly drunk when
they left. She became desperately anxious for the night
to end.

Looking in the opposite direction, she noticed the
increasingly popular young poet Lord Byron, his face
pale and surrounded by a riot of chestnut curls, his
whole attitude tonight being one of disdain. She let her
eyes wander to the lady seated beside him, recognising
her immediately as being the outrageous Lady Caroline

Lamb, whose scandalous behaviour and indiscreet affairs had made her the most notorious, talked-about woman in London, to which she didn't object in the slightest—in fact, she adored being the centre of attention, positively thriving on it.

But then Clarissa froze, for sitting right next to her was the stranger she had seen earlier in the gallery, and again he was looking directly at her, the look in his dark eyes unnerving. A crooked smile curved his lips and she noticed his long and slender hands toying with his napkin on the table.

Immediately she dropped her gaze and tried not to look in his direction again. All through the first course of turtle soup she fought to ignore him, uncomfortably conscious of his eyes on her constantly, burning into her flesh, but during the second course of saddle of mutton her curiosity got the better of her and she spoke quietly to Letty.

'Who's that man, Letty? The one at the end of the table—seated next to Lady Caroline Lamb?'

Letty glanced down the table, knowing immediately who she meant. 'Oh—you mean the one who keeps looking at you.' she said quite candidly.

Clarissa nearly choked on a piece of meat at the directness of her reply.

Letty smiled mischievously, her green eyes dancing merrily. 'Come on, love. He hasn't taken his eyes off you all night. And you mean to say you don't know who he is? Why, you must be the only person here who doesn't. That's Christopher Cordell—Lord Buckley's nephew, recently come over from America. He's devil-ishly attractive, isn't he? And he owns one of those huge plantations in South Carolina and grows cotton.' She leaned closer to Clarissa, whispering confidentially, 'Rumour has it that he's here to look for a wife,' and, looking down the table, she shamelessly flashed him a dazzling smile. 'Isn't he wonderfully virile—despite that polite exterior? I wouldn't mind if he chose me, I can tell you,' she sighed dreamily. 'He's as handsome as Narcissus and, I've heard, as rich as King Midas.'

'And we all know what happened to them,' quipped Clarissa drily. 'Narcissus was so vain that on gazing into a pool he fell hopelessly in love with his own reflection and, being unable to endure to possess and yet not possess himself, he plunged a dagger into his heart. And as for King Midas, his end was little better. After nearly starving to death because everything he touched turned to gold—including his food—and then being given ass's ears, unable to live with the disgrace, he died miserably. No, Letty. I wouldn't liken this Christopher Cordell to either of them.'

'Perhaps not—but you can't blame me for wondering what could happen if he were looking at me instead of you. Oh, Clarissa—don't you ever dream that one day——?'

'No,' cut in Clarissa crossly, her expression hard, suspecting that Letty was about to embark on one of her daydreams about love and romance. 'I don't dream any more, Letty. I stopped dreaming of romance when Edward died. He took my heart with him to the grave and there it will remain.'

Letty's eyes filled with remorse and she silently cursed herself for her careless, thoughtless words—although she had never shared Clarissa's admiration for Edward Montgomery, thinking it wise to keep her opinion of him to herself. Reaching out, she squeezed Clarissa's hand. 'I'm sorry, love—truly. I didn't mean to hurt you. It was unforgivable of me.'

Clarissa sighed and smiled weakly, placing her free hand over Letty's. 'It's all right, Letty. It's not your fault that I'm so edgy tonight, but—well—it's not just thinking of Edward that hurts—it's Father.' She glanced in his direction just in time to see him pour another glass of wine down his throat.

When dinner ended it was with relief that Clarissa saw nothing more of the American, and at two o'clock in the morning she went in search of her father, knowing where he would be and making straight for the gaming-room. She passed a long mirror and caught her reflection, pausing for just a moment to gaze at the shimmering apparition she presented in her lavender dress, enhanced by the candle-light. She looked lovely, she knew, but her beauty gave her no joy. What was the use of it when Edward was not here to see it? The eyes staring out of the glass were the cold blue eyes of a stranger and bore no resemblance to how they had looked all those months ago when they had sparkled and been filled with love, when her tender heart had beat with all the passions of being in love and which held nothing now but emptiness.

She sighed and turned away, moving towards the gaming-room, wondering what was to become of them all because of her father's drinking and gambling, and she was filled with a terrible deep sadness when she remembered how different things had once been. But she was also filled with a new kind of fear that was gnawing away at her inside, fear of the unknown if they were to suddenly find themselves penniless and without a roof over their heads.

While ever there was hope she had refused to see the truth staring her in the face, but now it was no longer possible for her to deny what was happening. In his grief over the death of his eldest son her father had sought solace in drink. He was seldom sober any more, and when he wasn't drinking he was silent and morose. Heaven knew, he had always gambled, but now he did it to excess, especially since coming up to London. It

was as if he didn't care any more, as if he wanted rid
of Ashton Park and all its memories.

On many occasions he wouldn't come home from
Brook's or White's—just two of the gentlemen's clubs
he frequented, where women were forbidden—until
daybreak. Somehow he would manage to make it up to
his room, sodden with drink and often thousands of
pounds poorer, where his valet would put him to bed.
Clarissa had seen men lose up to twenty thousand
pounds in one night at the tables, and often the shake
of a dice would decide the fate of some of England's
most noble country estates.

She wanted to rage at him when the debts began to
mount and when she saw how unkempt he was becoming, with his bloodshot eyes staring out from beneath
heavy lids, but nothing she said could penetrate his
fuddled mind. He was bringing shame on them all but
he couldn't see it, and he could not afford to lose any
more money. Already most of the Milton jewels were
gone and, fingering the pearls at her throat, she wondered how long it would be before they too met the
same fate.

Clarissa refused to sit back and wait for the final
insult—for the time when Ashton Park had gone too—
and so she squared her shoulders, determined that they
would not go under, refusing to let him bring ruin and
disgrace upon the family because of his irresponsibility.
Ashton Park was Richard's now and it was only right
that he should inherit. Besides, he loved the old family
home in a way that Simon never had. All his life
Richard had lived in the shadow of his older brother,
always aware that his father did not possess for him
that same fierce pride he did for Simon. He had never
made any secret of his preference for his eldest son,
who was so much like himself, his life dominated by
the pleasure principle, preferring to spend his time in

London, where he could indulge his expensive passion of socialising and gambling, whereas Richard was serious and quiet, like Clarissa and their mother, and was content to remain at Ashton Park.

Whatever sacrifice Clarissa had to make, and if it killed her, she would see to it that Richard got what was his by right, but she was also doing it for herself. The world that she had known and loved had fallen apart. Everything she had cherished had gone except for Ashton Park. She would not lose that too.

She entered the gaming-room, the air thick with tobacco smoke. Glancing quickly about the room, she saw her father seated at one of the card tables, the all too familiar glass of liquor at hand, ready to be refilled by a hovering waiter.

Why does he have to drink so much? she thought angrily. If he has to gamble then why can't he do it with a clear head? At least then he might stand a better chance of winning some of his money back. But she was relieved to see that he was not as drunk as he usually was on these occasions, and with any luck she would get him home without his making too much of a fool of himself.

His fellow players were sprawled around the green baize table, temporarily out of the game, watching with intensity the one that was taking place between her father and his partner. Somehow it came as no surprise to her that that partner should be Christopher Cordell, the American, and she was not in the least surprised either to see that, unlike her father, he had no drink beside him. His presence contrasted sharply with the pink-faced, over-dressed fops and aristocratic land-owners around the table.

As Clarissa came to stand behind Lord Milton she caught all of Christopher's attention. She appeared like a beautiful pale vision, and his breath caught in his throat. Close to she was even more lovely, her skin smooth and flawless with delectable soft lips. Her eyes were as bright as jewels. But there was no inner warmth in them—they were charged with mystery, and this aroused his curiosity about her even further. Her beauty was ice-cold and it seemed that nothing could penetrate that frozen exterior. It was as if she were made of stone. What could have happened to make her like this? But despite her air of aloofness he felt a defencelessness about her, a fragility that disturbed him, and he believed that behind that cold façade there beat the heart of a warm and passionate woman.

Clarissa moved to stand by her father's chair at the same time as the game ended, and she sensed, by the slump of his shoulders and the beads of perspiration on his brow, and also by the subdued murmur of his fellow players and the shake of their heads, that he had lost heavily. Everyone but the American and her father moved away from the table, and before he had the chance to become immersed in another game she placed a hand gently but firmly on his shoulder and spoke softly.

'Come, Father. It's late. I think it's time we left.'

Only then did he become aware of her presence and he scowled up at her, his red eyes full of displeasure and annoyance by her presence here in the gaming-room. Did her meddling know no bounds? Since coming to London she had given him no peace. Should've stayed behind at Ashton Park. Lord knew, he was fond of the girl, but it was high time she was married. Pity about young Montgomery. If he hadn't been killed in Spain they'd be married by now and she'd be off his hands and living in Bedfordshire.

'Go?' he growled, slurring his words. 'I can't leave yet, and the hour is not late. Besides—I must try to win back some of my money.' Time held no meaning when he was absorbed in a game of cards.

'Perhaps tomorrow,' persisted Clarissa, braving his wrath.

'No. And I will not be dictated to by you, Clarissa. Now run along if you must. I'll be home later.'

Obstinately Clarissa stood her ground, and it was the anger he saw spark in her eyes that prompted the American to rise to his feet, realising for the first time that this delightful creature must be the daughter of Harry Milton, the man who had just lost one thousand guineas to him. He cursed himself for allowing himself to be drawn into a game with this man. Had he known from the outset who she was he would have refused, for one thing was certain—the fact that he had taken money off her father would not endear him to her in the least. However, at last he had the opportunity of making her acquaintance and he was determined to make the most of it. When he spoke his words were directed at Lord Milton, but his eyes were fixed firmly on Clarissa.

'Will you not introduce me to your daughter, Lord Milton?'

Harry looked at him, a trifle nonplussed. 'Humph—— Oh—of course—forgive me. This is my daughter, Clarissa. Clarissa—Mr Christopher Cordell, recently come from America. Lord Buckley's nephew.'

Christopher bowed his head slightly but without taking his eyes from hers. 'Your servant, Miss Milton.'

His voice was deep and incredibly seductive, as smooth as silk, and he exuded a potent masculine allure that was almost impossible to ignore, and, however much Clarissa told herself she was immune to it and despite all her efforts, she could not prevent the colour from tinting her cheeks.

Christopher noticed and one corner of his mouth lifted in a little smile, which Clarissa found infuriating.

'I think your daughter is right, Lord Milton. The hour is late and I too must be leaving.'

'Nonsense. There are a good few hours left yet.'

'Not for me, I'm afraid.'

Glancing around the emptying room, Harry reluctantly, and with some difficulty, rose from the table. 'Oh, very well,' he said grumpily, 'but tomorrow night you'll find me at Brook's. Come along, won't you? Give me the opportunity to win back the thousand guineas you've just taken from me.'

Christopher smiled and did not reply immediately. Instead he looked again at Clarissa, who had blanched at the mention of the enormous sum, and anger was sparking from her eyes. He was not in the least discouraged.

'We shall see. Now if you will permit me I will escort you to your carriage.'

Good manners obliged Clarissa to allow him to lead them out of the room but, walking beside him, she struggled with a helpless rage welling up inside her. Rage against him and his cool self-assurance. He had just taken one thousand guineas from her father and yet he behaved as if it were a mere twopence. Before they reached the doorway, where Lady Holland was bidding her guests goodnight and where Betsy was waiting for her, she had already placed him in the category along with all the others to whom her father had lost his money—architects who were responsible for all her wretchedness.

'Ah, Harry,' said Lady Holland, her face flushed with pleasure. 'I see you're leaving and that you've met our American.'

'Yes. Just taken a thousand guineas off me, the young rascal,' and he turned to Christopher before

going down the steps. 'Tomorrow night at Brook's,
young man. Don't forget. Oh,' he said as an after-
thought as he was about to turn away, 'and give my
regards to your uncle when you see him, will you?'

'Of course. Goodnight, sir.'

Clarissa would have liked to follow him as he went
down the steps accompanied by Betsy, but the tall
figure of Christopher Cordell barred her way. She
turned to Lady Holland. 'Goodnight, Lady Holland,
and thank you for a lovely evening.'

'Lovely?' she said not unkindly, reaching out and
touching her arm in an affectionate gesture. 'I think
not, Clarissa. At least not for you. I know just how
painful these parties are for you—having to watch
Harry throw more of his money away while all the time
your heart is pining to be back at Ashton Park. Harry
has a hopeless passion for gambling,' she said to
Christopher, 'and if Clarissa weren't here to keep an
eye on him then he'd soon have nothing left. But—
anyway,' she said, glancing sharply from one to the
other, 'I'm glad you two have met. Might put a sparkle
back into her eyes, Christopher. Clarissa has too many
worries for one so young. It's not good for her. By the
way,' she said, eyeing him quizzically, seeming reluctant to let either of them go, 'what are you doing here
in London? Aren't we supposed to be at war with
America?'

'No—not yet, and let us hope it doesn't come to
that. I am here because I have business to attend to.'

'Cotton business, I don't doubt.'

'But of course. What else?'

Lady Holland's eyes twinkled mischievously. 'What
else, indeed?' she chuckled meaningfully. 'And you're
still not wed?'

He laughed. 'No—I have not put my mind to the
matter yet. But I shall.'

'Yes—you should—and soon. If you run true to form, with your looks, you shouldn't have any difficulty finding a wife. If my memory serves me correctly, women never used to be a problem. Rumour has it that this is the reason why you're here—to look for one.'

'No. That is only one of the reasons.'

Lady Holland gave an exaggerated sigh and looked at Clarissa. 'If only I were younger, Clarissa, and not already married to Henry—but you,' she said, smiling, a mischievous twinkle dancing in her shrewd eyes, 'now you would make someone like Christopher an excellent wife.'

'But perhaps Miss Milton does not wish to marry anyone,' said Christopher, his smile challenging and his brown eyes darkening so they were almost black, resting on Clarissa's tight face.

Clarissa had listened to the brief interchange between them and was neither shocked nor surprised. She was not at all disconcerted by Lady Holland's words, whose laughter made light of them. But Clarissa was no fool and knew what lay behind them, that Lady Holland thought it high time she stopped thinking of Edward and what might have been and began looking to the future. Perhaps she was right. Again she looked directly at the American, at the merry gleam dancing in his brown eyes, one of his winged brows arched as he waited expectantly for her reply. She looked at him with new interest and found herself remembering Letty's words and her reference to King Midas, and wondered if he really was that rich. She told herself to stop it, not to think like this, but she couldn't help it and the reply was already on her lips before she realised what she was saying.

'Sir,' she said coolly, 'I would marry the devil himself if he would settle the debts on Ashton Park.' She saw the startled look that appeared on his face, quickly followed by a thin smile curving his lips, and she caught a glimpse of very white teeth. 'Now, if you will excuse me, I will bid you goodnight,' and without further ado she turned, following her father down the steps to the waiting carriage.

'Well, now,' said Lady Holland, a smile of approval for the way Clarissa had responded to their teasing curving her lips. 'There's a challenge if ever there was. A challenge not to be ignored, I'd say.'

Watching the Milton carriage drive away, Christopher nodded thoughtfully. Her reply had been brief but to the point, and it had certainly given him food for thought. It was as if she had thrown down a gauntlet and he was forced to pick it up.

'You're right, Lady Holland. I have no intention of ignoring it. Ashton Park, I take it, is her family seat?'

'That's correct. In the heart of Kent—although if Harry doesn't watch himself I'm afraid it will have to be sold to cover his debts.'

CHAPTER TWO

IT WAS on the following day that Christopher joined his uncle in the gloomy comfort of his club in St James's Street. They sat surrounded by heavily carved mahogany furniture with dark red upholstery. The atmosphere was heavy, the aroma of tobacco lingering in the air. They were seated in his favourite corner, where he always sat to savour his port and read his newspaper and indulge in conversation with his companions.

Christopher had come to know and be extremely fond of his uncle, his mother's brother, when he had come to London to study law at the Inns of Court several years ago. His hair was fine and white and he was tall and lean, holding himself extremely erect for all his sixty years. His grey eyes were shrewd and steady and had lost none of their youthful sparkle. He gave the impression of superiority with his quick, penetrating mind.

They had discussed at length the growing discord between the United States and Britain, and Christopher was only here now because, for the first time in almost four years, peace, of a sort, had been restored between the two countries, albeit an uneasy one.

Ever since England and France had been at war both countries had been dependent upon the United States and were able to manipulate her trade and use it as a weapon against the other. England had ordered that no neutral ship could trade with France or her allies, and France had issued orders that no neutral ship could

trade with England. American ships had tried to break
the blockade and, as a result, hundreds were captured.
Almost four years ago the then President of the United
States, Thomas Jefferson, in his economic thinking,
instead of taking sides with one or the other, had
chosen to withdraw. After obtaining an embargo from
Congress, prohibiting the exportation of any goods
whatever from the United States, for a time virtually
cutting off all American trade with Europe, he had
hoped to starve England into a change of policy. For
fifty years Britain had depended upon America to feed
and clothe her people, but now, with the European
continent closed to her because of the Emperor
Napoleon's blockade, the embargo had cut off the
supply at the source, and through privation America
had hoped to bring her to heel. But the embargo had
also struck a deadly blow at America's national industry, prohibiting the departure of any vessel from
American ports to any foreign port, especially those
dependent on the British market.

During the embargo Christopher had been forced to
store his cotton in warehouses and sold as much as he
could to merchants in the north, in New England, for
whatever they would pay, and, like many more
southern planters whose whole existence depended
upon the sea as a safe highway for exporting their raw
cotton to the hungry mills of England, he had uttered
a sigh of relief when it was lifted; taking advantage of
this, he had come to England both on business and to
see his uncle concerning the death of his mother, for
while tempers were still running high among the inhabi-
tants of America against Britain there was no telling
how long it would last.

But business was not his only reason for coming to
England; there was another, more pressing reason, and
Lady Holland had been correct when she had said it

was to look for a wife—although his masculine pride had prevented him from admitting just how important it was that he find one—and soon, for since the death of his mother six months ago Tamasee desperately needed a mistress and he a wife. Leaving the plantation in the capable hands of his main overseer, Ralph Benton, he had booked a passage on a ship bound for England.

A silence had fallen between Christopher and his uncle. Lord Buckley observed his nephew fondly, remembering those few short years during which he had come to know him, when, as a young man, Christopher, full of enthusiasm for all life had to offer, had left his beloved America to take up his studies in London, secure in the knowledge that Tamasee was being well taken care of by his father and older brother, Andrew. Having no immediate family of his own, never having married, Lord Buckley had been delighted when Christopher had come to stay with him. His refreshing, exhilarating company had knocked years off his age, reminding him so very much of his own youth, when he too had studied at the Inns of Court.

But then Christopher had been devastated when, shortly after he had passed the bar, his mother had written, telling him of the deaths of both his father and brother in a tragic river-boat accident, and the enormous task of running Tamasee had suddenly been thrust upon him. Lord Buckley had no doubt that if this had not happened, being confident and ambitious for his country, Christopher would have gone far in the politics of America.

Looking at him now, after ten years, he realised just how much of a man he had become, no more the young student all set to put the world and its problems to rights. His build and his features were those of his father, but there was that about his bearing which

reminded him so very much of his dear, departed
sister, and he wondered, because of the tragic circumstances that had forced him to abandon his dreams of
a political future, when he had found out that life was
no simple thing, how often he had been obliged to look
into himself and realise the bitterness of his situation.

'I have a distinct feeling that there are other things
you wish to discuss that have nothing to do with the
price of cotton, Christopher.'

Christopher sighed and relaxed into his chair, his
long booted legs stretched out in front of him. 'Yes,
there is something else I would like to ask you. What
can you tell me about Lord Milton's daughter?'

Surprise registered in his uncle's eyes. 'Clarissa?'

He nodded. 'Yes.'

'You've met her, I take it?'

'Yes, last night at Lady Holland's dinner party.'

'Then what do you wish to know?'

'What she's really like.'

'You've seen her. Surely that should speak for itself.'

'I know, and she's a beauty—there's no denying.
But—I want to know what she's like beneath that.'

Lord Buckley smiled slowly. 'This is not just a
passing interest?'

'No. She impressed me a great deal and I wish to
know more about her.'

'Well, I will tell you all I can, and will begin by
telling you that she is not like her father—whom I have
known personally for a good many years—or her
brother, Simon—the one who was killed in Spain. No,
she is more like her mother and young Richard. Simon,
like his father, was a notorious lover of pleasure. Hated
being at Ashton Park—that's their family home in
Kent. Beautiful place it is, but he preferred to live here
in London. He existed for the army, too. His father
didn't want him to go to Spain, being the oldest son

and all that, but he was set on it. Unlike them, Clarissa deplores London and likes nothing better than to bury herself in the country with her horses and dogs. She is quite extraordinary, enduringly devoted to those she cares about. A highly intelligent young lady with a certain wilfulness about her—a certain headstrong quality. She was to have married Lord Montgomery's son, Edward. Known each other for years, and devoted to him she was—although I never cared much for him myself. Too much of a gad about town for my liking, like her brother, Simon. He was reported killed at Albuera, along with Simon. It's hit her hard. Some say she'll never get over it.'

So that was it, thought Christopher, understanding at last the reason why Clarissa looked so distant, a mournful solemnity in her lovely eyes. She was suffering from a broken heart. But he had no intention of being deterred by this and believed that time would heal her wounds. She had built up a resistance around her inner core, and he had every intention of breaking it down. However long it took, he believed it would be worth it.

'Nevertheless, Uncle, young Montgomery must have been someone quite exceptional to have inspired such love. One only has to look at her to see her suffering. But what did you mean when you said he was reported killed?'

'His body was never found. So many were killed at Albuera—a blood-bath it was, and eye-witnesses have reported seeing him shot down. His father received a letter from his commanding officer, informing him that Edward had fallen on the field of battle—seen it himself. Unfortunately it could not be ascertained whether or not his body had been buried along with many others who had fallen, nor was his name on the list of prisoners.'

'I see,' said Christopher calmly. 'Then is there any possibility that he might not be dead—that he might have been picked up by peasants or the partisans?'

Lord Buckley nodded. 'There is that possibility, but I doubt it. After Albuera, reports were confused, but I believe something would have been heard before now.'

'Then tell me—why does Clarissa come to London if she dislikes it so much?'

'Because if she didn't keep an eye on Harry and his gambling they'd have nothing left and, if rumour is correct, she has cause to be worried. He loses staggering amounts at the tables nightly. They're heavily in debt. Since the death of her mother two years ago Clarissa has had nothing but heartache, and to add to her worries she now has poverty staring her in the face. But—if my judgement of her is correct—she will fight tooth and nail to keep Ashton Park because if that goes it will break her heart. No—I feel nothing but admiration for the way she has coped with the arduous task of Harry and his gambling. I am sure she'll come through in the end. She is a very resilient young lady.' He paused and studied Christopher's face. 'There is a great deal more to this than just a casual interest in Clarissa Milton, isn't there, Christopher?'

'Yes,' he said, trying to sound casual, but Lord Buckley could tell that she had caught more than his eye.

'And I am correct when I say that you are here to look for a wife?'

'It is one of the reasons. I must admit that since Mother died I do need someone to manage the house and servants. I have my work cut out running the plantation.'

'And what about the young lady whose company you have been keeping for the past two years—the one in

Charleston?' asked his uncle, glancing sideways at him, a meaningful, mischievous look in his half-closed eyes.

Christopher grinned. 'There's not much that escapes you, is there, Uncle?' and into his mind flashed a picture of voluptuous, lovely raven-haired Marie, untamed, like a cat, but possessing all the softness—and the claws. Unlike Clarissa, whose beauty was delicate and passive and so spiritually passionate, Marie's was of the devil's kind, with a strong seductive power, whose every look offered men pleasure. He remembered the warmth and pleasure he derived from her and how she twined her naked body about him—but not his heart. 'Men do not marry women like Marie, Uncle. As a mistress she is perfect, but as my wife—no. She has none of the qualities and virtues I would wish my wife to have, and, anyway, our relationship ended before I left for England.'

'But surely there are countless southern ladies who would meet your requirements and leap at the chance of becoming your wife and mistress of Tamasee? Women who would fit into plantation life perfectly. More so than one from England who will find your way of life strange and different—not to mention that infernal climate of yours she will be forced to endure.'

'Yes,' replied Christopher wryly, 'that's just the trouble. There are too many. Over the months there has been a constant procession of young ladies— empty-headed, most of them—and all have been paraded before me by scheming, ambitious mothers.' He sighed. 'I want none of them, Uncle, and I will not marry just anyone. Tamasee deserves better than that,' he said quietly. 'So—I thought that while I was here I would look for a wife. Don't forget that my father did exactly the same. He came to England and he found an ideal wife.'

'Ah, but if I remember correctly my sister—God rest

her soul—had already caught his eye months before he actually proposed. It was no sudden decision. Theirs was a match made in heaven. Never were two people more ideally suited. It may be a long time before you find anyone quite like your mother, Christopher.'

Christopher shook his head slowly, his voice low and serious when he spoke. 'I'm not looking for a woman like her—but I do believe I have found the one I want. As you know, I am the last of the Cordells and I don't want any ordinary woman to be my wife. You see, she will not only be my wife but also the mother of my children. I want someone who will be able to teach them the finer things of life that I can't teach them. America is still new, still being built and the opportunities greater now than when my great-grandfather, Jonathan Cordell, went out there. I want my sons to have a part in the building of America. Whether they be planters or statesmen, whatever power and influence they may rise to they will choose, but I want to make sure I give them that chance, and to do that I must marry the right woman.'

His uncle nodded, understanding, knowing Christopher well enough to be sure that he must have thought about this seriously, and he certainly approved of his choice. 'Then, if she'll have you, marry her, Christopher. You'll not regret it. She may be nursing the hurt of young Montgomery's death, but she's young, she'll get over it, and if I know anything you're just the man to make her forget. It may cost you a pretty penny, but you can afford it. Yes—it will be a perfect match. Whoever gets Clarissa Milton will be a lucky man.'

From the moment the maid had shown Mr Palmer, the family lawyer, into the drawing-room, where Clarissa received him with her father, an icy hand had gripped her heart, and her feeling of dread deepened as immediately she feared the worst. When he finally went away he left her staring at the closed door in a state of shock. She remembered very little of the conversation but she had retained a confused impression of what Mr Palmer had said. She had a vague recollection that she had deliberately tried to close her mind to what he was saying by pretending that if she didn't hear him then it couldn't be true. It could not be true that he was telling them that the whole estate would have to be sold. Even this fine, fashionable house in St James's Square would have to go. It was the only possible way they could hope to pay off their enormous debts.

Clarissa was aware of a deadening of her senses, and her heart was pounding so hard that she could scarcely breathe. All around them the house was silent. When she looked at her father a bitter taste filled her mouth and she wanted to shout hurtful words at him for bringing them to this, this state of ruin and degradation. But when she saw the look on his face her conscience smote her and the cruel words died on her lips. What could she say, anyway, that would hurt him? He knew only too well what he had done and it was killing him.

Like a sleep-walker, Lord Milton moved towards a chair, supporting himself with trembling hands on the cushioned arms as he slowly lowered himself into it, a stunned, dazed expression on his face. It was as if he had lived through the past few months in a nightmare and had just woken up to reality. He was silent for a long time before he finally spoke, his voice full of anguish and self-castigation, his eyes awash with fear more profound than anything Clarissa had ever known. He stared at his daughter, her eyes enormous in her stricken face.

'Clarissa—oh, Clarissa. What have I done? That I should have brought us to this.'

Slowly he began to shake his head, his shoulders sagging as his head sank on to his chest. Clarissa couldn't move; she could only stand and stare at him as suddenly he seemed to shrink and become old before her eyes, his usually florid complexion the colour of parchment. He was defenceless, a beaten old man. There was a pain somewhere in the region of her heart as slowly she moved towards him, dropping to her knees beside his chair and gripping his arm to try to still the trembling. The emptiness and despair that engulfed him smote her heart and the Milton pride that had always been so much a part of him had gone forever.

'Don't distress yourself, Father. It may not be as bad as Mr Palmer has led us to believe.'

'Nay, Clarissa. Let us not deceive ourselves. 'Tis worse—far worse. I never imagined it was so bad, and I thank God your mother isn't here to see what I've done.' He lifted his head and looked at her, his face marked with sorrow. 'I have no excuse for what I've done. In my blind stupidity I believed I could go on and on—like a fool, thinking nothing meant anything to me any more—but I was wrong. In trying to obliterate the misery Simon's death caused me I have betrayed that which was most dear: my family—you and Richard—and your trust.'

Clarissa's heart went out to him. 'Don't—you mustn't say that. We'll come through, Father, you'll see. There must be somewhere we can get the money to pay off the debts—something to sell. We still have some of the Milton jewels.'

Her father shook his head. 'No—it's gone too far for that, and you and Richard must keep what is left of the jewels now that Simon's gone. He was very dear to me,

Clarissa—you know that—and I mourn him. We were so much alike. When he died I tried so hard to forget, and it was only when I was at the tables and out of my mind with drink that I was able to. I never stopped to think of what I must be doing to you and Richard—how you, too, must be suffering. Especially you, because your loss was double my own. A brother and your betrothed. Ah, Clarissa—what a terrible burden this is to bear.'

'But a burden we can share,' she said, trying to infuse some hope into him—although she had none herself. 'Oh, Father, we'll manage—you'll see. Somehow we'll find a way to come out of this. You've always been so strong——'

He shook his head resignedly. 'No, not any more. My strength went with your mother.'

He fell silent and with a deep sigh got to his feet. Still on her knees, Clarissa watched him move slowly towards the door, where he stopped, and for a moment there was some semblance of the man he had once been as he straightened his back and lifted his head, assuming an air of dignity she had not seen in him since he had played host at Ashton Park when she had been a little girl. He turned back to her, a strange look on his face. For the first time in months his eyes were clear—as if a veil had been lifted from them, but when he spoke his voice seemed far away.

'It's as if I've been dead for a long time and now I am alive, only to see how cruel life can be—because now I know I cannot live with what I have done. Forgive me, Clarissa.'

He turned and went out, leaving Clarissa staring after him with burning eyes, weighted down with despair, wondering at his words and what he had meant. A hard lump had risen in her throat, which she swallowed down angrily. She wouldn't cry—she mustn't. Now was not the time, and, anyway, what good would it do—it would only weaken her and make her feel worse. No, she must accept what Mr Palmer had told them without tears or emotion and do all in her power to find a way of keeping Ashton Park. It was up to her now and she would not recognise defeat. With that she took a deep breath and, getting to her feet, squared her shoulders. She paced the room, desperately trying to sort out in her mind what she could do. There must be someone who would lend them the money. But then, if someone did lend them the money, how could they ever hope to repay it?

In the dim grey light of the drawing-room she paused by the window and gazed out at the spacious simplicity of the square, letting her eyes linger on the bronze statue of King William III astride his horse with the last rays of the afternoon sun glinting on it. Over and over, again and again she asked herself what she could do, where she could turn. What was to become of them and where would they live? Mr Palmer had tactfully suggested that perhaps she and Richard could go and live with their aunt Celia in Buckinghamshire. This suggestion she had fiercely rejected. No—never would they go and live on Aunt Celia's charity, nor that of anyone else in the family, like poor relations. Never. Not while there was breath in her body.

It was then—like a thunderbolt—that she remembered what Letty had told her, and for the first time since that moment when Mr Palmer had told them just how serious their situation was she felt a faint dawning of hope. If what Letty had said was true then she knew only one man in the whole of London who was rich enough to lend them the money—Christopher Cordell.

When she thought of him and their brief meeting at Lady Holland's party she recalled the way he had looked at her, his smouldering brown eyes boldly appraising, and at the memory a strange tingling swept over her and a soft flush tinted her cheeks. Yes—she believed he would lend them the money, but at what price to herself? And then an idea entered her mind which she considered with cold, practical logic. Lady Holland had said he was here to look for a wife, and if that was true and he wanted her then she would marry him. After all, she had nothing to lose but everything to gain. Yes, marriage to the American would benefit them all.

For one brief moment she tried to imagine what it would be like married to a man like Christopher Cordell, what he would expect of her, but when the memory of Edward flashed into her mind and how appalled he would be at a match between herself and this strange, savage American she thrust all intimate thoughts like that away.

But the awful feeling of guilt and betrayal disappeared when she thought in cold desperation that Edward was dead and she must go on, and that if marrying Christopher Cordell would ensure that she could go to bed at night and sleep peacefully without having to worry about money, knowing both Richard and Ashton Park were safe, then she would do it.

But then a sickening chill crept over her as something else occurred to her. Christopher Cordell was no fool, and he would already know what desparate straits they were in. Knowing this, he might not want to marry her, and then what would they do?

It was much later and the many candles in gilt sconces had been lit in the Milton household when the maid knocked on Clarissa's bedroom door and told her that Mr Cordell was downstairs asking to see her. It took Clarissa several moments before she could bring herself to reply and tell her to show him into the drawing-room, that she would be down shortly, but strangely it

came as no surprise to her that the American had
come. Deep down she had expected him—although
perhaps not quite so soon.

Casting all melancholy thoughts aside, she went
down the stairs with a firm resolve inside her—to face
Christopher Cordell and what he had to offer squarely.
Whatever price she had to pay, she would pay it to get
the money to secure Ashton Park.

She entered the drawing-room quietly and, although
the candles had been lit, the heavy curtains were not
yet drawn, and Christopher was staring out at the
deserted square, his hands joined loosely behind his
back. The soft rustle of her deep pink silk dress
betrayed her presence and he turned sharply. For all
the room was large and high-ceilinged, his tall, broad-
shouldered frame appeared to make it smaller. He was
as immaculately dressed as he had been at Lady
Holland's party with the exception that his long, muscular legs were now encased in polished black knee-
boots. In the candle-light his tanned, strikingly handsome face had taken on a curiously softer look than
she remembered of the night before. But despite this
and his polite, correct manner Clarissa sensed something purposeful and intent about him which troubled
her and made her feel uneasy.

As she glided almost soundlessly over the thick-piled
carpet towards him, slender and long-limbed,
Christopher was enchanted by her and gave a slight
bow, his brown eyes making an instant appraisal. His
breath caught sharply in his throat. Never had he seen
a woman with so much beauty—an ethereal beauty—
and it was as if he were seeing it for the first time in his
life. She was different from any other woman he had
ever known and he could not take his eyes off her, but
today the smooth skin of her face was marred by mauve

shadows circling her eyes, which, he suspected, were the result of worry and a sleepless night.

But one thing had not changed about her and at this he felt a pang of dismay: there was still no warmth in those glorious blue eyes, which stared out of her pale face with a solemnity that touched him. But instinctively he knew that no matter how sad she was her sorrow only enhanced her magical power, and that if he was not careful it would enslave him forever.

When she was close there came to him the faint, heady scent of crushed rose petals, a scent he would forever more associate with her. They looked at each other steadily for a long moment before Clarissa spoke, seeming ill at ease, and Christopher had an animal instinct for sensing that all was far from well with her. Seeing her again, he knew last night had been no illusion. He wanted her more than he had ever wanted any other woman and he meant to have her, but more important was the fact that he wanted her to want him, and if he hoped to win her affections then he was going to have to hold his emotions under restraint—which would be no simple matter.

'Why, Mr Cordell—this is a surprise,' said Clarissa with a cool composure she was far from feeling. 'If you wish to see my father I'm afraid he is indisposed.'

'It isn't your father I've come to see,' he said in his deep, lazy voice. 'It's you.'

'Oh?'

'Yes, and I wouldn't have blamed you in the slightest if you had refused to see me.'

'Why should I do that?' she enquired, remembering their conversation of the previous evening and hoping he was too much of a gentleman to mention it, but she need not have worried.

'A matter of a thousand guineas,' he replied, having no intention of making any reference to her parting

words regarding Ashton Park. Perhaps later, when
they knew each other better and he had gained her
confidence.

'That is between you and my father. It is not my
concern,' she said firmly, conveying by the tone of her
voice and the look in her eyes that she did not wish to
discuss the matter further.

Christopher understood and was full of admiration
for her steadfast loyalty to the man who had brought
her to near ruin. But he was her father, and whatever
he was guilty of she would cloak his sins and utter no
words that would dishonour him in any way.

'Nevertheless, please believe me when I say that I
regret the circumstances of our meeting and it would
give me great pleasure if you would permit me to make
amends.' He would have liked to offer to return the
thousand guineas but he knew she would be offended
by the gesture and too proud to accept it and, besides,
their debts were too numerous now for it to make any
difference. 'Tell me—have you eaten?'

'No,' she said, slightly nonplussed.

'Then if your father is indisposed perhaps you would
consider having supper with me.'

Clarissa stared at him in amazement. What he had
suggested was quite unexpected. Supper? Never had
she been out to supper with a gentleman alone in her
life before—not even Edward. Thoughts of Edward
stirred powerful, painful memories and emotions,
emotions she would rather have left in the past—
especially now while in the presence of this American,
who she hoped would provide the solution to all her
worries and when it was imperative that she keep all
her wits about her.

'Why, Mr Cordell—I hardly think I know you well
enough for that.'

At her reaction he smiled, a long, slow smile, not in

the least discouraged. 'Then I think we should remedy that, and why don't we start by you calling me Christopher? No doubt you consider what I have suggested highly improper. I merely came to apologise for last night, but now I'm here I can think of nothing that would give me greater pleasure than for you to accept my invitation—and, besides, I do so hate dining alone.'

A serious note had entered his voice and he wasn't smiling any more as his eyes held hers. Startled by his frankness, curiously Clarissa felt her nervousness subsiding, and she wasn't at all displeased by his suggestion that they have supper together. And why should she be? she thought wryly. Wasn't this just what she wanted—an opportunity for them to get to know each other better? But it was out of the question. It would be highly improper for her to have supper alone with him.

'Won't you agree to have supper with me—or is it that you have a prior engagement?'

'Oh, no—it isn't that, only. . .' she faltered, unable to go on. Last night in the midst of Lady Holland's guests she had felt protected and full of a cool self-assurance, but here, in the intimate privacy of the drawing-room, where the only sounds to be heard were the clatter of carriage wheels out in the square and the somnolent tick of the clock on the mantelpiece, she was uncomfortably conscious of the overwhelming presence of this man who had come so suddenly into her life and at a time when she was lonely and so very vulnerable, when her spirits had sunk to such a low ebb that it would be so easy for her to turn to anyone who offered comfort.

At her hesitation he laughed, a soft, velvety sound. 'You're not afraid of having supper alone with me, are you?' he asked, his eyes and voice challenging.

Clarissa looked at him steadily for a long moment, at his darkly handsome face, conscious of the fact that if she did indeed agree to have supper with him then there would be no going back. Fate was moving quicker than she had anticipated. 'No, I'm not afraid of you,' she said steadily.

'Then perhaps you hesitate because it is not the way it's done over here. Is that it?'

She sighed, her manner relaxing, and the ghost of a smile hovered on her lips. 'Yes.'

He grinned broadly with mischievous delight. 'I'm an American, Clarissa, and we do things differently over there. We do not stand on ceremony like you English. Now—I have a carriage waiting outside and I know a very select little eating house not far from here where the food is exquisite.'

Looking deep into his eyes, she saw he was sincere and, unable to resist his charm, she melted just a little and her smile widened, revealing her small white teeth.

'You know,' said Christopher, frowning, a serious note entering his voice, 'you really should smile more often.'

She flushed, lowering her eyes beneath his intense gaze. 'I've had very little to smile about of late.'

'Then all the more reason why you should have supper with me,' he said softly.

'You are extremely persuasive, sir. But—you were right. It would be highly improper for me to dine alone with you, so instead will you join my companion, Betsy, and me for supper here? We shall be dining shortly and you are most welcome.'

Disappointment flickered in Christopher's eyes and he frowned at the thought of her companion being present at what he had hoped would be a private, intimate supper for two, but, determined to retain her company a little longer, he smiled. 'Thank you. It will be a pleasure.' His eyes darkened and he looked at her intently. 'Tomorrow I leave for Portsmouth, Clarissa. I'm not sure how long I shall be away but it was very important to me that I saw you before I left. I'm glad you didn't deny me that. Please forgive my haste but no power on earth would have prevented me from seeing you today.'

There was a moment of silence between them, the implication of his words all too clear. Clarissa lowered her eyes as she was seized by panic and also an indescribable fear that the situation developing between them, between herself and this man whose existence she had not been aware of until yesterday, was becoming all too real.

Noticing the confusion his words had caused her, Christopher laughed softly, wanting so much to put her at ease, but before he could say anything further the door opened and Betsy came in to tell them supper was ready.

CHAPTER THREE

THE dining-room at the Milton house in St James's Square glittered with light from a single crystal chandelier, the hundreds of tiny prisms shimmering, catching and holding the light from the many candles. Clarissa, Betsy and Christopher were seated at a table in the centre of which was a china bowl full of pink roses, each one soft and velvety and perfect, giving off the most gentle, heavenly perfume. Christopher was both polite and attentive throughout the meal, keeping the conversation impersonal. The more Clarissa relaxed, the more she looked at him, letting her gaze linger, which did not go unnoticed by Betsy, who was full of curiosity about Christopher Cordell. It was a long time since a gentleman had come calling on Clarissa—too long, she thought—and never one quite so handsome. No—not even Edward Montgomery.

Clarissa was beginning to feel all the power of Christopher's gaze and, although she had sworn never to become romantically involved with any man again, the memory of Edward still too painful, she was not immune to his dazzling good looks. But she did ask herself if she would have been quite so eager to invite him to supper if it were not for his wealth.

After the meal Betsy tactfully took up her sewing close to a lamp away from them, hoping that this would be the first of many visits from this handsome American who was obviously attracted by Clarissa, who hadn't looked so happy or relaxed for a long time.

Clarissa relaxed for the first time in weeks as she seated herself opposite Christopher by the fire. Worry

and nervousness were forgotten as she slowly stirred
her coffee. Christopher watched her, a half-smile curving his firm lips as he swirled his brandy around the
bowl of his glass. Clarissa asked him about his visit to
Portsmouth, curious to know more about him.

'I'm going to stay with a friend of mine and his
family. He is someone I was at law school with, here in
London. Many years ago now, it seems.'

'You are a lawyer?' asked Clarissa, unable to keep
the surprise out of her voice.

He smiled grimly. 'Yes. It was what I always
intended to be and maybe, later, to go into politics—
but life is under no obligation to give us the things we
want.'

She looked at him curiously. 'What happened?'

'My father and older brother were killed in a river-
boat accident,' he said quietly. 'That was when I
suddenly found myself the owner of a plantation with
no time for such things as law and politics.'

'Oh—I'm so sorry,' she said softly. 'How awful it
must have been for you.'

'Yes—at the time. You see, before they died,
Tamasee—that's the name of my home—didn't need
me. With father and Andrew to run things, I was free
to come to England to study law, but I was impatient
for the years to come when I would be able to immerse
myself in the politics of America.' He sighed deeply,
and Clarissa could detect a faint hint of bitterness in
his tone. 'But—it was not to be. At first I did think of
selling Tamasee and going to live in New England, but
Mother didn't want me to. She couldn't bear the
thought of selling—and so I had no choice but to
accept with as good grace as possible to be a planter.'

'Was that very difficult?'

'It was. I had no more brothers or sisters. There was
only me—and Mother, of course, but she died some

months back.' He sighed, taking a sip of his brandy, and, sitting back in his chair, crossed one booted leg over the other before going on. 'At first I was haunted by those days when I was here in London, but then, as the years progressed and because I wanted so much to do well—to make my father, had he lived, proud of me—I became determined to put those early years behind me—not to look back, because,' he said, suddenly seeming to look at something beyond Clarissa and speaking softly, almost to himself, 'if you do it drags you down so that you're incapable of picking yourself up.' He smiled ruefully. 'Since then I have lived and breathed cotton and become thankful for what I have. Nothing else has mattered—until now.'

He stopped speaking and they looked for a long, quiet moment into each other's eyes, and something of his mood conveyed itself to Clarissa, but the implication of his words again caused her to lower her eyes.

'H-have you ever been to Portsmouth before?' she asked, quickly changing the subject.

'No. I'm looking forward to seeing my friend and his family, but I had hoped to go north, to take a look at your cotton factories. However, I regret I do not have the time.'

'Oh—you surprise me. I admit that I know very little about the textile industry, but I thought we kept our machines and what goes on in our factories a jealously guarded secret,' she smiled.

'That might have been so ten years ago, but not any more. Your Parliament could not hope to keep the plans for the machines invented over here a secret forever. Wanting to keep the advantage over other manufacturing countries, they may have refused to export the machines or the plans of them, but people crossed the Atlantic, Clarissa, with plans and ideas carried in their heads, and as a result we now have our own mills in the northern states.'

'Why not in the south? Would it not be to your advantage to have them where the cotton is grown?'

'Yes, I agree it would, but there are many in the south who do not want change or industrialisation. Besides, all our time is turned to the raising of raw cotton.'

'Don't you grow anything else but cotton?'

'Yes, tobacco, and grain for our own use. We also leave some land fallow, rotating the crops every year, otherwise the land will become exhausted. But the main crop is cotton. There is an ever-increasing need for it because it's so cheap and easy for us in the south to grow. The climate and conditions are perfect. Believe me, Clarissa, raising cotton is the most profitable business in America, and this is only the beginning.'

Later, when it was time for Christopher to leave, Clarissa walked with him through the hall and out on to the top of the steps, noticing a carriage waiting below. A haze of moonlight filled the square and, looking up, she studied his face in the silver light, deeply touched by what he had told her of his life in America. How dreadful it must have been for him to have to abandon his life's dreams and ambitions in such tragic circumstances, and she wondered if, regardless of his firm resolution to become a planter, he still clung to those dreams, and she was saddened, but understood all the disappointment and bitterness he must have felt.

He looked down at her upturned face, as pale as the moonlight that washed over her. 'Thank you for supper, Clarissa. You were a wonderful hostess.'

'I'm glad you were able to stay.'

'I think I was the most fortunate man in London tonight,' he said softly.

At his words she smiled but said nothing.

'I must go.'

'What time do you have to leave for Portsmouth?'

'I have to be away early.'

'I hope you have a good journey.'

'When I return to London, Clarissa, will you permit me to call on you?'

'Of course,' she said without hesitation, feeling a sharp pang of dismay that he was leaving so soon, and this puzzled her. 'How long do you think you'll be gone?'

'I don't know. That depends upon a number of things,' he said meaningfully. He saw the questioning look in her eyes and he had an impulse to reach out and touch her, to caress the softness of her lips with his own, and he thought with yearning of the time when they would know each other better. To divert his thoughts from what was at the moment an impossible dream, he took her hand in his own and raised it to his lips, placing them gently on her cool fingers, but his eyes remained fixed on hers, a warm glow in their depths.

Clarissa trembled slightly at the feel of his lips on her fingers, and she experienced strange sensations and emotions and was sorry when he released her hand and stepped back, his voice low and husky when he spoke.

'Goodnight, Clarissa,' and then he turned sharply and went down the steps. He turned and looked at her just once more before climbing into the carriage and disappearing into the night.

Clarissa was only faintly aware of Betsy as she moved, as if in a trance, back into the hall, so preoccupied was she with her thoughts and the strange evening.

Betsy smiled at Clarissa's entranced state and moved

to close the door, which she had absent-mindedly left open. 'What a nice gentleman,' she said.

Clarissa looked at her and frowned, considering the word. 'Nice? No. Nice is not a word I would apply to Mr Cordell. Perhaps to someone like Richard or Mother, but no—certainly not to the American.' Smiling, she turned to go up the stairs, only to be jolted back to reality when told by a maid that her father had left the house while they were having dinner. He had gone to his club.

She went to bed with a heavy heart, unable to sleep, troubled about her father and the day's events—but also about Christopher Cordell, and when she thought of him it was such a host of contradictory feelings that she was quite lost.

It was in the cold grey light of dawn that her father's valet came to fetch her to her father's room, and it was with heavy, mechanical footsteps that Clarissa walked along the landing. The door was open and she went inside. It was totally quiet, the smell of death filling the room. Her eyes were drawn to and focused on the limp form of her father strewn grotesquely across the bedclothes. She stared as one hypnotised. His face was a mask of blood, his head lying in a sticky pool, showing rusty brown against the stark white of the bedclothes. His pistol was still in his hand. Slowly Clarissa crumpled to her knees, her hand rising to her lips to stifle the scream that rose in her throat. Now she knew what he had meant yesterday. Oh—she should have known. Unable to live with what he had done, her father had shot himself.

It was late when Christopher passed beneath the broken sign of the unwelcoming-looking inn outside Winchester and went inside. The taproom was small and low-ceilinged, and if the hour had not been late he would have travelled on to look for another. It took a while for his eyes to adjust to the dim light from a couple of oil lights hung from the ceiling. He was met by the nauseating reek of tobacco smoke and alcohol combined with the unappetising odour of cooked food. A fire struggled to survive in the hearth, black with soot, and the scrubbed wooden tables, their greasy surfaces slopped with pools of ale, were occupied by what he would only describe as a drunken rabble and two soldiers in a similar state, in uniforms of scarlet coats and tight white breeches, having seen much service, creased and unwashed, obviously on their way home from the Peninsular War, their cocked hats and sabres on the bench beside them.

Christopher sat down at a table near the wide chimney piece and a young serving maid came to him. She was small, lacking the lusty sensuality of the other serving girls. He saw that she had caught the eye of one of the soldiers, who reached out to try to touch her as she moved past his table. His advances were unwelcome, and swiftly she darted away; as Christopher ordered food and a room for the night her pretty young face beneath the starched white cap was scarlet with embarrassment and shame, and her large, liquid brown eyes held the same kind of fear he had seen in those of a frightened young doe facing death.

After he had eaten he settled into the corner of his seat, slowly savouring his brandy, shutting out the coarse drunken singing and shouting, his thoughts turning to Clarissa—in fact, he had thought of little else since leaving London, and how bewitchingly lovely she had looked when he had left her on the steps of Milton House. She had become an enigma to him and he had no intention of remaining for the four weeks in

Portsmouth as he had originally intended, however disappointed David might be.

His attention was again drawn to the young serving girl, still trying to avoid the clawing hands of the soldier who had been making a play for her all night, his face flushed with drink, his scarlet tunic stained with it. Christopher studied him. He had the superior attitude and the trimmings and facings on his uniform of a young officer. He recognised that he belonged to the privileged class, to that arrogant breed of English aristocracy, the type who wasted both time and money, his life, more than likely, given over to the pleasures of women and gaming—the type he despised.

His thick pale blond hair fell in a heavy wave over his boyishly handsome face and his eyes were grey with heavy lids, giving him a lazy, insolent look. His fleshy pink lips were parted as he leered and groped for the serving girl.

At first Christopher watched with amusement as the young girl eluded his clawing hands as best she could, but gradually he became irritated and then angry by the distress the soldier's persistence was causing her. Suddenly, with a yell of triumph, and much to the glee of everyone present, the soldier at last succeeded in pulling the girl on to his knee and thrusting his hand down the front of her low-necked dress, his hand gripping her firm young breast, but with a wordless cry and unusual strength for one so young the girl pushed his hands away and scrambled from his knees; reaching out, she grasped his tankard full of frothing ale and flung it in his face before turning and fleeing from the inn.

At this, silence fell and all eyes became fixed on the young soldier. His manner changed immediately and his eyes became splintered with ice. It was clear to Christopher that here was a young man who was not used to being rejected or bested by someone he would consider his inferior.

The whole place suddenly erupted in a volley of shouts and coarse jokes as the soldier rose, his hair dripping with ale, which he made no attempt to wipe away. His voice, full of a desperate violence, thundered above the din.

'I'll wager any man here that she's a virgin, and I'll tell you now that I intend to find out.'

At this a roar of approval went up, and the soldier staggered drunkenly towards the door, dragging one of his legs, which indicated that he'd been wounded in the war with France.

Christopher watched and listened, suddenly remembering the fearful look he had seen in the eyes of the girl, thinking she couldn't be more than fifteen years old at the most, and, as he was all too aware of the soldier's evil intent, it wasn't long before he followed him outside.

The night was dark and cold when he stepped into the yard but he paid no heed to it, hearing the strangled cry of the girl pierce the air, cut off as a hand was clapped over her mouth. He turned towards the sound and quickly went across towards the stables, where a light spilled out from the open doorway, pointing on the ground like a long orange finger.

The soldier had seized the terrified girl and dragged her inside, where he had brutally flung her to the ground, pushing her back on to a pile of straw, crashing down on top of her and pinning her beneath him, ripping the thin fabric of her dress from neck to waist, exposing her small, immature breasts. Though she screamed and managed to struggle frantically against him as if her very life depended on it, it was no use. She was no match for his brute strength, his muscles honed to perfection on the battlefields of Spain.

At first her resistance surprised him, but then it excited him and he laughed, a low, merciless sound. 'Fight me all you like, my little beauty. I like a girl with spirit—but I'll have you in the end,' and, gripping her chin with fingers like steel, he pressed his lips on to hers.

Struggle as she might, she was forced to submit to his loathsome kiss while his hand fumbled greedily under her skirts, exposing the soft flesh of her white legs. Her last reserves of strength were almost exhausted when Christopher's tall shadow fell across them from where he stood in the doorway.

In surprise the soldier paused for a moment and turned, favouring him with a mocking grin, a glazed expression in his eyes. 'Come to watch the sport, have you? Well, you can have her when I'm done.'

'Enough,' said Christopher with an ominous coolness, noticing the mute appeal in the girl's terrified eyes. Something in his tone made the solider turn again and look at him.

'Indeed, it is not,' he growled. 'Enough, you say—for what reason? Perhaps it is that you want this baggage now—for yourself. Well, I will tell you this—I do not care for anyone to interrupt me in my pleasures. So—whoever you are—be gone. Find your own amusement—or wait till I'm done.'

Undeterred, Christopher stepped closer, glowering down at him. 'Then allow me to present myself—Christopher Cordell, at your service, and I told you to release the young lady. She has made it quite plain that your over-amorous advances are not welcome.'

Recognising his soft southern-American accent and that each word was enunciated slowly and carefully, the soldier staggered to his feet, his clothes dishevelled and his expression deadly. He stood and faced Christopher, several inches taller than himself, who was making a visible effort to control his anger, a faint, scornful smile on his lips that only added to the soldier's rage.

'This is not your affair and I resent your interference.'

'Really?' he mocked. 'But you are bothering the young lady and I am making it my affair.'

'Young lady?' sneered the soldier. 'She is nothing but a common trull.'

There was a faint, animal-like whimper from the straw as the girl, as pale as death and shaking from head to foot, struggled to get up, modesty causing her to pull her torn skirts over her naked flesh with trembling fingers. The soldier turned as if to go back to her.

'Touch her again and I'll break your neck,' drawled Christopher.

The threatening quality in his voice caused the soldier to look at him again, anger blazing from his eyes, and suddenly, unable to restrain himself, he sprang at Christopher with clenched fists; perhaps, if his brain had not been fogged with drink, he might not have missed his target, but, as he raised them to strike, Christopher deftly side-stepped and struck out, hitting the soldier on the side of the face. His eyes rolled in his head and he staggered and fell to the ground, his face bleeding from a cut caused by the blow. All vestige of pride was stripped from the soldier, who was enraged to find himself so humiliated by the American. His body shook with the intensity of his anger and sheer hatred blazed from his eyes.

'Get out,' said Christopher, his voice like steel.

The soldier struggled to his feet and in the doorway he turned. 'If ever I have the misfortune to meet you again I'll make you pay for that. I'll get even—I swear it.'

'Oh, I doubt our paths will cross again, but perhaps you'll think twice the next time you're intent on raping anyone.'

Muttering curses beneath his breath, the soldier turned and stumbled out into the night, dragging his injured leg behind him.

When he'd gone Christopher sighed and, reaching out, put his arm about the girl's shaking shoulders. 'Are you all right?'

She nodded, smiling at him gratefully, too shocked to speak. A woman suddenly appeared by her side.

'Oh, Sal——' and, taking in her torn clothes, she looked at Christopher in alarm. 'Is she all right?'

He nodded. 'Yes. I came in time.'

She sighed with relief. 'Thank the Lord. Come on, love—I'll take you home.' She looked up at Christopher. 'She came instead of her sister tonight. She's ill, you see, and they need the money bad.'

Christopher nodded, understanding. 'Tell me—how old is she?'

'Thirteen.'

He looked at her, horrified. 'Then this is no place for her. Take her home, and here,' he said, pressing some coins into her hand. 'This should more than cover her night's work. Make sure she doesn't come back.'

The following morning Christopher continued his journey to Portsmouth, but no sooner had he arrived than he heard of the death of Lord Milton. He returned to London immediately.

For Clarissa the days following her father's death passed like a nightmare. There was a dull lethargy about her so that for a time, after the dreadful shock, she couldn't think clearly, her mind was numb, but she knew that later, as the numbness wore off and her nerves struggled to make themselves felt, there would come the sharp, searing pain of reality.

The fact that she would have to travel to Ashton Park and break the news to Richard about their father and tell him that the house would have to be sold was tearing her apart. How could either of them bear to lose it? But there was nothing else for it. Ashton Park would have to go. At last she had to admit defeat, to bow to the inevitable. She had pinned her one hope on Christopher Cordell, that, given time, he would offer her marriage, but now that was not to be. He had left London and would not be back in time to be of any help.

With Betsy's help she somehow managed to function, to do all the things she should, even arranging for her father's body to be taken back to Ashton Park, where it would be laid beside her mother in the village church at Ashton, but it was as if it were happening to someone else. No one came to offer their condolences. It was as if she had suddenly become shipwrecked upon some desert island as the outside world retained an embarrassed silence over her father's death. The only person she saw, apart from Mr Palmer, was Letty, and she thanked God for that. Without her support and Betsy's she couldn't have carried on.

CHAPTER FOUR

IT WAS the following evening, after a journey that had seemed endless to Clarissa, that the carriage passed through the huge iron gates of Ashton Park with their heraldic bearings, indicating that they were entering the grounds of a noble family.

She walked wearily into the house, into the lofty hall with its fine, gracefully arched timber roof, where servants were rushing about in haste because of her unexpected arrival. Thankfully she sank into a chair beside the hearth, where a welcoming fire blazed.

She was cold, but only now did she realise it and, taking comfort from the fire's warmth, she gazed into the hot coals while she waited for Richard, feeling the heat seep through her veins and the great house wrapping itself about her, acting like a balm, soothing her troubled heart.

As quickly as she could she told Richard why she had come home, regardless of the pain it caused her to do so, knowing she was about to bring his whole world tumbling down. She told him about their father's gambling and his enormous debts and about the way he had killed himself. For a while Richard was at a loss for words. Horror flared in his eyes over the manner of his father's death, but as the full meaning of her words sank in he looked pale and shaken, his whole attitude being one of despair.

'Dear God,' he said weakly, staring into Clarissa's eyes. 'I didn't know. I had no idea things were as bad as that. Why didn't you tell me?'

'I was going to—if and when I could get him to come home.'

'Is there nothing we can do? What about his holdings in the tin and coal mines and all the others?'

Clarissa shook her head resignedly. 'No. They're all gone.'

A deathly pallor spread over Richard's face as the implication of her words sank in. 'All?'

She nodded. 'We have nothing left, Richard. After we have sold the house in London and the rest of Father's properties—including Ashton Park—and paid off the creditors we may just have enough left to buy somewhere small to live and enough to live on until we can find work.'

'How long have we got?'

'Not long. Some of the creditors have agreed to wait, but they won't wait forever.'

He stared at her in disbelief. 'It's as bad as that?'

'Yes. The only alternative is that we go and live in Buckinghamshire with Aunt Celia.'

Angry emotion flared in Richard's eyes. 'Never—never that. I will not accept her charity.'

He was not ignorant of his father's passion for gambling and his presence at the endless gaming parties, where huge fortunes changed hands and where many were lost, but it had never occurred to him that his own father would indulge in such follies—to sink so low as to allow himself to lose all he owned and then shoot himself. His hurt tone when he spoke tore at Clarissa's heart.

'How could he do it, Clarissa?' he cried with a forlorn desperation in his voice. 'How can anyone lose so much at the tables?'

'Father could have told you,' she said bitterly.

'But to throw away everything like that. I always knew I could never mean the same to him as Simon—

but to do this. In the name of God, Clarissa—how could he do it? He has destroyed us both with his drunkenness and gambling—his weakness and stupidity.' His eyes were suddenly blinded by a scalding rush of angry tears. 'Well—I'll be damned and in hell itself before I see Ashton Park sold to someone else. The Miltons have lived here for generations. They have been the only family to live here.'

Clarissa rose from her seat and went to him, placing her hand tenderly on his arm. 'I know, but there is nothing else we can do,' she said gently. 'I have been over it all with Mr Palmer. He will be coming down to see us after—after the funeral, to tell us what has to be done. There is no other way we can pay off the debts—believe me, Richard.'

He turned and looked at her, a mixture of anger and grief filling his eyes, but his voice held a kind of bitterness she had not heard from him before; bitterness over the fact that he had been cheated out of what was his by right now that Simon was gone. 'Oh, I do—I believe you, Clarissa, and you are right. In the end Ashton Park—our home—will have to go unless I can find some way of raising the money, which is damn near impossible. But then,' he said, his lips twisting scornfully, 'I suppose I could look for a rich wife—an heiress. But no doubt it would have to be someone old and ugly, who has been passed over, to even consider taking me on with such enormous debts.'

'Don't. Please don't,' whispered Clarissa. His suffering was almost too much for her to bear. 'What—what about Laura? Tell me about her.'

At the mention of Laura's name his expression suddenly softened, and he sighed, running his shaking fingers through his untidy hair. 'Laura, poor love, has no means. I'm afraid she's as poor as a church mouse.

Her father is our new minister at Ashton. No doubt
you will meet him shortly.'

'But you love her—don't you, Richard?'

'Yes—yes, I do. Very much.'

Clarissa sighed and looked back into the flames,
feeling the heat on her face and all the sadness of her
own lost love. 'Then be content with that and marry
her. You know—I did consider marrying someone
myself. Someone who is immensely rich—an
American, who is over here looking for a wife.'

Richard gave her a puzzled look. 'But I thought—
you—you said when Edward died that you'd never
marry.'

'I know. I said a lot of things when he was killed and
I meant every word I said—then. But now I have the
future to think about and, like you, I cannot think of a
future without Ashton Park.'

'What happened to your American? Where is he
now?'

'In Portsmouth,' she said quietly. 'He will have no
idea about all this—not that it would make any difference if he did. You see, we had only just met and
didn't have the chance to become well acquainted, but
for a time all my hopes for the future were in him.
However distasteful the prospect, Richard, I thought
that, if I must marry, if it's not for love then it must be
to someone I could respect. But the most important
thing of all was that he must be rich. Christopher
Cordell was all that, but he won't be returning to
London for quite some time. I fear it will be too late
for him to help us.'

Richard didn't ask her any more questions about the
American, but he was sure he detected a note of regret
in her voice.

* * *

Harry Milton's body was brought from London, and it was with a leaden heart that Clarissa saw him placed beside her mother and other ancestors in the family vault in Ashton church, feeling that already a part of her life was receding into the past as his body was sealed in the darkness of the tomb.

Afterwards she remembered little of the service conducted by the new minister, the Reverend Mr Greenwood. The little church had been filled with their tenants, although they had not come to pay their respects to a Lord they scarcely knew, who had spent most of his time away in London, but to his son, who they considered was the mainspring at Ashton Park, who was the embodiment of all the qualities of a young gentleman, who, regardless of an extremely efficient bailiff, shouldered most of the responsibilities of the estate, making their troubles his own, the welfare of the workers and tenants being important to him. They all held him in the highest esteem, but none could know that the suffering and anguish etched in deep lines on his young face were not those of grief over the death of his father but over the inevitable loss of Ashton Park—which was like a death in itself.

It was over a week later, and Mr Palmer had just left Ashton Park to return to London, where he would begin selling off what was left of Lord Milton's property.

Driven by a compelling need to be by herself, Clarissa quickly changed into her riding habit and, after saddling her horse, Melody, was soon riding through the park. As she dug in her heels her horse bounded forward, and she galloped hard, trying to ease the misery and hurt that filled her, that was real and definite, echoing with the thunder of her horse's hoofs in her ears as it pounded over the turf.

It was late afternoon and already the last of the sun

had gone, and a band of darkness spanned the horizon. The wind had risen and overhead were swirling black clouds, which had been gathering all that day, and at last it began to rain, sharp and cold, stinging her cheeks already awash with her tears. Her hair became undone from its pins and began to blow about her face. She rode with reckless abandon over the springy wet turf, unable to determine in which direction she rode, so intolerable were her thoughts. The harder she rode, the more the wind screamed past her ears, and in her desperate need to escape her tortured mind she became forgetful of time and stopped thinking altogether.

This was how Christopher found her, seeing her through a dark veil of rain, her horse galloping at full stretch.

Clarissa was first aware of his presence when she heard the distant sound of his horse's hoofs galloping behind her. She pulled her horse to a halt and turned, listening to the rhythmic drumming coming closer, sounding louder, and then, in a moment, her sharp eyes saw the dark, ghostly shape of a rider looming, enormous, out of the rain, shrouded in a black cape with the stiff collar turned up and his hat pulled down so that his face was in shadow. She strained her eyes to see who it could be but he was too far away for her to see his features. Suddenly her attention became riveted on him and for a moment she thought she must be seeing things, brought on by some kind of a delusion, recognising the strong set of his broad shoulders and, as he came closer, the dark bronzed features of his face.

Quite inexplicably her heart gave a joyful leap when she saw it was indeed the American—Christopher Cordell—and for a brief moment all her terrors were forgotten. He drew rein beside her and she stared at him, at a complete loss for words. He pulled his hat back from his face and she looked into those dark brown eyes.

He smiled, his lips curving in a crooked smile as he took in her appearance. Her wet hair was drawn with a severity from her face, which only served to heighten her beauty, drawing attention to the fine lines of her cheekbones, the brilliance of her eyes and the proud curve of her lips. She sat straight and slim in the saddle. Her severely cut habit was soaked, her small waist and the round swell of her hips emphasising her femininity far more than all her dresses of satin and lace.

'Hello, Clarissa.'

'You—you must forgive me,' she stammered. 'I did not expect you. How did you know where to find me?'

'Your brother told me.' He had to shout to make himself heard over the noise of the wind. 'I want to talk to you. Isn't there somewhere we can go out of this infernal rain?'

She turned and pointed towards the dome of a summer-house which rose above the trees, one of several that dotted the park. 'Over there.'

Together they rode quickly towards the small round building, its walls bare but for the dust and festoons of spiders' webs that hung from the roof. It was not the most welcoming of places, being cold and damp, with the smell of decay from the sodden undergrowth, but at least it was a shelter from the rain. Clarissa shuddered, feeling a trickle of icy water run beneath her collar and down her back, and, clasping her arms about her, she was suddenly conscious of the extreme cold caused by her wet clothes.

To Christopher she seemed drained of all her strength and, touched by her sorry state, he immediately removed his cape and wrapped it about her, his hands oddly gentle as they rested on her shoulders. She began to relax, feeling its comforting warmth, and stood facing him, her eyes captured and held by his. He looked at her long and hard, catching a glimpse of her almost desperate sorrow. Neither of them spoke for several moments. Curiously Clarissa felt an insidious feeling of peace stealing over her. Christopher sighed and shook his head slowly, keeping his eyes fixed on hers, plumbing their innermost depths.

'How are you, Clarissa?'

'I am well—considering what has happened. Why are you here, Christopher? Why have you come?'

'I believe you know why,' he said, his voice low and serious. 'And I think you know that I want more from you than friendship.'

She nodded. 'Yes—although why I can't imagine. You scarcely know me.'

'As I told you before, that can soon be remedied. You must forgive my haste, but I did not have the time to remain in London kicking my heels indefinitely. I do not intend remaining in England for more than a few weeks. I learned of your father's death only when I reached Portsmouth. I'm very sorry, Clarissa. It must have been harrowing for you.'

'Yes—yes, it was,' and Christopher sensed a bitter note in her voice. 'But Father did not just die. It was suicide—there is a difference—but I think you already know that, don't you? Anyway, it's over now—or it will be when. . .when. . .' She faltered, unable to go on, and turned from his penetrating gaze as hot tears welled up in her eyes. Angrily she dashed them away with her clenched fist and moved towards the door, looking out over the park, but everything was a blur.

Christopher moved towards her, wanting so much to reach out and draw her into his arms. Her suffering almost broke his heart.

'Tell me why you're here,' she asked quietly. 'What do you want of me?'

'I came to ask you to be my wife,' he replied simply.

At his words she closed her eyes tightly, remaining frozen, like a beautiful marble statue. 'Wife?' she whispered. 'You would not ask me to be your wife if you knew what marriage to me would mean.'

Gently he placed his hands on her shoulders and turned her to face him, his eyes grave but calm, his fingers brushing away the wet strands of hair clinging to her cheeks. 'Oh—I believe I do,' he said softly, 'and please believe me when I say that it was not my intention to pry into your circumstances, but it is no secret that since your brother's death in Spain your father has squandered money in every direction, leaving you hopelessly in debt, that in order to survive you will have to sell that which you hold most dear— Ashton Park.'

She nodded dumbly.

'Clarissa, I am offering you a chance to be happy—a future. I promise you that if you marry me I will secure your home—if it is so precious to you, and if it is to be a condition of your acceptance.' He saw the relief flood her eyes and sighed. 'So—I was right. Ashton Park does mean that much to you.'

'Yes—everything,' she replied quietly. 'But why should you want to marry me?'

'Because, as Lady Holland told you, I need a wife.'

'But there are thousands of women in London. Why me? With all my debts, I can only be an encumbrance to you.'

'Because you are the only one who interests me. The only one I want—debts and all,' he smiled. 'I want to make you smile, to laugh, and I want you to savour all I have to offer.'

She looked at him, at the serious expression in his eyes, and thought how unfortunate it was that she did not love him. She owed it to him to be completely honest. 'I must be frank with you, Christopher, although I suspect you already know what I am about to tell you. After all—you do seem to know everything else about me,' she said not unkindly. 'But until a short time ago I was betrothed to someone I loved a great deal. He—he too was killed in Spain, shortly before we were to have been married,' she finished quietly.

Christopher nodded, noting how her face changed when she spoke of him, bringing to it a softness, a mistiness in her wide eyes, and he felt a sudden rush of resentment towards this unknown love of hers. His face remained impassive when he next spoke. 'Yes, I did know. But time is a great healer, Clarissa. You were both very young—you will forget.' Immediately he had said the words he regretted them, for her eyes were suddenly charged with anger.

'No. Never,' she said fiercely. 'I may not have the benefit of your experience, but I know that I shall never forget—ever.' Her anger melted and she sighed, lowering her eyes. 'I shall never love you, Christopher. I shall never love any man—and so if you,' she said, her face white and tense, 'knowing this, still want to marry me and if you will promise to secure Ashton Park, then. . . I accept.' As she said these words a sudden peace and an enormous feeling of relief that soon her problems would become his descended on her spirit, but she had every intention of paying back the money it would take to pay off the debts. 'You must realise that whatever it costs it must be considered a loan. Richard, I am sure, will pay it all back, given time—and good harvests.'

Christopher smiled, a strange, crooked smile, and placed his fingers gently beneath her chin, tilting her head, forcing her to meet his gaze. 'I am sure he will, Clarissa, but believe me when I say that marriage to you will be payment enough. You do realise that if you marry me you will have to go with me to America, don't you? That we cannot live here, at Ashton Park? But I assure you that my home, Tamasee, is a place that will be worthy of you.'

She nodded as she looked at him, feeling strange emotions stirring in her breast. 'Yes,' she answered. 'I do know that, but I hope that I shall be worthy of Tamasee. I shan't mind going to America, knowing Ashton Park is safe, and I promise to do my best—to make you a good wife.'

Christopher's lips twisted in a thin smile. 'I am sure you will, but I have to admit that it does nothing for my pride or self-esteem, knowing it's my wealth and not my charming self you want. However—I do think we both have something to give.'

His face suddenly became a hard, inscrutable mask, and something Clarissa could not recognise flickered behind his dark eyes, and again she sensed in him something purposeful, something vital that made her feel uneasy, and it came to her that Christopher Cordell was not a man to run afoul of. Ignoring this moment of insight and preferring to think instead of the kindness he had shown her and his obvious sincerity, she fixed him with a steady gaze. Yes, she would marry him. With everything collapsing about her ears, she had no choice. But how different it had been when she had loved Edward, with all the passionate intensity of her youth. How she had yearned to marry him, to learn all the overwhelming joys that love had to offer. But this was to be a different kind of marriage—positive and cold. It was to be a union of two people drawn together by circumstances. She wouldn't think about what would come later but be content for now, knowing Ashton Park was safe.

'Come,' he said, taking her hand and moving outside. 'It isn't raining quite so hard now. Let's go back to the house—otherwise, if you don't get out of those wet clothes, you'll be in no fit condition to marry anyone.'

CHAPTER FIVE

RICHARD could not believe their good fortune when Clarissa told him she was to marry the American Christopher Cordell, and that he had agreed to loan them enough money to secure Ashton Park after the remainder of his father's property had been sold. His relief was enormous and he lost no time in making it quite clear to his sister that he thought she had done well for herself. Better, he thought, than if she had married Edward. His feelings regarding Clarissa's one-time betrothed had been far from favourable and, like Letty, he had kept his opinion to himself.

The gloom and despondency hanging over the house was lifted, and as the days passed and the two men got to know each other a strong friendship developed between them. It was with pride that Richard showed the estate to Christopher, who, on observing the shining brown earth of fallow fields awaiting spring for the planting of the corn, jokingly told him that it was a pity they couldn't grow cotton. Their financial worries would be at an end.

In the days after she had told Christopher she would marry him Clarissa's life had taken on a strange feeling of unreality. But why, she asked herself, why should he want to marry her? It couldn't possibly be because he loved her—not on so short an acquaintance—nor could it be because he felt sorry for her or out of kindness, for he was not the kind of man to tie himself to anyone out of pity. But whatever the reason she was acutely aware of how attractive he was and found herself watching for him, listening for his footfall on the hard tiles of the hall floor, which would set her pulses racing, and when she thought of him, of the way she often found him watching her, his gaze dark and intent, she couldn't stop the trembling that came over her.

The wedding was to take place two weeks hence, just one week before they would have to leave Ashton Park for America, this date now earlier than Christopher had intended after hearing of the meeting of Congress, which had been brought forward by a month.

The younger, more aggressive members of the ageing, peaceable President Madison's party, mainly southerners and westerners who had newly entered Congress, with all their passionate ardour had enumerated the many grievances against Britain, among them being the continuing indignities inflicted upon the American flag by arrogant British sea captains and the injuries done to American commerce. But greatest of all was their anger over Britain's continuing insistence upon the navy's right to board neutral vessels, impressing into their service any British subjects found on them. Unfortunately they were often unable to distinguish between an Englishman and an American and there was no doubt that many of them were unquestionably American.

And so these newly appointed members of Congress—the 'War Hawks', as they were called—clamoured for revenge, for America to clad itself in armour, becoming determined to rid themselves of the British from the north-American continent—including Canada, Britain's most prized colony. But sentiments against further hostilities with Britain were high in the north-east, in New York and New England, where the Federalists were bent on avoiding war, knowing all too well that it would end a trade from which they profited enormously if just a few ships, their holds crammed with raw cotton and other supplies, they sent across the Atlantic escaped seizure by the British.

It was with reluctance that Christopher made his decision to leave for London to arrange for their departure to America. He was to return to Ashton Park the day before the wedding.

It was the evening before his departure that he and Clarissa talked at length of what going to live in America would mean to her, of what she could expect and the many duties and responsibilities that would be hers at Tamasee. They had just finished dinner and were in the drawing-room. Christopher was grateful to Richard for tactfully arranging to be elsewhere so they could be alone.

It was only then that Clarissa began to realise what marriage to Christopher would really mean and that there was a gulf between them wider than the Atlantic Ocean, their backgrounds being completely different. He came from a world she could not begin to imagine with its semi-tropical weather, where life revolved around the plantation with its rolling acres of cotton, where ideas and customs would be alien to her and where the economic and social survival of the southern states depended solely upon the blood, sweat and tears of the Negro slave.

This was a system Clarissa had only heard about and considered a crippling evil. Nothing Christopher said to her would ever be able to justify it, but some deep feminine instinct told her to keep her thoughts to herself. Whatever doubts she might have regarding any aspect of what her life in America would be like, she must learn to put them behind her, to accept it, because the survival of Ashton Park was as important to her as was the survival and preservation of their way of life to the plantation owners of the southern states of America.

But Christopher had read those confused and often angry emotions clouding her eyes when he talked of the slaves, and it might have surprised her to know that he understood and sympathised with what he knew she must be thinking, but he was glad she had the good sense to keep her opinions to herself upon a subject she was not yet personally acquainted with.

With his back to the fire and his hands folded loosely behind him, he gazed down to where she sat on the sofa, her eyes upturned to his. He smiled gently. 'You do understand why I have to return to London so soon, don't you, Clarissa?'

'Yes, of course I do.'

'I had hoped for us to spend the weeks before our wedding getting to know one another better.'

'Never mind,' she said, smiling softly. 'I do have plenty to occupy my time, not only for the wedding but also in preparation for our going to America. Letty is coming in a few days, so she will help me. You probably don't remember her, but she was with me at Lady Holland's party—the night we met.'

'And a night I shall never forget,' said Christopher softly, meaningfully. 'And I do remember her. We met briefly when I got back to London and called to see you. One of your maids directed me to her house. She told me you had come down here. And I must say,' he said, his lips twisting in a smile, 'she did seem very keen that I come and see you.'

'Oh, yes, she would,' remarked Clarissa, smiling a little to herself in amusement when she pictured how startled and surprised Letty must have been when Christopher had called on her. Letty's curiosity about what he wanted with her had obviously got the better of her because only yesterday a letter had arrived, informing her of her intended visit to Ashton Park. There had been no mention of her meeting with Christopher, but Clarissa could well imagine her reaction when she learned they were to be married—and so soon. Her gaze settled on Christopher again. 'You do realise, don't you, Christopher, that because it is so close to Father's funeral it must be a modest wedding? I don't want any fuss. Normally so short an engagement would be unthinkable, but because we must leave England quickly there is nothing else for it.'

'I do understand, believe me, Clarissa, and it suits me perfectly—although if you were at Tamasee everyone in the state of South Carolina would expect to be invited and would be mortally offended if they weren't.'

Clarissa looked at him, horrified. 'Everyone?'

'I'm afraid so,' he said softly, a glint of teasing laughter shining briefly in his eyes. 'And those who weren't invited would come anyway.'

'Even after a bereavement?'

'No—perhaps not. When a member of a family dies then the plantation is in mourning for months.'

'Will you be bringing your uncle, Lord Buckley, back with you for the wedding?'

'Would you mind?'

'Of course not. He is your closest relative and was a good friend of my father's. I would like him to be here. I—I just wish we had more time—that we didn't have to leave quite so soon after the wedding.'

All trace of amusement vanished from Christopher's expression and his voice sounded grave. 'I know, but if we delay much longer we may have difficulty getting back.'

'What do you think will happen, Christopher? Do you think there will be war?'

At her question his face became tense and his tall

figure seemed to dominate the room. 'Yes, I do, and once it begins it will have to be fought. But America is so unprepared. It is a war that will be fought largely at sea. No one can dispute the quality of our navy—it is superb—but it has so few vessels, twenty at the most, nothing that can compete with the might of your British ships. It will be fortunate for us that Britain will be unable to concentrate her full force on America because she is still at war with France.' He sighed and looked at Clarissa, who had paled at his words. 'But how will you feel, Clarissa, if war does break out between our two countries? Will you not think it an act of betrayal, leaving England for a country that has declared war on her?'

'I don't know. In truth I haven't thought about it. My mind has been so full of other things of late. The French wars have been a fact of life since I was a child, but,' she said softly, looking away from him into the heart of the fire as her thoughts suddenly evoked painful memories of the past, 'it is only in the past few months that, as a family, we have been touched by the cruelties of it. I can't envisage a world without a country being on a war footing. At the moment I have to admit that war with America doesn't make any difference to me one way or the other, although how I shall feel when I get there I cannot say.'

'And it won't make you change your mind?'

She stared at him with surprise. 'What—as regards my marrying you?'

He nodded, watching her face closely.

'No, of course not.'

'How will you feel when the time comes for you to leave Ashton Park? It will be a terrible wrench.'

'I know, but I don't think it will be long before the house has a new mistress, and I'm glad it's to be Laura. But you will let me come back, won't you?'

'Of course you can come back. I don't wish to give you any reason to regret marrying me.'

'I don't think you'll do that. I only hope I don't give you cause for regrets. I do promise to make you a good wife and pray that we shall be tolerably happy.' She smiled wryly. 'After all you've done for me, the last thing I want is to prove a poor investment.'

Christopher looked at her sharply and his eyes suddenly flamed with anger, at which Clarissa immediately regretted her thoughtless, impulsive words, and for the first time since she had known him she felt fear in her heart. He moved quickly and sat beside her, taking both her hands in his own hard grip. His eyes were dark and compelling, forcing her to look into them, and his voice was stern when he spoke.

'Tolerably? An investment? I intend for us to be more than tolerably happy and I never for one moment considered you an investment. I am not given to pretty speeches, Clarissa, and, unlike young Edward Montgomery—whom you professed to love more than life itself—I cannot offer you a title, but what I can offer you is a home and an estate, the like of which you have never seen.'

'If you knew me you would know that none of that matters,' she whispered with a sinking heart, wishing he had not made that reference to Edward. She hadn't even known that Christopher knew the name of the man she would have married had the war not taken him from her. Was there nothing about her he didn't know?

'Perhaps, but you must understand that I asked you to be my wife because it was you I wanted and for no other reason. The fact that your family was hopelessly in debt was unimportant. You have told me that you will never love me, that your heart went with the soldier you were betrothed to to the grave, and I accept that—for now—but time heals many wounds, Clarissa, including the invisible ones, and when it does you will love again. When you become my wife, when you bear my name, which to me is as proud and noble as any of your ancient aristocratic ones, I shall expect some affection from you and respect, but more than anything else I want you to be happy.' His voice softened when he looked at her sad, downcast face, and he placed his fingers gently beneath her chin. 'Look at me, Clarissa.'

Slowly she raised her eyes to his, the candle-light shining into their sapphire-blue depths. Despite himself, Christopher was touched by the grief he saw there, which brought a bitter taste to his mouth. He sighed deeply, shaking his head slowly, his eyes never leaving hers.

'I am a fool,' he murmured, 'and I have a distinct feeling that I am going to make an even bigger fool of myself where you are concerned, but you cannot live your life searching for something that is gone, that is dead. It is like chasing the wind. You have to let go, Clarissa. Do you think you will be punished if, instead, you look for happiness among the living? That you will have to pay penance? For I can tell you that no amount of tears can bring back the dead.'

Clarissa stared at him, lulled into a curious sense of well-being by his words as a rush of warmth and gratitude completely pervaded her and her lovely eyes became blurred, shining like stars with her tears.

'I really do not deserve you,' she whispered, 'and I know you are right—only. . .it's just not that easy to let go.'

'Then perhaps this will help,' he murmured, and very slowly he lifted his lean brown hands and placed them on either side of her face. His brown eyes darkened so that they were almost black as he leaned forward, and at his touch Clarissa trembled slightly—with fear or excitement, she didn't know which, but she did not draw away as he placed his mouth on her soft, quivering lips, cherishing them with his own, slow and so very tender. His gentleness kindled a response and a warm glow spread over her, but also a fear began to possess her, a fear not of him but of herself and the dark, hidden feelings he aroused.

When he finally drew away she remained unmoving, as though still suspended in that kiss, her lips moist and slightly parted. She gazed wonderingly into his eyes and for the first time since he had known her some of the grief had gone from hers, which were very bright with tears. They spilled over her lashes, rolling slowly down her flushed cheeks and over his hands, which still held her face. Tenderly he wiped them away with the tips of his fingers. She was utterly lovely, breathtakingly so, and he was moved by emotions almost beyond his control, wanting so very much to kiss her again but this time with all the hunger and passion that threatened to engulf him. He controlled himself with an effort lest he betray how deeply he felt.

Early the next morning it was with reluctance that Christopher left for London, and a few days later Letty arrived. She swept up the steps, her bunches of auburn ringlets bouncing wildly as she moved, her bright eyes shining. Clarissa ushered her inside, out of the cold.

'It's lovely to see you, Letty, but I must say that your letter was something of a surprise. How are things in London?'

'Oh, much the same. As you know, nothing of interest happens until the season gets under way.' She paused and studied Clarissa with concern and was relieved to see that the strain of the past weeks had left her face. Now there was a somewhat settled air about her, a new strength of purpose that had not been there before, and she suspected that Christopher Cordell could have something to do with that. She made up her mind not to tell her about Edward until she discovered what had transpired between them. 'I know you told me not to come down to Ashton Park but I thought, now the funeral is over, you might be glad of some company.'

Clarissa smiled and squeezed her friend's hand fondly. 'Thank you. I am, Letty, and I'm so glad you've come. Now, take off your cloak and come into the drawing-room. You must be dying for some refreshment after your journey.'

Over tea they talked of inconsequential things, neither of them mentioning Christopher until Letty could stand the suspense no longer, suspecting that Clarissa was deliberately avoiding the subject. And so, unable to wait any longer and taking the bit between the teeth, she set her cup firmly on its saucer and fixed her eyes on Clarissa.

'Well—where is he?'

'Who?'

'Why—the exquisite Christopher Cordell, of course. I know he came down here to see you.'

'Oh, him,' said Clarissa, making a pretence of indifference and trying to stop her lips from quivering into a smile. 'You're too late, I'm afraid. He went back to London a few days ago.'

Letty's face fell with disappointment. 'Oh—he didn't?'

'Mm, he did—but don't worry, he'll be back.'

'He will?'

'He'd better be. We're getting married in less than two weeks.' At last her face broke into a smile.

Letty's jaw dropped in astonishment; then she gave a little squeal of delight and clasped Clarissa to her.

'Oh—love—I don't believe it,' but then she held her at arm's length. 'It is true, isn't it? You're not jesting?'

'Would I jest about so serious a matter?'

'I guess not. I knew he was coming to see you. Did you know that on learning of your father's death while in Portsmouth he immediately went straight back to London to see you?'

'Yes, he told me.'

Letty sighed, a kind of wonder in her green eyes as she looked at Clarissa, hardly able to believe that what she had told her was true, and now she knew that she could not tell her that Edward was alive. May God and Clarissa forgive her but she could not tell her, not until after she was safely married to Christopher. She would pray that Edward wouldn't change his mind and decide to come down to Ashton Park sooner than he intended. But her instinct told her that what she was doing was right. Clarissa would be far happier with Christopher than she ever would with Edward. If he had been anything like decent she would not be deceiving her in this way and, besides, she thought as renewed anger possessed her when she remembered how he had assaulted and tried to rape her, it would serve him right when he finally condescended to come down to Ashton Park and found Clarissa had married someone else, someone richer even than his own arrogant, conceited self, and with any luck she would be on her way to America.

'I can hardly believe it. To think that just three weeks ago you were on the point of penury and now—well, look at you. Your position is most enviable.'

It was almost dark when they strolled on the terraced lawns, their arms linked together and a light cold wind blowing their cloaks and hair. Soon the gardens, their beds and borders bereft of flowers, would be bathed in moonlight. Only the tall black evergreens showed any sign of life, casting their velvety shadows on the lawns. Their eyes strayed beyond to the park and they paused, each aware of the complete silence that wrapped itself about them.

Letty sighed wistfully. 'I do love Ashton Park, Clarissa. You are so lucky.'

'Don't I know it. But I didn't realise just how much it meant to me until it was almost gone. I have a lot to thank Christopher for. What he has offered me is a lifeline, Letty. I have to take it. He's been so kind, so considerate, and I believe he is genuinely fond of me. Why else would he have asked me to marry him?'

'Why else indeed? You know, you've changed, Clarissa.'

'Changed? I dare say I have changed a little. You see, I've made up my mind to put the past and whatever dreams I once had behind me and look to the future.'

'I'm glad to hear it, but I have to admit that I'm going to miss you when you go to America.'

'I know, and I'll miss you too, but you must come over and visit.' She sighed and again let her eyes stray lovingly over the countryside. 'I'm going to miss all this, but I know it will be well taken care of with Richard. It's his now, his and Laura's when they marry. I'm only sorry I can't be here for their wedding.'

'Laura? Who is she?'

'Our new minister's daughter, and she and Richard are hopelessly in love. I like her and I know she'll be good for Richard. I'm sure you'll agree with me when you meet her tomorrow. It does make going away that much easier—although theirs will be a different kind of marriage from mine.'

Letty frowned. 'Why do you say that?'

'Mine will not be clouded with romantic thoughts like theirs and, if I can help it, I don't intend being a captive of my emotions ever again. I've known love and lost it, so I must learn to come to terms with it. From now on all my aspirations must be realistic, but you know, Letty, it is important that I marry someone I can trust, someone I can lean on, who will protect me, and if Christopher can do that then I shall try very hard to love him, although I have to admit that when I think of America and being his wife it scares me.'

'You'll soon get used to it, and you'll have Betsy with you.'

'I know, and thank goodness she's agreed to come with us—in fact, she's positively looking forward to it. Oh,' she sighed, 'I'm being silly. I do realise just how lucky I am, but everything has a price—even happiness, and if I have to leave Ashton Park in order to preserve it then I am ready to pay that price.'

The wedding took place the day after Christopher returned from London, at noon on a cold January day and, because Clarissa wanted as little fuss as possible, the only people present in the little church at Ashton, which had so recently witnessed the interment of her father, were Richard and Laura and Letty, who acted as maid of honour. Only a few of the servants from Ashton Park occupied the pews and, much to Clarissa's regret, due to a severe chill, Lord Buckley had been unable to be there, but sent his good wishes.

Clarissa was a vision in a simple gown of white brocade, embroidered with tiny seed-pearls that matched to perfection the glorious creamy pearls around her throat, a wedding gift from Christopher. A fine veil was drawn over her face. She took her place beside him; he was handsome and impressive, his black coat hugging his broad shoulders and narrow waist with not a crease anywhere. His dark good looks were a striking contrast to her delicate beauty. He turned and looked at her, and his throat constricted at the picture she presented. Pray God, he thought, let me be worthy of her. Before she had been lovely, but today, as his bride, she was exquisitely perfect.

Along the walls of the church lay effigies on the tombs of long-dead Miltons, there to witness the marriage of one of their own, offering little comfort in the cold, dank church. After the ritual sacred vows had been said and the Reverend Mr Greenwood had pronounced the final blessing, it was with relief that Clarissa, now enveloped in a warm velvet cloak, left the church with her husband—and with Letty dabbing at her eyes with a lace handkerchief.

She soon found herself alone with Christopher in the coach taking them back to Ashton Park. The whole day had taken on an air of unreality and she found it almost impossible to believe that the man sitting next to her was now her husband. She had married him but did not know him. She glanced obliquely at him, telling herself how fortunate she was when she gazed at his bronze, clean-cut profile and proud features, and realised, not for the first time, how incredibly handsome he was, and began to think of the physical side of their marriage, of her duty, and all that would come later, and she experienced a curious mixture of terror and excitement and prayed she wouldn't disappoint him.

She remembered his kiss and how he had made her feel suddenly alive, rekindling desires she had suppressed for so long, desires that she had told herself she would never experience again, which proved how little she knew her own body. The memory of that kiss brought colour flooding to her cheeks and she looked away, but too late, for at that moment Christopher looked at her and laughed softly. Taking her cold hand in his own, he lightly touched the narrow golden ring on her finger before raising it to his lips.

This simple act of reassurance released her from her anxiety and she began to relax. The icy numbness that had gripped her from the moment she had left home for the church began to melt, and the feel of his lips on her fingers sent a strange thrill soaring through her.

'Tell me what you were thinking—that made you look away?'

'Oh—nothing really, only how lucky I am.'

'Are you happy?'

She nodded. 'Yes.'

'No regrets?'

'No—none that I can think of.'

He contemplated her for a moment and Clarissa was riveted by his gaze. 'Did I tell you that you look adorable?'

'Yes, before we left for the church.'

'Then I will tell you again. You are beautiful, Clarissa—like some perfect work of art.'

She laughed shyly. 'I'm sure every groom says that to his bride on their wedding-day. I am no more beautiful than any other.'

His eyebrows rose. 'I think I should be the judge of that, and perhaps they don't all mean it as sincerely as I.' His eyes darkened as they fastened on her soft pink lips, moist and slightly parted, revealing her small white teeth. His voice was husky when he spoke, which sent a tremor through Clarissa. 'Would you mind if I kissed my wife now we are alone, for I fear that when we arrive back at the house I shall not have you to myself for—let me see—at least eight hours?'

Clarissa's eyes widened in mock amazement and her mouth formed a silent 'Oh'. 'That long?' and she smiled softly. 'Then in that case I think you should.'

Christopher's gaze was intent and he was looking at her in a way he had never dared look at her before lest he betray how he really felt, and he prayed by all he held sacred that he would be able to bring her all the joy and happiness she was meant for.

Sliding his hand beneath her cloak and around her waist, he pulled her towards him, his eyes dark and full of tenderness. He did not kiss her at once but studied her face, close to his, with a kind of wonder, his eyes gazing intently into hers before settling on her parted lips, which he at last covered with his own, his arm about her waist tightening, drawing her closer, until their bodies were moulded together and Clarissa could feel the hardness of his muscular body. Her heart was beating so hard that she was sure he must feel it. His lips, moist and warm, caressed hers, becoming firm and insistent as he felt her respond, kindling a fire inside her with such exquisite slowness, a whole new world exploding inside her. She raised her arms, fastening them around his neck, returning his kiss, her lips soft and clinging, moving upon his in a caress that seemed to last for an eternity.

Christopher's lips left hers and he buried them in the soft hollow of her throat. He heard the sharp intake of her breath but she did not pull away from him, and when he lifted his head and looked at her his eyes burned with naked desire. Clarissa trembled inside, feeling as if she was on the threshold of something unknown, which caused fear to course through her but also something else, a longing so strong that she wanted to pull him towards her, for him to kiss her with all the savage intensity of his desire.

She had been kissed before by Edward, but never like this. His kisses had not aroused the passion that Christopher's did, a passion so primitive, which swept through her, a passion almost beyond her control, evoking feelings she had never felt before, and this new awareness of her own desire shook her to her very core.

Seeing the hunger in her eyes, Christopher sighed deeply. 'So—I was right.'

'Right?' she whispered. 'What do you mean?'

'That first time I saw you, to me, as a stranger, you seemed to have everything—beauty, wealth, every young man in London at your feet—but you seemed to want none of it. You seemed so cold, so remote, as if only part of you was alive. You became an enigma to me, Clarissa, and I was determined to get to know you better, convinced that behind your cold façade there beat the heart of a warm and passionate woman—and, it seems, I was right. I hope you will never regret your decision to marry me.'

'How could I? You have given me everything I could possibly want.'

His dark brows knit together as he considered her thoughtfully, a shadow of doubt darkening his eyes. 'Everything?'

Just for a moment her eyes clouded but quickly they became clear, as if she had suddenly come to a decision, and she looked at him directly, a determined tilt to her chin. 'Yes—everything,' and, smiling, she leaned forward and kissed him gently on the lips, just as the carriage came to a halt at the bottom of the steps of Ashton Park.

CHAPTER SIX

THE wedding breakfast at Ashton Park was a prolonged and happy affair, a festive air prevailing throughout. The food was exquisite, the champagne cold and delicious, the toasts numerous. Christopher was charming, regaling them with fascinating stories of his native America, smiling softly when he caught Clarissa's eye, silently reminding her of their kiss and the night to come. Richard acted the perfect host, an adoring Laura looking rather fetching by his side.

They chatted and laughed and sipped champagne until, what seemed like hours later, they sat back in their chairs, replete and exhausted. Richard left to escort Laura and her father home. Clarissa sighed and looked at Letty, who had seemed unusually preoccupied and quiet throughout the meal, nervously toying with her napkin, and on reflection Clarissa thought she had behaved rather oddly all week. She had blithely helped with the arrangements for the wedding, but at times she had been nervous and slightly agitated. Something was wrong, she could sense it, and she reproached herself for being too consumed with her own affairs not to notice.

Christopher poured himself another brandy, and Clarissa stood up.

'Come on, Letty, let's take our coffee into the drawing-room, shall we, and then I'll go and change?' She smiled at Christopher. 'Join us when you've finished your brandy.'

Clarissa relaxed on the sofa, watching Letty with concern as she slowly paced up and down, sipping her coffee. They made small talk for several minutes about the wedding and preparations that had to be made for going to America, until Clarissa could no longer ignore what was on her mind.

'What's wrong, Letty?'

'Wrong?' she asked, somewhat surprised.

'Yes, something's amiss—I can tell.'

'Nonsense. Nothing's wrong,' she replied, trying to sound casual.

Clarissa rose and went to stand beside her, studying her face closely. 'Come, Letty. It's me—remember? I know you too well. You cannot deceive me. You've been on edge ever since you got here. What is it?'

She shrugged. 'Nothing. But if you think I've been a little on edge then it's probably just excitement over the wedding. It came as quite a shock, you know.'

'Are you sure that's it?' asked Clarissa, not convinced. 'And that it doesn't concern me?'

'You? Of course not.'

Clarissa shook her head and sighed. If there was something wrong and Letty didn't want to tell her then she couldn't make her. 'Well—if you're sure——'

'Yes, I am sure—don't trouble your head about me; you have other things to think of now and I think you should be with your husband—not me. He's a wonderful man, Clarissa. You're so lucky.' She lowered her eyes, hating herself for her deceit. She would tell Clarissa about Edward before she left for London, but not just yet. It would be too cruel to tell her now. She would not be responsible for spoiling her first night of love and, besides, perhaps tomorrow, after a night spent in the arms of the American, Clarissa would not care one way or the other whether Edward was alive or dead. But how Letty wished that Clarissa could sail away to America and never find out the truth.

'Yes—you're right, I am lucky, aren't I? But

although you say otherwise I am still not convinced there isn't something you have to tell me.' She turned and glanced out of the window at the gathering dusk, noticing the long shadows slanting through the branches of the tall elms, and she sighed, about to turn away, but her eye was drawn to a large carriage travelling up the drive. She watched it come closer, the horses lathered and the carriage travel-stained with dust, indicating that it had come a long way. 'If there is something, Letty, then I'm afraid it will have to wait. I think we have a visitor—although I have no idea who it can be. I'll go and see.'

Clarissa went out into the hall, followed by Letty. She too had seen the carriage and an awful premonition as to who it could be filled her with foreboding. Clarissa flung open the big double doors and stepped outside, the wind catching hold of her skirts and whipping them about her ankles. The carriage came to a halt, an elegant black carriage, and Clarissa suddenly went icy cold when she recognised the familiar coat of arms emblazoned on the door panel. It was the Montgomery crest.

She stared at it, unable to believe what she saw, but then she told herself that it must be Edward's father and reproached herself for not having written to tell him of her marriage. She watched one of the footmen step down from the front of the carriage and open the door, and she moved, as if to walk down the steps, but then froze, one hand rising to her throat, the colour draining from her face, her lips, and her eyes fastened on the man who emerged from the dark interior, a gold-handled walking cane in his hand.

He was quite tall and stepped out of the carriage with a languid, aristocratic grace, his attire elegant, to say the least. He wore a dark blue coat with paler pantaloons encasing his muscular legs, embroidered silk waistcoat, and there was white linen spilling from his neck and wrists.

Clarissa stared at him, unable to believe her eyes, remembering so vividly the pale blond hair falling in a heavy wave over his forehead and the handsome features, the cynical smile on his lips and hooded, lazy grey eyes. She stared at him with all the incredulous horror of one who had seen a ghost, unable to believe it. She must be dreaming. It could not be true. How could fate play such a cruel trick? Edward was dead and she was married to someone else.

He looked up at her and smiled lazily. Clarissa's face was whiter than death, one hand frozen at her throat, and she watched, feeling a terrible, agonising wrench at her heart. She scarcely breathed as he slowly climbed the steps, and then she knew her eyes were not deceiving her, that this was no dream.

'Edward,' she breathed, a hazy mist floating before her eyes, darkness threatening to engulf her. 'It cannot be you. They told me you were dead.'

'Dead? I assure you, Clarissa, that—as you can see—I am very much alive.'

It was then that Clarissa gave a desperate cry and crumpled on to the steps at Letty's feet. Alarmed, Letty fell to her knees beside her, taking her cold hand in her own while raising her face to Edward, complete and utter hatred blazing from her eyes.

'Why? Why did you have to come here? Why couldn't you leave her alone?'

Very slowly he smiled, a thin, cruel smile, his eyes like ice. 'I shouldn't have thought it necessary for me to have to explain my reasons to you, Letty, and, besides, London is a trifle dull just now—as well you know. Why did you not tell Clarissa I am alive?'

'Because I didn't want her to know. I hoped and

prayed to God she'd never find out. She's better off without you.'

'How could she not find out that I'm alive? Unless—God forbid—she intends staying down here forever and, anyway, shouldn't she be the judge of whether or not she's better off without me? I doubt she would agree with you,' he drawled.

On his way to join Clarissa in the drawing-room, Christopher heard Clarissa's strangled cry and halted in shock. Seeing the open door, he hurried outside, to find her lying in a crumpled heap on the top of the steps with Letty by her side. His dark face clouded with concern.

'Clarissa!'

'She's all right,' said Letty quickly. 'She's fainted, that's all.'

'Let me take her inside,' and, bending down, he picked her up effortlessly, cradling her in his arms, her head resting against his shoulder. It was only then, as he straightened up, that he became aware of the man who had paused halfway up the steps.

At first, taken unawares, Edward was startled by the tall man's sudden appearance and the familiarity he showed to Clarissa, and it was when their eyes met that recognition came to each man simultaneously.

'Permit me to introduce you,' said Letty, standing beside Christopher.

'I think the social distinctions can be ignored, thank you, Letty. We are already acquainted.'

'So,' said Edward, his cold grey eyes narrowed with murderous fury, 'it is you. The American I had the misfortune to encounter on my journey back to London.'

'The same, and I observe you have discarded your uniform.'

'Temporarily, I assure you,' he replied, his voice like

steel. 'We have an account to settle, you and I. You cannot have forgotten.'

'I have not forgotten, and neither have I forgotten the sordidness of the situation in which we met. As I remember it, the account was settled. Now—permit me to take Clarissa inside. It appears she has received quite a shock, and I suggest you leave this house before I do something I would not regret.'

'Wait,' cried Letty as he was about to turn away, her face a picture of confusion, wishing she knew what they were talking about. 'Wait, Christopher. Have you no idea who this is?'

'No, and nor do I wish to.'

She ignored his cutting remark. 'It is Edward. Edward Montgomery. He was betrothed to Clarissa before he went to Spain and was reported killed.' She looked from one to the other, feeling the tension between them, aware of an ominous, eerie silence wrapping itself about them.

Christopher did not reply at once; he just stared at Edward, showing neither shock nor surprise, his face a hard, inscrutable mask, the muscles tight. 'Dear God,' he said when he finally did speak, his voice not without contempt. 'How unfortunate for Clarissa.'

Still holding Clarissa, who was beginning to stir in his arms, he walked inside and into the drawing-room. Gently he laid her on the sofa and stood looking down at her, relieved to see that some of the colour had returned to her face. He was well aware of all the torment, the suffering she would feel when she came to, and it tore at his heart.

The first person she saw when her eyes fluttered open was Christopher, his dark form staring down at her, his eyes full of pain and concern but also something else, which puzzled her—understanding and pity. Letty stood beside him, anxiously worrying a handker-

chief in her fingers. Clarissa blinked her eyes to clear
the mist, wondering what she was doing, lying on the
sofa, and then she remembered Edward and that he
had come back to her, and her heart leaped and began
racing as her eyes moved round the room, searching
for him.

He stood, seeming very much at ease at the far side
of the room. She stared at him, unable to speak for
what seemed to be an eternity, and her eyes shone with
the unbelievable comfort of knowing he was alive, and
yet why, when he looked the same, did she feel that
she was looking into the face of a man she did not
know—a stranger?

Seeing her open eyes, he moved towards her, ignoring Christopher, whose face wore a hard mask of
disapproval. With Letty he stepped back to observe
the reunion between his wife and her one-time
betrothed.

Aware of and slightly amused by his audience,
Edward dropped to one knee beside the sofa and took
Clarissa's hand in his own. Slowly she reached out with
the other and gently touched his cheek with the tips of
her fingers to convince herself that it really was him.

'It is you,' she whispered. 'It really is you.'

'Yes. I must apologise if my sudden appearance
came as a shock, but I came as soon as I could.'

There was an impulse in Letty to rush forward and
drag him away from Clarissa, and Edward heard her
sharp intake of breath at this barefaced lie, but he
ignored it.

'I'm sure you did, but—but you were reported
killed.'

'That I didn't know until later.'

'What happened? Please—tell me.'

'It was during the battle at Albuera that my horse
was shot from under me, and afterwards grapeshot

shattered my leg. I was also injured in the chest. I lost consciousness, and I knew nothing else until I came to, only to find myself a prisoner of the French.'

A deathly pallor spread over Clarissa's face. So often she had pictured him lying wounded on the field of battle, his life's blood ebbing away. She couldn't bear to think of it. 'How did you get back to your regiment? Did you escape?'

'No, it was later, when I began to recover, that I was rescued by the partisans.' At this he remembered how they had come under cover of darkness and freed several prisoners. They were an odd-looking bunch, the partisans, dressed in a variety of uniforms, armed with carbine, pistol and lance, red flags tied to them, and it was with a stirring in his loins that he remembered in particular the black-haired beauty who had wielded lance and carbine like a man but who had also made his time spent in their camp more pleasurable. 'They returned me to my regiment,' he continued, 'but it was only to find that most of it had been wiped out.'

'How awful. Are you going back?'

'Yes. I was sent home to recuperate and shall return when the officers who returned with me to England have recruited fresh men.'

'I—I missed you so much, Edward. You and Simon.' Even as she said this she was vividly aware of Christopher standing behind Edward as if turned to stone, his hands clenched by his sides, but she did not look at him; she dared not.

'Yes, I know about Simon,' he replied, and the memory of Clarissa's brother touched a forgotten chord in his selfish heart. 'I'm sorry, Clarissa.' He looked at her pale face resting against the cushions, thinking she looked different somehow, different from when he had last seen her, before he had gone to fight with Wellington's army in Spain. Perhaps it was because of

the deprivations over the past months that he noticed,
although he had seen to it that he had not been without
female distractions. His attitude to love and women
had always been easygoing, take it or leave it, but,
looking at Clarissa now, he was almost bowled over by
his desire for her.

It had been his father who had insisted that he marry
Clarissa. He was a fiercely proud man and would not
have the ancient line of Montgomerys sullied by having
his heir marry just any woman. Clarissa Milton, the
daughter of his good friend Lord Milton, was the kind
of woman he wanted him to marry, to bear his grand-
children, not one of those unsavoury doxies he kept
company with in London. Edward had taken his father's advice and also taken advantage of Clarissa's
naïveté and innocence and wooed her, having to admit
that his father was right. She would make a perfect
wife. One he could keep tucked away in the country
while he continued to pursue the kind of life he had
become accustomed to in London. Yes—they would
get on well, providing she did not interfere with his
passion for women and entertaining his friends and the
green baize tables. He raised her fingers to his lips.

'Would you agree for us to be married before I
return to Spain?'

Before she had time to reply Christopher's voice
lashed the air like the crack of a whip. 'I think not,' he
said, unable to watch a moment longer this intimate,
touching scene and the possessive way Edward was
holding Clarissa's hand. 'And I would be obliged if you
would take your hands off her.'

Edward turned and stood up, fixing him with a cold
stare, wondering, not for the first time, as to this
American's presence here at Ashton Park. At first he
had thought he must be a friend of Letty's—after all,
she had a reputation for keeping an odd collection of

friends. 'Oh, no—not this time. Clarissa is mine. We are to be married.'

Christopher stepped forward and he smiled, an absolutely chilling smile, his eyes gleaming with a deadly purpose, his voice cold and lethal. 'I don't think so. Clarissa is no longer free to marry you. She is my wife. We were married today.'

Christopher's words hung like a pall in the air, and an unearthly silence fell on the room. The moment was tense. The expression on Edward's face did not change, but his skin paled and a tiny muscle began to throb at the side of his eye. There was a cold glitter in his grey eyes when he fixed them on Christopher.

'You lie,' he spat.

'I am not in the habit of lying.'

Edward spun round to Clarissa, who had risen to a sitting position on the sofa, and his eyes, when they rested on hers, were merciless, his tone cutting. 'Is this true? Is this—this man your husband?' When she hesitated his voice rang out impatiently. 'Come, Clarissa—what have you to say?'

She nodded, gazing up at him, all her wretchedness and pain staring out of tear-filled eyes. 'Yes,' she whispered. 'It is true. But—I thought you were dead.'

'Dead or alive, I can see you lost no time in filling my place. How long is it—eight months? Were you in such a hurry to be rid of me? The next thing you'll be telling me is how much you love him,' he sneered, 'how you couldn't wait the decent interval of at least one year to marry. Well—for God's sake, spare me that.'

'Edward, please,' cried Clarissa in a terrible anguish, rising to her feet, one hand stretched out to him in her need to make him understand. 'You don't under-stand——'

Cutting short her protestations, Edward dashed away her hand. Christopher stepped towards them. The tone of this over-dandified Englishman had been deliberately offensive and had provoked his anger further, and he was torn by Clarissa's piteous defencelessness.

'Whether he understands or not is of no consequence. Six months or a year is neither here nor there. You were not married to him, so what does it matter? Clarissa is *my* wife.'

Edward's face was set hard, and a terrible hatred and jealousy directed at this American smouldered just beneath the surface that threatened to burst like a raging volcano, but an inborn caution told him to stay calm, to overcome the overwhelming lust to reach out and tear the man apart with his bare hands. 'Damn you for forcing your attentions on her, knowing she was spoken for.'

'You were dead,' he drawled flatly, 'or so everyone thought.'

'I am very much alive.'

'So I see. The devil has a way of taking care of his own, and if you intend to remain that way then I suggest you stay away from me—and especially Clarissa. So let that be an end to it.'

'An end to it? As far as I am concerned, there will never be an end to it. You have offended my honour— I have a mind to call you out. I want revenge and I will stop at nothing until I have obtained it.'

Clarissa gasped with horror at his words. 'No— Edward—please, you must not.'

Both men ignored her pleas and their eyes clashed with all the violence born of hatred. Christopher was all too well aware that beneath Edward Montgomery's cool exterior there was a ruthless vindictiveness that would know no bounds.

'Honour,' he scorned. 'I dispute that. There isn't an honourable bone in your body, and do not try and fool me. We both know that the revenge you talk of is not, as you would have me believe, for my marrying Clarissa. As I remember, you have the disgusting morals of a tom cat, and you make me sorry I didn't kill you when I had the chance. Your sort can only go one way and I thank God that by marrying Clarissa I have prevented her from being dragged down into the mire.'

Clarissa's eyes passed from one to the other in puzzlement as she tried to comprehend what they were talking about. None of it made any sense. That they should feel prejudice towards each other was understandable, but Christopher was talking of another matter which had nothing whatsoever to do with her or their marriage.

'You know each other, don't you?' she asked in shocked disbelief.

'Yes, we have met,' said Christopher. 'But I shall not offend your ears by telling you of the circumstances.'

Letty, who had stood apart, watching and listening to all that was being said, went cold when she saw Edward's eyes light on her for the first time in minutes, suddenly smiling, a thin, knowing smile, and now she braced herself. The moment of truth, the moment she had dreaded had come. He would take malicious pleasure in telling Clarissa of her deception. Oh, yes, he would glory in telling her. When he next spoke it was to Clarissa, but his eyes were fixed on her.

'Tell me, Clarissa, would you have gone ahead and married him—this American. . .?' and he flashed Christopher a mocking smile. 'Forgive me, but I do not remember your name. You did tell me, but it has slipped my mind. Would you have married him if you had known I was alive?'

The echo of his words lingered in the stillness of the room as all eyes became riveted expectantly on her. It was a question she had preferred not to ask herself because she could not endure knowing he might have refused her when he discovered she didn't have a penny to her name.

'I—I don't know,' she faltered. 'Please—don't ask me that.'

Slowly and with a deadly purpose Edward sauntered to where Letty stood, his limp not quite as pronounced as it had been. Considering the severity of his injured leg, he was lucky in the fact that he had kept his where others had lost theirs. His smashed bones had knit with remarkable speed due to the punishing series of exercises he had put himself through, determined to regain full strength quickly. He fixed Letty with a cunning stare, aware of what the impact of his words would be.

'Why didn't you tell her, Letty? Why didn't you tell Clarissa that I was alive and back in London? That you saw and spoke with me yourself and that my intention was to come down here to Ashton Park?'

Clarissa's heart suddenly missed a beat and she thought she was going mad. She stared at Letty in disbelief. 'No—no, Letty. Tell me it isn't true. Tell me Edward is lying.'

Letty looked into her eyes, seeing the hurt, the pain, and knowing the accusations would come later, but she firmly believed that what she had done was right. She squared her shoulders, meeting her gaze unflinchingly. 'No. He is telling the truth.'

'So,' breathed Clarissa. 'That is what you've been keeping from me. I knew there was something.'

Edward laughed, a low, cruel sound. 'And you are supposed to be Clarissa's friend—her closest and dearest friend,' he sneered. 'What kind of friend is it that would practise such deceit?'

Letty looked at him steadily, reading the mockery on his face, but her gaze did not falter. 'I am her friend,' she said coldly. 'That is precisely why I did not tell her. You are a liar and a cheat, Edward, and many more things besides. I couldn't begin to list them all. You are a man without morals or principles, and dishonour the very name you bear. You could have written to Clarissa, letting her know you were still alive. You had your chances, and then when you returned to London—at least three weeks ago—you could have written or come straight down here, but you chose not to,' and her eyes glittered with contempt. 'I don't know who it was that kept you in town—but I hope she was worth it.' She heard Clarissa gasp and moved towards her. 'God knows, I wanted to tell you, Clarissa, but I couldn't. I truly believed—and I still do, I might tell you—that he would have brought you nothing but heartache. For you to marry the likes of him would be like casting pearls before swine.'

'That is not true,' snapped Edward, beginning to lose some of his control. 'She is lying.'

'Stop—stop—please stop,' cried Clarissa, covering her ears with her hands. 'I cannot bear it. Oh, Edward—you should have written. You can't know what it was like for me. I have lain awake night after night, fighting battle after battle, not knowing whether you were alive or dead. Thousands were killed or wounded, yet I heard nothing of you—never a word. All I could do was wonder and pray and—and then your father. . .he. . .he told me you had been reported killed. I was devastated, but I had to come to terms with that. You must understand.'

'You came to terms with it a mite too quickly for my liking, Clarissa,' he said with brutal sarcasm. 'However,' and he turned from her sharply, 'I do realise the impropriety of my coming here today. I am well aware that this is your wedding-night and I should hate to rob you of a single minute of it, so I shall leave you to get on with it.'

'But where will you go?' cried Clarissa. 'You cannot go back to London tonight.' She suddenly looked imploringly at Christopher, her eyes bright with tears. 'Christopher—please——' But there the words froze on her lips and she suddenly felt very afraid. His dark face had paled and his narrowed eyes held a frightening glitter, and she realised that what he felt for Edward went deeper than anger, deeper even than hate. It was something she did not recognise and therefore could not understand.

But Christopher had read her mind, that she wanted him to stay at Ashton Park for the night, and the look he gave her was hard and unyielding, his tone low with contempt. 'No, Clarissa. How dare you ask that of me? He will not share the same roof as me tonight—or any other night. He can go and rot in hell for all I care.'

Edward laughed, a light, brittle sound, but there was no hiding his underlying tension. 'Worry not, Clarissa. I shall stay at the Black Boar here in Ashton tonight and should this. . .husband of yours not reach your expectations then you will know where to find me,' and he turned and strode out into the hall.

Clarissa noticed his limp and was brutally reminded of all he must have suffered in Spain, and her tender heart went out to him. A tearing sob broke from her. He couldn't leave, not now that she had found him again, and, gathering up her skirts, she hurried after him, avoiding Christopher's hand when he reached out to stop her. 'Edward—wait. For pity's sake, please—wait.'

He stopped and turned, and she came to a halt in front of him, her face awash with tears. 'I'm sorry,' she gulped. 'I know how much I must have hurt you. Please—you must forgive me.'

He looked at her hard for several moments and his eyes travelled with a lazy insolence over her white wedding dress, from the warm glow of the pearls around her slender neck down to her slippered feet before fastening on her face. 'Tell me, Clarissa, is that the dress you would have worn at our wedding?'

She stared at him in horror. 'Oh, no—no—that would not have been fair.'

'Fair on whom?' he said scathingly. 'Me or your American husband?' He looked back at Christopher, a cynical curl to his lips. 'As you will know, I am a gambling man,' he said slowly, 'and I will lay odds that Clarissa will come back to me in the end.'

Christopher's sleek black brows rose mockingly. 'I am a gambler of some skill myself, and I would not bet on that,' he replied.

'Oh—I would. You see—I hold the trump card.'

'And that is?'

'It is me she still loves. Think of that when you lie with her tonight. I shall have her in the end.' With a satisfied smile he turned and left the house.

Clarissa watched him go, without a smile or a word of affection or even farewell, and she bowed her head, thinking that he might just as well be dead to her. The sound of the closing door and his feet dying away down the steps was like a death-knell to her already breaking heart. She stared at the closed door for several moments until, filled with panic that she might never see him again, she hurled herself forward. She couldn't let him go—not like this.

'Edward,' she called, crushed with misery, but suddenly hands caught her, holding her in a hard grip, pulling her back, and she was enraged to find herself helpless.

'Clarissa, are you out of your mind? Let him go,' Christopher commanded sharply.

'No,' she cried, whirling round in his arms, a wild expression in her eyes. 'No—I have to make him understand why I married you. I cannot let him go like this. I may never see him again.'

'And for that I will thank God,' he growled.

'That's unfair, Christopher,' she said, her voice quivering with anger. 'We were to have been married. Can you blame him for being angry, coming home after what he's been through, only to discover that the woman he should have married has married someone else? I don't know what he's done to make you speak of him as you do, but whatever it is it cannot possibly justify this terrible hatred you feel for him.'

Christopher remained silent, his expression hard, his hands clenched by his sides, wanting to tell her what had taken place between them at Winchester but at the same time not wanting to be the one to shatter her illusions.

She stepped back and looked at them both, her eyes full of pain and accusation. 'You deceived me—both of you. You should have told me.'

'Oh, Clarissa,' said Letty. 'I wanted to—you've no idea how much—but I just couldn't. Do you really believe Edward would have married you when he found out about your father and the fact that you no longer have a penny to your name? He wouldn't. He would have dropped you like a stone.'

Clarissa's lips curled scornfully. 'What a low opinion you have of him, Letty. What can he possibly have done to make you hate him so? And yes—yes, I tell you, he would have married me, but you tricked me, both of you, and you had no right. I shall never forgive you for keeping this from me—either of you. I had a right to know so that I could choose for myself,' and with a choked sob and a swirl of skirts she turned sharply and fled up the stairs to seek the sanctuary of her room, but not before Christopher had seen fresh tears shining in her eyes.

CHAPTER SEVEN

CHRISTOPHER entered Clarissa's room and moved towards the bed, where she lay face down, with utter disregard to the ruin she was doing to her wedding finery, her face buried in the pillows and sobbing as though her heart would break. He looked down at her and his throat constricted with pain at her sheer loveliness. As she lay there in the flickering golden glow of the fire and candle-light, her pale blonde hair a wild tangle about her, he thought no one in the whole world was as lovely as she and he cursed Edward Montgomery with every fibre of his being. His very presence had withdrawn her a distance of a thousand miles, and what was in Christopher's heart was like death itself.

As he saw her despair, rage rose inside him against Montgomery, and he wondered what manner of man he was that could inspire such a love as hers, but also so much devastating misery. He let his gaze wander around the tastefully furnished room, this room he was to have shared for the few nights they were to remain at Ashton Park, an essentially feminine room, but, he thought bitterly, that was unlikely now. His gaze rested on the tantalising fine white lace nightdress Clarissa's maid had left draped over a velvet armchair near the fire, and he groaned inwardly, knowing he would not make her his wife in the true sense of the word until she had cleansed her heart of Edward Montgomery.

Sensing his presence, she turned her tear-drenched face and peered up at him, huge droplets hanging on her lashes like diamonds. He was so still, watching her, his face a hard, unreadable mask, and, seeing him, she felt renewed anger surge through her and her tears became frozen on her flushed cheeks.

'What do you want?' she asked coldly.

'Want?' he drawled with a hint of sarcasm, her anger inciting his own. 'Do I have to have a reason for entering my wife's bedroom?'

'Wife?' she scorned, feeding her anger with her words. 'I might not be your wife if you'd been honest with me.'

'What do you mean?'

'You know perfectly well what I mean. No wonder you were in such a hurry for the wedding to take place, having me believe it was because you wanted to get back to America when all the time it was because you knew Edward was alive and he——'

'Enough,' he snapped coldly. 'Hear me out first, Clarissa. Your accusations are unjust. I do not deny that I met him just the once, and I swear to you that I did not know who he was until today.'

'And I am expected to believe that?'

'Believe what you like but, as I told him, I do not lie. What a low creature you must think me, Clarissa— but not as low as Edward Montgomery. But this I do know. Letty spoke the truth when she said he was a cheat and a liar. He is utterly corrupt, rotten to the very core—and this worthless libertine is the man you say you love and wanted to marry.'

Clarissa leapt quickly off the bed, beside herself with fury, and her eyes blazed into his. 'How dare you make the one thing I have loved so vile?' she flared. 'I will not listen to your accusations. I do not believe you.'

'Because you don't want to believe me. You cannot get it into your head that your beloved Edward is anything other than what you know of him—which, it seems, is very little.'

'Little?' she flared. 'I knew him well enough to say I'd marry him.'

'I doubt that—but, just supposing you had married him, do you think for one minute that he would have loaned Richard the money to save this place, your home? Because if you think that then you are a fool.'

His mention of Ashton Park and the cold disdain with which he uttered the words were like having a bucket of cold water poured over her, and she was suddenly reminded of all he had done for her and was full of contrition. He had offered her strength, security and understanding, which she had accepted gladly. She couldn't throw it back in his face. She sighed deeply, some of her anger evaporating.

'I'm sorry, Christopher, and perhaps I am a fool. You must think me extremely ungrateful.'

'The last thing I want is your gratitude,' he said coldly.

'Is it true—that you didn't know Edward was alive?'

'Yes.'

'But Letty knew. She could have told me.'

'Letty loves you more than anyone else in the world and she would not hurt you intentionally. Because of her past knowledge of your so-called betrothed— which, I might add, seems anything but honourable— she considered that what she was doing was right. She went through hell, keeping it from you, but she truly believed she was doing it for your own good.' Smiling crookedly, he moved away from her, pausing halfway to the door and turning to look at her again. 'You should thank me, Clarissa, for by marrying you I have saved you from an infinitely worse fate than death.'

'Where are you going?' she asked as he again turned away from her.

'To my room. And you needn't worry,' he said, his lips twisting cruelly. 'I shan't be bothering you tonight.'

'What do you mean?' she whispered in bewilderment.

'You know what I mean plain enough,' and when he turned and looked at her again his dark eyes began to gleam oddly and one sleek black brow went up. 'You can keep your chaste sanctity, my dear. Do you think I would stay with you tonight as, I might remind you, is my right, lie with you, touch you, all the while knowing you were wishing it was your precious Edward who was beside you?' He looked at her long and cool. 'It is obvious by the way you rush to his defence that you still care for him a great deal, so until the time when it is otherwise I will bid you goodnight.'

He went out, leaving Clarissa staring at the closed door, feeling so utterly bereft, thinking what an awful mess everything was.

A merciful numbness filled her mind as she listened to his footsteps dying away on the landing and she wanted to run after him, to appeal to his emotions, but she knew that while ever Edward was uppermost in her heart he would remain implacable; he would not yield from his cool verdict and she would continue to sleep alone. He had been angry and with good reason, and as she stared into the dying embers of the fire she took stock of all that had happened since she had returned home as his wife, suddenly feeling so very tired and drained of all emotion. Her feelings towards Edward were all confused and her mind seemed to be going round in circles. Why had she been so ready to believe him dead? Why hadn't she waited before rushing into marriage with someone else? But, she told herself, she couldn't have waited if she'd wanted to. Not with her father's creditors baying at the door.

Her thoughts turned to Christopher. Of her own free will she had married him, nothing could change that, and, she thought sadly, it was too late to weep for

Edward and what might have been. She and Christopher were man and wife and she would honour that, but what her feelings were towards him she couldn't say—only that they were different from those she felt for Edward. Christopher had asked her if she believed Edward would have married her, knowing of her circumstances, without a dowry and with the added shame of her father's suicide. And would Edward have secured Ashton Park as he had done? For her own peace of mind she had to know so that she could put things right, and to do this she must see him tonight, for tomorrow he would return to London and she might never see him again. It was a problem only she could resolve.

Christopher, lying fully clothed on the bed and hearing the soft thud of horse's hoofs, crossed over to the window and, looking out, saw the dark silhouette of a horse and rider galloping hard across the park. Moonlight picked out the silver flanks of the horse, which he recognised immediately as Clarissa's horse Melody, and he was filled with a dreadful suspicion that she was in the saddle. Cursing softly, he hurried to her room, flinging the door wide open. On finding it empty, he became consumed with a cold, blinding fury, knowing then, without doubt, that the rider had indeed been his wife and that she was going to the Black Boar to see Edward Montgomery. He paused only to don his cloak and it wasn't long before he was riding after her.

The wind had risen, plucking strands of hair from beneath Clarissa's hat, whipping them about her face as she rode her horse hard, driven by a compelling need to see Edward for one last time. The confusion in her heart drove her on through the park until at last she saw the dark buildings of the village of Ashton, and looming above the houses was the square, battlemented tower of the church, standing stark and ghostly against the night sky—the church where she had been married that very day. She rode up the straggling street until she came to the Black Boar.

Only a few men were inside the inn, seated on the crude wooden benches that flanked the long tables. Edward was one of them, sitting with his back towards her. He turned, feeling the cold draught from the open door, and she moved into the centre of the room, the soft glow from the oil light shining full on her. He recognised her at once and surprise caused his eyes to widen, but then he smiled thinly, a smug, self-satisfied smile, and he rose, sauntering to where she stood.

He looked untidy without his jacket, his shirt open at the collar, the fine white linen stained with alcohol. Clarissa was disappointed, never having seen him like this; he had always been so immaculate. It came as some surprise to her to find he had lost some of that magical power to stir the old attraction that had kept her love attached to him for so long. He had also drunk a considerable amount, for his eyes were bloodshot, his aristocratic countenance flushed. She had always been aware of his capacity to absorb large amounts of alcohol—what man didn't? But this was the first time she had seen him lose some of his dignity. When he spoke his voice was slow and a little thick. He gave her a profoundly mocking bow.

'Why, Clarissa—this is an unexpected pleasure. I did not expect you quite so soon.'

His lack of elementary politeness irked her somewhat. He had not tried to hide the sarcasm in his tone. 'Why were you so sure I would come?'

'Because I knew you would be unable to resist the temptation of seeing me before I left for London in the morning. But isn't this a little irregular—I mean, isn't it supposed to be your wedding-night?'

An embarrassed flush spread over her face when she noticed the men at the tables had ceased their talking. She had become the object of curiosity and, whether they recognised her or not, she didn't want to stand there long enough to find out. 'Isn't there somewhere we can talk, Edward? Somewhere less public?'

A sly smile curled his lips. 'Of course—that is, if you don't mind my room.'

'No—anywhere.'

Still smiling, he led her up the narrow stairs and along a dimly lit landing. She entered his room, taking little notice of its shabbiness and the big four-poster bed that dominated it. Edward went over to the fire, kicking the logs alive, their orange sparks shooting up the blackened chimney. He turned and faced her.

'Well, Clarissa,' he said softly, a strange light entering his eyes as they travelled insolently over her slender form, over her close-fitting habit, emphasising the slimness of her body. S'truth, he thought, what a shape, and he realised, as the blood pounded in his temples, that she had more to offer than he had realised. 'Tell me why you are here. Can it be that your husband does not live up to your expectations?'

'Please, Edward—don't,' she said, choosing to ignore the implication of his words. 'He has no idea that I'm here.'

'Of course he hasn't—otherwise you wouldn't be. But why are you here?'

'You know why.'

'No. Tell me. Is it because now, after finding out that I am alive, you are sorry you married your American?'

'I don't know—truly.'

'But then, perhaps if I had been dead it would have saved you the embarrassment of your betrayal, your treachery.'

She gasped, angered by his accusation. 'Treachery? No—never that.'

He moved closer to her, his eyes fixed on her face, having narrowed to thin slits. 'I find it hard to believe how easily you forgot me, Clarissa.'

'I never forgot you,' she said emphatically. 'You have no idea how I wanted so much for the reports of your death to be lies. I tried not to believe it and you can have no idea how I dreamed of your coming home—so that we could be married, but. . .' She sighed, lowering her eyes. 'Oh—what's the use in talking now? It's too late. I am no longer free.'

A cunning glint appeared in Edward's eyes. The American had made a fool of him, had touched his honour in a way no other man ever had, not only when he had intervened in the matter of that young trollop at the inn in Winchester but also by taking Clarissa from him—which was too much to be borne. He knew that his success in winning her back, therefore exacting his revenge, depended upon all his powers of persuasion. 'A sermon doesn't make a marriage, Clarissa. You can be free of him—the wedding can be annulled if you swear it has not been consummated.'

For a moment she dispassionately studied this man she had once sworn to love forever, and shook her head slowly. 'No, Edward. Nothing is the same as when you left. I am not the same—although I am only now becoming aware of it. My marriage cannot be annulled. The vows I made are sacred. I married Christopher of my own free will and I will not betray him. He is my husband in the sight of man and God.'

At her words there was a sudden change in Edward's manner and his features became taut with a strange glow in the depths of his eyes, which was beginning to make Clarissa feel uneasy. She moved away from him, remembering why she had come, the question she must ask for her own peace of mind.

'Edward, there is a reason why I had to see you—something I have to know. Since—since coming home, what do you know of my circumstances?'

'What do you mean?'

She looked at him directly. 'Would you have married me—without a dowry?'

He looked slightly nonplussed. 'Dowry?' He ran his fingers through his untidy hair, irritated by her question. What had her dowry got to do with anything? 'What are you talking about, Clarissa?'

'When my father died he left Richard and myself nothing but a mountain of debts. He lost all his money gambling. Everything had to be sold to pay off his creditors.'

A look of genuine shock and amazement spread over Edward's face. So, thought Clarissa with a sinking heart, he didn't know.

'Good Lord. I had no idea. I knew he had debts—what gambler doesn't? But to be fool enough to lose everything——'

'Yes—everything,' she replied, fixing him with an unwavering stare. 'And do you know how my father died? Did no one tell you? Because I find it hard to believe you have not heard the scandal—which rocked London at the time.'

'No. I knew he was dead—Letty Davenport told me—but I haven't been home to Buckinghamshire for longer than a couple of days——' He faltered, having no wish to disclose how he'd spent his time in London with the highly delectable young actress, Lucy Marchant, who was appearing at the Theatre Royal in Drury Lane. They had hardly left her rooms in two weeks. 'Father was in Brighton, you see, and——'

'My father shot himself, Edward,' she said quietly, cutting him short. 'He committed suicide.'

Edward was stunned, and she watched the play of emotions on his handsome face.

'Well, Edward,' she continued, giving him no time to put his thoughts in order, 'would you have still married me—penniless and with the shame of my father's suicide? I need to know. Did you love me enough to do that?'

He was taken aback by her question and for a moment they looked at each other as if both were carved from stone.

'Marriage,' he murmured at last. 'Good Lord— why—of—of course I would. ' But his voice died away, flat and unconvincing.

Clarissa wanted to believe him, but she knew with a sickening sense of reality that he was lying, and the face that looked into hers was not that handsome, beloved face it had once been. That was a sweet fantasy, a cherished illusion that had been shattered forever. Edward did not love her, had never loved her, not in the way she had wanted to be loved. He would have used her to serve his own interests, nothing more. It should hurt, but, strangely, it didn't, and if it didn't hurt then could it be that she didn't love him either?

She smiled bitterly. 'Don't try and fool me any more, Edward. I can see the truth in your eyes. You wouldn't have married me—even had you wanted to—and I very much doubt that now. Your father would never have allowed you to marry me anyway.'

He remained silent, looking at her hard, swaying slightly on his feet, the unspoken truth staring from his eyes. She turned from him, suddenly eager to leave this sordid room, the oil lamp making grotesque, monstrous shapes on the whitewashed walls. She wanted to get back to Ashton Park as quickly as possible—and to Christopher, and she prayed he would never find out that she had come here tonight. He would never forgive her.

'I don't think there's anything more to be said between us—do you?' and she moved towards the door, but in an instant he covered the distance between them, as light and fleet as a cat. He stood in front of her menacingly, blocking her path to the door. There was a dangerous, threatening glint in his cold grey eyes and she could not repress the icy fear that crept through her. When he spoke his voice was low and each word he uttered precise, but underlying them she could sense a violence that threatened to erupt at any moment.

'Before you go, Clarissa, tell me about your American and how it was that he came to marry you. Did you have to lie about your circumstances to him?'

'No, I didn't have to. Christopher and I have always been perfectly honest with each other. He has loaned Richard enough money to secure Ashton Park.'

For a moment his face did not change its expression, but suddenly what she had told him caused him to laugh mirthlessly. 'You mean, he bought you? You sold yourself to the highest bidder?'

'There were no other bidders,' she said drily. 'Only Christopher.'

'And he promised to pay all your father's debts for your own sweet self,' he scoffed. 'How very touching, and how unworthy of you.'

'Unworthy? No—I don't think so. I had no choice.'

'And—do you love him?'

'He—he has been very good to me.'

'I asked you if you love him,' he persisted.

'He is a wonderful man——'

'But you don't love him,' he said with an odious smile of triumph, with such finality that she stared at him unbelievingly, noting the immense satisfaction he derived from this knowledge, and she wished with her whole heart that she could have said otherwise.

'Please—move out of my way, Edward. The way you talk, you cannot blame me for thinking you are jealous of Christopher.'

Suddenly his face changed and his lips curled viciously. 'Jealous? And why shouldn't I be jealous? He's taken the woman I would have married.'

'No,' she replied coldly. 'Only the woman you did not love. And now,' she said, breathing deeply, seeing the fire in his eyes, that she knew spelt danger, knowing it had indeed been madness to come here, 'please move out of my way. I am leaving for America within the week. I doubt we shall meet again.'

'Then I tell you that this, our last night together, will be one to remember. I know you still love me, Clarissa, not that—that American you've so foolishly married, so come, why not show it?'

He moved closer to her and she could feel his breath hot on her face and the smell of spirits, which made her stomach churn. She stepped back, her face showing revulsion.

'No. What you suggest is an adulterous love—the sort I despise,' and she smiled scornfully. 'You talk of love, of my love, of not being loyal and accusing me of treachery—but what of your love, Edward? Not once in all the time I have known you have you mentioned that.'

'Haven't I? Then permit me to show you. I'm going to love you, Clarissa. I'm going to make you so happy that you'll never want to leave me to go back to your American. You'll beg me on your knees to let you stay.'

'No—never,' she cried angrily. 'I wish to leave now. Let me go.'

'No.'

'Do you intend to hold me here by force?'

'Only if I have to.'

Panic and fear overcame Clarissa and she began to tremble. He noticed and smiled with smug satisfaction.

'Why—you're trembling. Come, Clarissa,' he drawled, his voice thick with passion, 'you think I don't love you—but I do.' He placed his hands heavily on her shoulders, looking deeply into her eyes. At his touch she struggled, trying to free herself from his grip, but they tightened, refusing to relinquish their hold. 'So,' he hissed, 'you want to fight me—well, all the better. I like a woman with spirit—one to match my own.'

Clarissa was suddenly filled with fear, but it was a different kind of fear from any she had ever known. Never, in all the time she had known him, had he been anything other than charming, and she had always believed that nothing could touch him, that nothing mattered, but as she faced him, his expression dark and ruthless, she knew that at last something had touched him enough to bring about this ill-mannered, drunken stranger. She was now in no doubt that it was Christopher who had brought about this change and, whatever had passed between them that first time they had met, it must have been something terrible. She knew with a sinking heart that she could have married anyone and he wouldn't have cared one iota—but because it was the American it was a different matter. He would destroy her if he could to get back at him.

The full consequence of what she had done by coming here swept over her and she was gripped by panic. Edward saw her fear, feeling her quivering body beneath his hands, but he only laughed, a deep, horrible, mocking sound that curled his lips, and a look of madness filled and dilated his eyes, which told her that his mere triumph over her, her very resistance, excited him much more than all her passive docility. He wanted her whatever the odds, and the very fact that she belonged to Christopher made him even more determined to possess her wholly. He would settle for nothing less than that she surrender herself to him completely—absolutely. She knew that she could expect no mercy from him. He would not be cheated out of his ultimate pleasure.

The very sight of Clarissa aroused a violent, unfamiliar desire in Edward, such as no woman had before, and his lust, combined with hatred, made him like a man possessed of the devil. Brutally he pushed her back towards the bed. She cried out and stumbled, but he caught her, throwing her on to the covers. An icy terror gripped her and she tried to get up, but he fell upon her, crushing her with his weight, his face close to hers, contorted with fury and passion as he began tearing at her clothes, his hands expert from long practice.

A fierce, merciless struggle began between them and he became like a mad beast tearing at its prey. Now that she was faced with the terrible prospect of being raped and possibly killed, renewed strength surged through Clarissa and she fought as if her life depended on it, like a wildcat turning on its tormentor, and in her blind fury her nails raked his face, his eyes, anywhere she could see his flesh, feeling an immense, unholy satisfaction when she drew blood.

He laughed, a fierce, demonical sound that sent a chill through her. 'That's it—fight, my beauty,' he hissed. 'Fight all you want. I shall soon have you crying and pleading for mercy. I shall enjoy teaching you to obey me—breaking that stubborn Milton pride.'

When she opened her mouth to scream his own covered hers, brutal and demanding, nothing left but lust and need, and he kissed her as he would a whore.

By some miracle she somehow managed to tear herself away and scramble to the edge of the bed, but he seized a handful of her thick hair, which had come loose, pulling her back with such force that she cried out, tears of helpless rage filling her eyes. Savagely he continued tearing at her clothes, and as he forced her legs apart he cursed loudly at the encumbrance of clothes. But she was finding it harder to defend herself, reality slipping further and further away, and despair overpowered her as she reached the limits of her strength and her struggles became feeble.

And then, abruptly, something happened and his weight left her. There was a dull thud and she ceased struggling, trembling in what remained of her clothes, the taste of blood in her mouth from a cut on her lip. Through a mist she looked up and discerned a terrifying, faceless figure looming over her. Instinct made her draw her defiled body into a ball and shove herself back against the head of the bed, where she huddled, quivering like a terrified child, clutching her torn bodice. In the wild tangle of her hair, her eyes, enormous and full of fear, accentuated the transparent whiteness of her face, streaked with blood.

She peered up at Christopher, who was in a towering jealous rage, his face contorted out of all recognition as he glared down at her, beside himself with fury. The spectacle of the vile and contemptible Edward Montgomery forcing his attentions on Clarissa and the pitiful state he had brutally reduced her to made him feel physically sick. He thanked God he had found her in time.

Clarissa did not ask herself by what miracle he happened to be there, to save her from what she had been about to suffer at Edward's hands; it was enough for her that he had come, regardless of the fury and anger he would be sure to vent on her. He glared down at her half-naked form bitterly. In the flickering glow of the lamp she was still lovely, although now tragically so, and he knew the sight of her should sicken him, but it didn't.

'You brainless little fool,' he hissed. 'Is there no room in that head of yours for sense? How dare you come here, looking for him? Did you think I would not find out? What did you imagine would happen when that animal got his hands on you? You could ask for nothing better—believe me.' His eyes took in her soft white flesh showing through the tattered remnants of her bodice and quickly he removed his cloak, throwing it to her contemptuously. 'Here—cover yourself.'

Clarissa seized it and clutched it to her. He turned and looked at Edward, who had got up from the floor, where, in his rage, Christopher had thrown him. He stood glowering at the tall American, his fists tightly clenched by his sides, and the trace Clarissa's finger-nails had left on his face trickled blood.

'Damn your filthy hide, Montgomery,' spat Christopher, his voice like a naked blade. 'She no longer has anything to do with you.'

'Perhaps not—but she did come looking for me, like a bitch on heat.'

Pure madness flamed in Christopher's eyes and he sprang at his adversary, grasping the front of his shirt and pulling his face close to his own, full of revulsion. 'And you should know all about that—being the dog that you are. Your methods of seduction leave a lot to be desired. I could kill you now but I will save that pleasure until later.'

Edward's lips twisted in an arrogant sneer, his grey eyes spitting venom as he knocked Christopher's hands away. 'Why, you are jealous—jealous because she preferred my bed to yours. But then, why shouldn't she? And how do you know she hasn't shared it with me before?'

Christopher eyed him with unconcealed scorn. 'Judging by what has happened here tonight, I doubt very much she would come back a second time.'

'At least I have given you a wedding-night to remember. You must have paid quite a price to get her to leave England and her home for that land of savages. Perhaps after tonight you'll consider she wasn't worth it.'

'Savages?' scoffed Christopher. 'That's a fine word, coming from you. You, who, it is said, belong to one of England's most noble families, are out of your class. You haven't an honourable, decent bone in your body. You are a low, stinking animal—not worthy of the blade with which I shall kill you.'

An ugly smile spread across Edward's features. 'No—it is I who will kill you. Nevertheless, if Clarissa had married me I would not have had to buy her as you have done. But then, you should know all about that—buying people.'

'What do you mean?'

'I've learnt quite a lot about you since this afternoon—and isn't that how you plantation owners in America get rich? By buying and selling human flesh, black flesh—slaves? Because as I see it there's nothing noble or honourable in that. How many Negro slaves do you own, eh? Fifty, a hundred, a thousand—or don't you know?'

'It's none of your damned business. Where I come from it's a perfectly normal practice.'

'I wonder if Clarissa will see it that way.'

'Whatever she thinks or feels has got nothing to do with you.' He turned back to Clarissa, who hadn't moved, and, pulling her towards him, wrapped his cloak about her trembling form before again facing

Edward. 'I'm taking my wife home, but be sure I shall return. You and I have a score to settle. I demand satisfaction for this night's work.'

Edward went very pale. 'You surprise me. I was under the impression that you Americans shot people in the back. However—you shall have it. It will give me immense pleasure to kill you. I shall not be cheated a third time.'

'Don't be too sure. Whatever you might think, we Americans are not all backwoodsmen. Like many of my fellow countrymen, I am an expert with pistol or blade, and I aim to make damned sure you rape no more defenceless women—high or low born.'

CHAPTER EIGHT

NOT a word was spoken between Clarissa and Christopher until they reached her room. She was oblivious to everything around her, utterly broken by all that had happened to her at Edward's hands. Her body felt bruised and defiled and weighted down with a terrible misery and despair, and the thought that she had to go on living after this night was inconceivable.

She stood in the centre of the room, still clutching Christopher's cloak about her, as if afraid to let it go. Christopher was suddenly overwhelmed with compassion. He wanted to go to her, to hold her, but he couldn't. He could not yet forgive her for going to Edward Montgomery. The memory of this night would live with him for a long time, longer than the sight of Clarissa's bruised and broken body. Because he had placed her on a pedestal her act of betrayal became harder for him to bear.

He turned from her and left the room to fetch Letty, and, when he returned with an anxious-looking Letty hard on his heels, Clarissa was still standing where he had left her, swaying slightly and pitiful to look at, wild and unkempt with her hair falling about her face, pale and frightened, her blue eyes wide open and staring.

'Oh, Clarissa,' breathed Letty. 'By all the saints—what has that monster done to you?' and, going to her, she gathered her in her arms, guiding her towards the bed, where she sat like an obedient child. Letty turned to Christopher, who was striding towards the door. 'Where are you going, Christopher? You're not leaving?'

He turned and looked at her, his face immobile. 'Yes. There is something I have to do. Something I have to take care of.'

Letty nodded, understanding, knowing without having to ask that he was returning to the Black Boar to settle the score with Edward. She couldn't blame him but thought, in his anger, that he had underestimated Edward. However confident Christopher might feel about his own prowess, Edward was a superb marksman and an expert with a sword.

His words penetrated Clarissa's tortured mind and realisation of where he was going and what he intended dawned on her. She tore herself from Letty's comforting arms and flung herself across the room, the cloak she had been so reluctant to relinquish falling to the floor, revealing the shameful ruin Edward had wreaked on her body. Her eyes were full of a desperate pleading when she looked into her husband's formidable face, gripping his arm fiercely.

'No,' she cried. 'Please don't go back there—you mustn't.'

He looked down at her, a cold glitter in his dark eyes. 'Don't try to stop me, Clarissa,' he said curtly. 'I have to. My honour is involved.'

'No, please—I know why you're going back, what you're going to do. Promise me you will not kill him. Whatever he has done, he does not deserve that.'

'No? Then perhaps you should have thought of that before you went looking for him.'

'H-how did you know I'd gone?'

'I heard you creep from your room and saw you ride off across the park towards Ashton. Where else would you be going if not to the Black Boar—and him? Did you think you could creep into his bed for a few hours and I would never find out? You underestimated me, Clarissa, if you thought that.'

'I—I'm so sorry——'

'The fact that you have betrayed me, have incurred my displeasure, does not seem to matter,' he said with heavy irony.

'Of course it does, and you have every right to be angry, but I did love him, Christopher, only I realise now that I did not know him, what he was capable of. . . I—I was so afraid——'

'Please—don't try explaining,' he scorned, 'and spare me the sordid details. What a pity I disturbed you before you could indulge your appetites for each other further.'

Clarissa stared at him in disbelief. 'It wasn't like that and you know it. You saw what the situation was, what he was doing to me. I had no idea he would behave as he did. It was as if some kind of monster had been unleashed.'

'And yet you want him to live. Clarissa, that man has abused you and damn near destroyed you. Don't ask me to ignore what he did tonight—I would rather hang.'

'And hang you shall if you kill him.'

He looked down at her, feeling her hand clinging to his arm with all her strength as tears began running unheeded down her cheeks. 'The minute he walked through the door earlier today he addled your wits. Come, now, tell me, if you had known he was still alive, would you have married me? Tell me, Clarissa— I have a right to know.'

'I don't know,' she cried miserably. 'Truly.'

'Do you still love him?' he went on remorselessly.

'Whatever love I had left he killed tonight.'

'I see,' he said, not totally convinced. 'However, because of your stupidity you have forced me to avenge you.'

'No,' she cried. 'I beg you not to. I no longer love

him but I cannot be the one to bring about his death.
If you kill him I shall blame myself. As surely as if I
had pulled the trigger I shall have killed him, and I
cannot live with that. The guilt would be too heavy for
me to bear. Please,' she whispered softly, 'if you kill
him his death will be between us forever.'

The anguish and pain on her pale face had their
effect, touching some hidden chord deep inside him.
He didn't know how to react to this terrible display of
grief, but he had to acknowledge the sense of her
words, fully aware that he had allowed his hurt masculine pride and anger to cloud his judgement.

'Haven't you thought what will happen if you do kill
him?'

He considered her intently and nodded slowly.
'Yes—I have. But put it another way, Clarissa. What
if Edward proves to be stronger than me? Have you
thought what will happen if he kills me?'

At his words she stared at him hard, not having
thought of this. Tonight her feelings had undergone a
considerable change so that she no longer knew what
to think, but when she thought of her life without
Christopher—her husband—on whom she had come
to depend like the very air she breathed, and whose
quiet strength she valued a great deal, she was bewil-
dered and confused. She covered her face with her
trembling hands. 'Dear God, no. Please, not that.
After all that has happened—after all I have lost—I
could not bear that too.'

Christopher sighed, deeply touched by her words.
'Very well, Clarissa. I promise you that I shall not kill
him—merely teach him a lesson he will not forget,'
and he turned from her and strode out of the room.

Back in his room, Christopher flung his jacket on to
the bed and, moving to the fireplace, rested his arms
on the mantelpiece, gazing into the fire.

He sighed, thinking over the night's events. Perhaps his anger had made him hasty. If he was honest with himself then he had to admit that he didn't want to kill Montgomery. He was a villain and he despised him, and it was right that he should be punished for what he had done, but he did not deserve to die for it. And Clarissa was partly to blame. She should never have gone looking for him. Anyway, the last thing he wanted was his death on his conscience. He would prefer to put the whole ugly episode behind him. But that was before one of the footmen brought him a note that had just been delivered to the house. It was from Edward, and the short missive told him that he would meet him at dawn in Huntsman's Quarry, where they would settle their differences with swords. Christopher uttered a sigh of resignation. So, he had no choice. He would have to fight. If he did not meet him he would be branded a coward, and that was unthinkable.

It was just before daybreak that he went to rouse Richard, urging him to get dressed quickly and meet him in the hall. It took him just a few minutes to tell him all that had happened.

The world as the two men rode through the park in a thick blanket of grey cloud was cold, everything about them dormant, gripped by a beautiful desolation. The ground was hard, the young shoots of spring held captive beneath a white, hoary frost, spread like a mantle over the land, showing tracks of rabbits and hoofprints of deer. The wind snaked a pathway round the naked trees, pointing their branches like gnarled fingers up to an as yet invisible sky.

They rode hard, staring straight ahead, grim-faced, the only sound being the blowing of their horses and the rhythmic pounding of their hoofs. As they approached Huntsman's Quarry nothing moved; it was oddly silent and deserted, the park hereabouts deeply wooded and, as Christopher looked into the semi-circular glade, he couldn't help thinking that it was aptly named and he remembered with an icy chill what Richard had told him before they had left the house, and could well imagine that this was where many a hunt had ceased. This was where, after spilling over the land like quicksilver, frenzied by excitement and their lust for blood, the liver- and white-coloured hounds, the death pack, trapped its quarry with a terrible ferocity, and with blood-curdling howls brought it to the ground, savagely tearing at the convulsive body.

They slowed their pace, advancing with caution deeper into the glade, the branches of the huge trees joining overhead, forming a tunnel. They scanned the dark shadows not only for Edward and his second but also for others, for the constables, for if the law had got wind that a duel was to be fought then it would spell disaster for them all.

Edward and his second, a servant who had accompanied him from London, were already there, and rode out of the dark shadows as they entered the glade. Quickly all four dismounted, Christopher divesting himself of his cloak and handing it to Richard, eyeing Edward carefully as he moved closer. In the cold light of dawn there was no trace of the drunken creature of last night, when the fumes of alcohol had clouded his mind. Now he met Christopher's gaze coldly.

'I trust you slept well,' he said with sarcasm, 'and that you said farewell to your bride, for I doubt you shall see her again.'

'No, I did not, for I do not expect to die.'

Edward smiled almost pleasantly. 'Then you were too confident, for, I promise you, you will not live to see another dawn.'

'We shall see,' said Christopher, taking off his jacket and throwing it on the ground.

The two men faced each other in shirts of fine lawn, and Christopher read clearly the evil intent to kill in Edward's eyes. Both men loosed their swords, freeing the naked blades from their sheaths. Edward saluted his opponent with a sardonic smile.

'*En garde.*'

They circled each other warily before their blades engaged, ferociously slicing the air. The swords clashed and at first neither bore the initiative, but they fought with all the violence born of hatred.

Richard watched fearfully, realising both men were evenly matched although Christopher was taller and appeared the most powerful of the two with his strong, muscular frame, but Edward possessed a lithe agility and fought with all the skill of an experienced duellist. As he watched he was certain that one of these men would not emerge from this encounter alive.

It was only after Edward stumbled slightly on stepping back, his injured leg letting him down, that Christopher seized his chance and immediately took the initiative, lunging, pressing home his attack. Enraged at finding himself at a disadvantage, Edward fought like a man possessed and their blades clashed faster and faster. A fierce, determined light shone in Christopher's eyes, but not a muscle in his dark face moved as his sword flashed, the clash of steel on steel rending the air. Edward began to fight dementedly, with everything to lose, but however hard he tried to attack he could not penetrate that unwavering guard and was constantly driven back as Christopher proved the stronger, his blade fiercely hissing the air.

Pure cold fury filled Edward's eyes at being held constantly at bay, and in desperation he began lunging wildly, carelessly, while Christopher retained his calm, and at last pressed home his advantage, sliding the point of his sword through the soft flesh of Edward's shoulder.

Edward's eyes opened wide in absolute surprise, his sword slipping from his hand, bright red blood staining the white purity of his shirt as he stumbled and fell, crumpling on to the ground. Christopher stepped back and stared down at him. Richard was beside him in a moment.

Edward cursed softly and attempted to get up but, his chest heaving, the effort proved too much and, smiling bitterly, he looked up at Christopher. 'Well, what are you waiting for? Aren't you going to finish me?'

'No—I shall not kill you, but only because before I came here Clarissa begged me not to. It is she you have to thank for your life, though God knows why after what she suffered at your hands. But be under no illusion, because it would give me immense pleasure to finish you for good.'

'Then do so,' hissed Edward. 'Because I swear that while ever there is breath in my body I shall hunt you down. I shall be avenged—I swear it. You shall regret not killing me—this I promise you.'

Christopher favoured him with one last contemptuous stare. 'I doubt that. Come, Richard, our business here is done. He is not dead and it was a fair fight. Whatever he threatens, I doubt he will bother us again,' and without paying further attention to the recumbent figure he turned and strode away, firmly believing as he did so that he would never set eyes on Edward Montgomery again.

At the house Clarissa waited anxiously for them to return. When Christopher stepped into the hall, having left Richard stabling the horses, he stopped for a moment and looked at her, so still that she might have been carved out of stone. Her face was white, one hand at her throat as she waited, taut with suspense, for him to tell her what had happened. Slowly she moved towards him and stared into his face, set in hard lines, his expression grim. She swallowed hard, reluctant to ask the question uppermost in her mind but knowing she must.

'Is he—is he dead?'

She trembled inwardly with fear at what he might tell her, and the intonation in her husband's voice was cold and distant—he might have been a stranger—as he replied, 'No. When I left him, I regret to tell you, he was very much alive.'

At the relief that flooded her eyes his face hardened and he was conscious of a sudden surge of anger.

'Thank you. Was—was he badly wounded?' she whispered, her voice dying away into the silence of the great hall.

Christopher looked at her incredulously. 'You astound me, Clarissa. Does it matter to you so much? Is it possible that, after all the harm he has done, you can still feel compassion? Your concern for him is quite touching, but did it not occur to you for one moment that I might not return? That I might be the one lying out there?' and then he smiled suddenly, a thin sardonic smile and his eyes narrowed cruelly. 'But then, how convenient for you if I had been. I shudder to think how quickly you would have flown to your precious Edward then.'

'No—no,' she gasped, staring at him in disbelief. 'I couldn't.'

'Why not?' he mocked. 'Do you mean because of last night? Did his violent lovemaking give you no pleasure?' and he laughed mirthlessly, a low, horrible sound. 'But isn't that how women like their lovers to be—violent? Don't they glean pleasure from the pain and humiliation inflicted on them?'

Clarissa shook her head. 'Christopher, don't—please don't talk like this.' She looked down at her hands. What could she say, she thought despairingly, to make him understand the torment she had been through after he had left her? How could she make him believe that she never wanted to see Edward again—ever—but that neither did she want him to die at the hands of her husband? And how could she make him believe that, after much soul-searching, she had realised that if one man had to forfeit his life during the course of the duel then she would rather it have been Edward? She stared up at him, unable to put her thoughts into words, and as she met his gaze miserably all she said was, 'This has been one of the most terrible nights of my life. I shall never forget it as long as I live.'

'Then you must forget it. For your sake—as well as for mine,' he replied cruelly. 'And I will tell you this, Clarissa: I never want to hear the name of Edward Montgomery mentioned again. Do you understand? You are my wife now and I expect you to behave as such. So the next time you feel the inclination to go running off in the middle of the night to meet your lover, perhaps you would be wise to think again. I will fight no more duels on your behalf.'

She was stung by his unjust accusation and the contempt in his voice, and some of Clarissa's fighting spirit rose to the fore and her eyes met his, flashing defiance. 'No—he was never that and you know it.'

Christopher's face became taut, his dark eyes boring into hers, plumbing their innermost depths, searching for some sign that would tell him she was lying, but there was none. He reached out and gripped her wrist as she was about to turn away, anger flushing her cheeks. 'Swear to me,' he rasped, glaring down at her mercilessly. 'Swear to me that what you say is true, because if he was and I had known earlier then I would have done all in my power to kill him.'

A violent, hidden force seemed to erupt inside him, and Clarissa was seeing a side to him she hadn't known existed. She felt afraid but her eyes did not fall beneath his gaze. Could this cold, angry stranger be her husband? The man she had married—who had asked her to go with him to America? The hideous events of the past twenty-four hours had unleashed in him all the fury of his passionate nature, and all the more terrible because she knew that due to her blind stupidity she was the one to blame. The pain his fingers caused her as they gripped her wrist suddenly made her cry out and tears start to her eyes.

'For pity's sake, Christopher. You're hurting me—please—let go——'

'Swear it,' he said between clenched teeth, forcing back a rage that threatened to consume him.

'Yes—yes, I do swear.'

He glared at her for a long hard moment, seeing the tears in her eyes, and only then did he release his terrible hold, flinging her hand away from him. 'Very well. But God help you if you are lying.' He took a deep breath. 'And now—perhaps you would be good enough to be ready to leave for London as soon as possible.'

At his words her eyes opened wide in alarm. 'Leave? But—but you said we could have a few days here at least before we had to leave.'

'I've changed my mind. I've wasted too much time already and have no wish to remain here a moment longer. Must I remind you that my country is on the brink of war and I have to get back?'

'But—but a few days,' she pleaded, rubbing her sore

wrist. 'We're not due to sail for a week—we could stay here a little longer.'

'No,' he said with such finality that she stepped back from him.

'Very well. If you insist then I shall instruct the maids to begin packing my things.'

She said this with such doleful resignation that Christopher sighed, some of the hardness leaving him, knowing just how difficult it would be for her to leave Ashton Park. But however much she pleaded he would not relent. The past twenty-four hours had made him heartily sick of the place and he was impatient to leave. They would spend the time left in London with his uncle before it was time to leave for Bristol, where they were to board a ship for Charleston.

'I'm sorry, Clarissa, but you have to leave some time—you knew that when you married me, so what does it matter whether it is today or tomorrow?'

She nodded and, swallowing back her tears, squared her shoulders, a determined little tilt to her chin as she looked at him directly. 'I know, and you are right—one day is much the same as any other.'

She turned from him and he watched her walk across the hall and disappear up the stairs to her room, aware of all the wretchedness she must be feeling, detesting himself for venting his anger on her, knowing that the manner in which he had spoken to her was unforgivable. He strode quickly into the dining-room, cursing angrily, and, taking a decanter, poured a generous helping of brandy into a glass; but not even when he drank deeply, feeling the fiery liquid course through his veins, did it lessen his self-loathing.

When Clarissa considered what her life would be from now on she felt that it would be like spinning about in some great vortex, without the stable influences of

Ashton Park, on which she had always depended and from which she was about to be wrenched, and she was totally unprepared for the scale of misery that engulfed her. She took refuge in silence, withdrawing inside herself, helping Betsy and Letty to pack her belongings with care, gazing at all that was familiar to her a little longer than usual, for whatever she saw now would be imprinted on her mind for all time.

It was the morning following the duel and she stood on the steps of Ashton Park, the wind blowing in sharp gusts across the wide expanse of the park, sending threatening black clouds scurrying across the sky. She looked up, feeling the wind brush her pale cheeks, and, breathing deeply, there came to her the pungent smell of pine needles. The first sharp drops of rain began to fall, stinging her skin, and she shuddered, feeling that the cold wind was like an act of terrible ill omen.

Servants, footmen and stablehands were all milling about and, straight-backed and dry-eyed, she said goodbye to them all, but it was with a heavy heart that she embraced Letty, who wet her with her tears, and Richard, who held her tight, hugging her to him so that she could feel the pounding of his heart, telling her to be happy. However much she wanted to, she did not cry; not even when she was in the carriage, sitting across from her husband and leaving the graceful lines of Ashton Park behind, wondering if she would ever come back, did she cry. But she would not allow herself to look back, for if she did it would break her heart.

CHAPTER NINE

THE American coastline was dotted with islands separated from the mainland by salt marshes, and the skyline over Charleston was dominated by numerous church steeples. Clarissa and Betsy, standing at the ship's rail, watched enchanted as the *Endeavour* drew closer to land, gliding through the tranquil waters, weaving its way between other vessels. They entered the broad, sparkling bay with snow-white sand and sailed up the harbour to the waterfront. It seemed an age before the *Endeavour* finally slid into her berth in this seemingly sleepy town, often called the mother city of the south, the focal point of social culture and economic and political activity of South Carolina, one of the smallest of the southern states. It occupied a narrow peninsula overlooking a large natural harbour created by the confluence of the Cooper and Ashley rivers.

It didn't take them long to disembark. Their baggage was to be brought ashore and sent on to the hotel here in Charleston where they were to stay overnight before travelling on to Tamasee. They soon found themselves in an open carriage, Clarissa's and Betsy's skin protected from the glare of the afternoon sun by lacy parasols. They travelled away from the docks, moving past warehouses piled high with bales of cotton, rice and tobacco, and Clarissa found herself wondering what would happen to it all if, as Christopher expected, a state of war was declared between England and America. He had told her gravely that if this happened then America's foreign trade would be almost destroyed. She wondered if most of it would go north to New England, where merchants were taking their capital and investing in new machinery, eager to manufacture their own goods and so reducing their imports from Europe. She sighed, wondering if she would ever understand the complexities of this strange new land, which, regardless of how she might feel, she must learn to adopt as her own.

After the winter in England she was quite unprepared for the light-hearted excitement of Charleston, with its sudden explosion of colour. It had been when the *Endeavour* had sailed closer to America, when the climate had changed considerably, that she and Betsy had taken to wearing their lighter dresses, more suited to the balmy clement weather. The warm sun and sultry air was filled with the sweet delicate perfume of tropical flowers and she was struck by the careless, languid atmosphere and the soft blur of the southern speech that fell pleasantly on her ears.

Pavements swarmed with people, people of all colours ranging from white, passing through every shade of brown to black. Their clothes were gaily coloured, their dark skins glowing as if they had been rubbed with oil. Clarissa looked at them curiously. The only black people she had seen before had been in London. Several of her acquaintances kept black servants, whom they dressed in brightly coloured silks with turbans on their heads. But all at once she was acutely aware of a cold, sickly feeling in the pit of her stomach, which told her that this was different. This was slavery, which, she told herself, she must learn to accept if she was to live here. It was this obscene trade in human flesh that kept the southern states and men like her husband rich. Her embarrassment was evident and she did not know how to react, hence it was with great difficulty that she avoided Christopher's questioning eyes, his close scrutiny, as he waited expectantly for her reaction, and so she remained silent.

The carriage came to a halt in front of their hotel and immediately three bell boys dressed in blue velvet emerged from inside to assist them. The manner in which the manager and the hotel staff greeted Christopher, ushering them inside, seeing to their every comfort at once, left Clarissa in no doubt as to his importance and the high regard in which they held him. It was almost as if he were royalty. But then, she thought, having learnt a great deal about South Carolina and its people from her fellow passengers on board the *Endeavour*, wasn't that what these southern planters considered themselves? Wasn't there a conspicuous upper-class gentry, an aristocracy, as some liked to call it, with old established names like Rutledge, Lauren and Pinckney? And she was in no doubt that the Cordells could be listed among them. In fact, these people, this planting upper class who had a right to this class, were relatively more numerous in South Carolina than in any other part of north America.

The room to which they were shown was large and cool and, she thought, quite correctly, probably the best the hotel had to offer. The creamy lace curtains moved gently with the soft, refreshing breeze blowing in through the open window. Betsy was to occupy the smaller, adjoining room, to which she disappeared immediately to change, and it was only then that Clarissa, staring at the large bed, felt a sudden dart of panic when she realised that Christopher was to share it with her.

He had followed her inside and, seeing her standing quite still in the centre of the room, staring at the bed, and noticing the sudden pallor of her face, he smiled thinly, angered by her reaction. 'Does it displease you to know this room is for both of us?'

She spun round, startled by the sound of his voice. 'No—no, of course not,' she stammered. 'Only—I—I thought——'

'Thought what?' he said brusquely. 'That I didn't wish to share a bed with my wife? Well, whatever thoughts might have passed through that pretty head of yours, Clarissa, I can tell you now that I find the possibility quite appealing, although on board ship was hardly the place to begin married life,' he said drily.

He moved to the window and stood looking down into the street. Clarissa stared at his stony profile, his jaw set firm, and a sudden surge of longing to go to him and run her hands over the broad set of his shoulders welled inside her, but she didn't move. She swallowed hard, sensing the tension inside him. This was the first time they had been alone, truly alone, since their marriage, which now felt as if it had happened in some other lifetime. But one thing was clear to her and that was that they couldn't go on like this. They would have to talk, to bring down this invisible wall he had erected between them. At last she moved towards him.

'Please, Christopher,' she said softly. 'We have to talk. We can't go on like this.'

'No—you're right, we can't. But tell me,' he said without turning, his voice low and controlled, 'why did you go to him that night? I have to know, Clarissa.'

He had told her he never wanted to hear Edward's name mentioned again and since the duel neither of them had, but she knew he remained uppermost in his mind.

'I went to him,' she said quietly, 'because I had to know if he would have married me—knowing my

circumstances. I had to know, before I went away, for
my own peace of mind.'

He turned sharply and looked at her, and she cringed
inwardly at his cold expression. 'And would he?'

She shook her head. 'No.'

'Then it was fortunate for you, after all, that I came
along, wasn't it?' he said cruelly.

'That wasn't fair,' she gasped, stung by his words.
'You knew my situation when you asked me to marry
you. I made no secret of what my feelings were for
Edward.'

'Of course,' he said, his lips twisting with sarcasm.
'You must forgive me for forgetting. But do you expect
me to believe that you went to him on our wedding-
night for no other reason than to talk to him?'

'Yes, I do.'

He shrugged. 'Whatever your reasons, you should
not have gone.'

Clarissa's cheeks suddenly flamed, and she raised
her head high as anger rose inside her, anger at his
stubborn male pride, his refusal to accept what she had
told him. 'Perhaps not, but if I remember correctly it
was you who left me. It was you who turned from me
on our wedding-night.'

'I will not make love to my wife, or any other
woman, come to that, while her heart lies elsewhere,'
and he threw her a mocking smile. 'Rather like having
three in a bed, don't you think?'

'As far as I am concerned, Edward is dead, and if
we are to find any happiness in our marriage then he
must be dead for you too. Nothing can change what
has happened, so we must learn to put it behind us. I
no longer love him—I think I realised that before I
went to see him at the inn—and, in fact, I don't know
if I ever did. This I have told you, so why can't that
stubborn pride of yours let you accept it?' She sighed

deeply, her anger of a moment ago leaving her.
'Please,' she murmured, placing her hand timidly on
his arm. Summoning up all her courage, she gazed
beseechingly into his angry eyes. 'Have you made up
your mind to hate me all your life? How much longer
will you continue to spurn me? Can you not find it in
your heart to forgive me? It hasn't been easy for me
either, you know.'

Christopher looked into the imploring softness of
her eyes, so bewitchingly beautiful, and he was moved
in spite of himself. She looked so piteous, so defenceless and she spoke so passionately that the hard gleam
went from his eyes and there was a softer tone to his
voice when he spoke. 'You little fool,' he said, taking
her hand from his arm and tenderly drawing her close.
'I don't hate you, Clarissa—don't ever think that. No
man in his right mind would spurn you intentionally.
You are far too lovely for that.' He smiled slowly. 'I've
been a selfish brute, haven't I? You deserved better
after what you've been through.'

She smiled with relief at the tenderness filling his
dark eyes, and she trembled with a quiet joy. 'Then we
are friends again?'

'More than that, I hope. But how does it feel to
know you have the power to make me suffer, to make
my life hell? You have bewitched me, Clarissa. No
other woman has ever done that.'

'I—I'm sorry, Christopher.'

'What for?'

'My stupidity. Did I hurt you very much?'

'More than you will ever know, but you are right.
We will put all that has happened behind us. We must
not allow it to poison our happiness and, besides, the
days ahead will be difficult enough for you without
that. It is very important to me that you learn to love
Tamasee as I do.' Gazing down into the magnificent

blue depths of her eyes, he raised her hand to his lips, feeling desire surge through him, and he was impatient for the time to come when he could make her his wife in flesh as well as in name. But, however soft and inviting the large bed looked, now was not the time. 'I have to leave you for a while,' he said huskily. 'Much as I hate to.'

Disappointment clouded her eyes. 'Oh—must you?'

'Yes. Ralph Benton, my overseer, should be here in Charleston. I have one or two things to attend to before we leave for Tamasee tomorrow.' He lowered his gaze, moving from her, unable to tell her that the things he had to attend to concerned the buying of slaves at the auction to be taken back to Tamasee.

'When will you be back?'

'Later. If I'm not back in time for dinner, you and Betsy go ahead and eat without me.' He turned back to her, drawing her once again into the warm circle of his arms. 'Don't worry, I'll be back later,' he said, bending his head and brushing her soft lips with his own. 'Wild horses won't be able to keep me from you tonight.'

Clarissa watched him go, her heart pounding as she awaited the night to come with all the sweet anticipation of a new bride.

Ralph Benton was a tall man in his mid-thirties, with a big muscular frame and a loud deep voice that gave the impression of his being more intimidating than he actually was. He'd been the main overseer at Tamasee for as long as Christopher had been the owner, and a great mutual respect and friendship had developed between them over the years.

Unlike many other plantation owners, Christopher abhorred unnecessary brutality where the slaves were concerned, and he had not hired Ralph for his skill in exhorting labour from the slaves with brutal methods. He was tough, and his commanding presence could galvanise any one of the Negroes at Tamasee into work without the use of the lash. Both men managed the plantation and Christopher only surrendered everything over to Ralph when he had to make business trips up north or to England.

The two men greeted each other warmly and, ordering refreshment, made themselves comfortable in the hotel lounge.

'How are things at Tamasee, Ralph?'

'Just fine. Young Mitchel's running things until we get back. Must say, your letter came as something of a surprise. Didn't expect you back so soon. Why the haste?'

Christopher lounged back in his chair indolently, crossing one booted leg over his knee. 'With the continuing unrest, I had no intention of being stuck on the wrong side of the Atlantic if war breaks out.'

'As it surely will if these new members of Congress have their way,' said Ralph.

'What's the situation here, Ralph?'

'Much the same as when you left. Many people in the south, and especially here in South Carolina, still clamour for war with the British—including that dynamic young pup from the back country, John Calhoun. He's one of these so-called "War Hawks".'

'Then they are fools,' said Christopher grimly. 'All of them.'

Ralph shook his head in disagreement. 'Are they? I'm not so sure. Ever since the Chesapeake incident in '07, when the British opened fire on her, you know yourself the demands for vengeance have been nationwide. Britain's continued harassment since has done nothing to reduce their anger.'

'Then they should learn to temper their ardour. Don't they realise that we shall be the losers?'

'It's no longer a matter of money, of dollars and cents, but one of national honour. War is inevitable. As I see it, we have two choices—fight or submit. We really do have to teach Britain a lesson. If we don't fight then everything we achieved during the revolution will be undone. She cannot go on treating us as one of her colonies. We are a free, independent nation, and the sooner she realises that and accepts it the better.'

Christopher sighed deeply. 'Yes, and I do agree, but war achieves nothing. I believe negotiations are the best way to sort things out. Surely people can't have forgotten so soon that the embargo we exacted on Britain three years ago all but ruined us? Don't they realise that if we are unable to ship our cotton to Europe then we will be totally dependent on merchants in New England, and they will take advantage of our helplessness and offer us such ridiculously low prices that we will be forced to accept? Unless,' he smiled with a touch of sarcasm, 'we learn to spin and weave it ourselves.'

'And would that be such a bad thing?' asked Ralph. 'Wouldn't it be a good thing for us to stop being what Britain wants us to be—exchanging our raw materials for their manufactured goods? Wouldn't it be a good thing for us to pour more of our labour into learning to make things for ourselves? We have nothing in the south but slaves and cotton. Ah, Christopher,' he sighed, 'you have the mind of a lawyer. By the way you think and talk, I reckon you're more in tune with the Federalists up north. Maybe you'd be better off selling Tamasee and opening a law practice in Washington.'

Christopher grinned, not in the least offended by Ralph's words. There was no one else in the world who could speak as openly to him as Ralph. 'And we both know I won't do that. I shall never sell. Tamasee is where I belong.' He looked across at his overseer and the serious expression on his face. However much they argued, they would never see eye to eye, and he laughed suddenly, knowing from past experience and the many nights they had sat in the library at Tamasee after a hard day's work in the fields, relaxing and drinking their port, how Ralph loved nothing more than embroiling himself in political discussion, and, reaching out, he slapped him good-humouredly on the shoulder. 'Have you never considered joining the "War Hawks" yourself, Ralph?' he joked light-heartedly. 'Bet they'd like to have someone with your political enthusiasm on board.'

Ralph frowned seriously. 'Nope. But I bet they'd welcome you.' He grinned, and his expression relaxed. 'As for me—well, I'm quite happy doin' what I'm doin' and letting others sort the nation out. Now,' he said, looking across at Christopher and squinting thought-fully, 'what about this other matter you mentioned in your letter? Didn't you write somethin' about a wife?'

Christopher nodded, the expression in his dark eyes softening when he thought of Clarissa. 'I did, and her name's Clarissa.'

'Well,' said Ralph, scratching his head. 'You could have bowled me over when I read that. Never thought you'd do it,' and he frowned suddenly, although a merry glint danced in his eye as an amusing thought struck him, and he looked at Christopher sideways. 'Does Marie know?'

Christopher looked at him long and hard, smiling slowly. 'No, not yet—but she will.'

'Then I sure hope I'm not there when she finds out. All hell will break loose—that's for sure.' He didn't tell Christopher that he had his doubts about him

bringing a girl out from England to live at Tamasee. If
he'd said he was looking for a wife and asked his advice
then he'd have told him to marry a girl from the south.
There were plenty just waiting to be asked. Girls who'd
been born and bred to plantation life and who would
manage Tamasee and the slaves in a way no girl from
England ever could. Still, he'd bide his judgement until
he'd met her, for, knowing Christopher, he wouldn't
have married her if he hadn't thought she'd be suitable.

There was a more pressing matter Ralph had to
mention to him, one that he knew would upset him,
and a serious note had entered his voice when he spoke
again. 'There's something I have to tell you, Chris, and
I'm not goin' to beat about the bush. Sam's run away.'

'Sam?' Christopher looked at him in amazement, but
as the full implication of his words struck him he paled
and he was filled with a cold dread. Sam was his valet
and meant a great deal to him. 'Why on earth would
Sam want to run away?'

'Because I sold Della. You remember, that young
Negress you bought in Georgetown just before you left
for England—the one from Louisiana.'

Christopher nodded slowly. He did remember her—
about twenty years of age, slender as a willow with
short-cropped hair about her well shaped head, held
high and proud, and he remembered the way she had
met his gaze defiantly, her dark eyes spitting hatred,
lacking the humility of other slaves. Oddly, this had
appealed to him and, lacking his better judgement, he
had bought her, intending to have her work in the
house to help Agatha, whose aged bones were almost
worn out. It had been obvious from the outset that the
two did not see eye to eye but, unable to do anything
about the situation because he was about to leave for
England, he'd deliberately put Della out of his mind,

hoping they would have resolved their differences by the time he returned home.

'I do remember her, but why should Sam run away because of her?'

'He became mighty smitten by the girl. I tell you, Chris, she was nothing but trouble. Even Agatha couldn't do anything with her in the house. She was forever complaining about her insolence and how uncooperative she was. Gave me the creeps, that one, with that strange practice these blacks have brought with them from Africa of worshipping the devil. As the Negroes say, she had the power to know things seen and unseen. She was both feared and respected. Sam certainly came under her spell—although I have to admit I didn't know he'd got it that bad.'

'He must have if getting rid of her caused him to run away. Nearly every plantation has one like her, Ralph. I don't think we need worry on that score. The Negroes at Tamasee aren't as deeply immersed in witchcraft as they are down in Louisiana and the Caribbean islands. Couldn't you have turned a blind eye?'

'No. There was too much general unrest, with strange rituals and incantations taking place at night, scaring the drivers out of their wits. She's different, that one, I tell you. Whatever you might think, her powers are not fanciful and nor can they be ignored.'

Christopher sighed. 'Nevertheless, it's years since a slave ran away from Tamasee. God help Sam if the slave patrol gets wind of this. Their brutality is renowned throughout the state. They'll show him no mercy, that's for sure. They've long had an eye on Tamasee, anxious to find an excuse to flog one of our "pampered slaves". We'll have to get to him first.' He glanced sharply at Ralph. 'I take it the patrol doesn't know about this yet?'

Ralph shook his head. 'I'm not sure. Slaves talk, and

when someone as important as Sam goes missing it's hard to keep it quiet.'

'I value Sam above any of the others, Ralph,' he said quietly. 'You know that. He was born at Tamasee on the same night as myself. My brother, Andrew, was so much older than me that I never really knew him as a child and, besides, he lived in Father's shadow. It was Sam I grew up with. If I manage to find him I want to make sure he'll have no reason to run away again— even if it means buying back the girl. Who bought her?'

'Robert Wheeler. His place is just north of here.'

'Yes, I know him and, from what I remember, he's a reasonable man. Perhaps if I offer him enough I might be able to buy her back.'

'If he's having the same trouble we had then he might be glad to be rid of her by now,' said Ralph wryly, but doubt filled his eyes. 'Do you think it'd be wise having her back? Everyone's breathed a lot easier since she went.'

'I don't know until I see her. Have you any idea where he might be?'

'I reckon he'll have headed for the Wheeler place— trying to get to her.'

'When did he leave Tamasee?'

'Two days ago.'

'How long will it take us to ride to the Wheeler plantation?'

'About an hour, I'd say.'

'Right, then have me a horse saddled and we'll leave here in half an hour. I'll go and change and tell Clarissa.'

They rode their horses hard, spurred on by thoughts of the slave patrol and what they would do to Sam if they got to him first. By the time they arrived at the Wheeler plantation the moon was already high in the sky, lighting up the driveway and the house. They rode towards the foot of the steps, but no one came out of the house to meet them. An uneasy, unnatural quiet hung over the place and just a few lights flickered through the windows; in fact, the whole house seemed devoid of life. The men glanced at each other apprehensively.

'Let's go round to the rear quarters,' said Ralph. 'There has to be someone about.'

Immediately he'd said these words the peace of the night was disturbed by the high, piercing scream of a woman, and suddenly the night became hideously unreal. A sinking feeling of dread knotted Christopher's insides. Hearing a commotion coming from the direction of the slave cabins, they set off quickly to investigate.

Away from the street of crude wooden slave huts was a large gathering of Negroes, with little isolated groups pressed against buildings, men, women and children, their eyes riveted on a huge wooden stake, to which a Negro was tied with ropes. They stood in silent obedience, but Christopher could smell the stench of fear emanating from every one of them. A dozen or so white men stood guard, some with guns trained on the Negroes, while one was administering the flogging of the man tied to the stake, his face twisted with sadistic pleasure as he brought the lash down slowly and with relish, to inflict the worst possible pain.

As the lash came down Christopher saw the body give one last agonising jerk before collapsing against the stake, his head flung back, the muscles of his arms bulging as they took the strain. A woman he recognised as Della was on her knees close by, her face in her hands, sobbing brokenly. In her despair she was the one who had screamed out her anguish into the night.

The man at the stake was filthy and bleeding profusely. The flesh had been reduced to a crimson jelly where the lash had fallen with such dreadful precision, but Christopher would have recognised him in any condition. It was Sam, and at the sight of him, a prisoner of these blood-thirsty slave catchers, he went white to his lips and could feel himself trembling with a terrible anger and indignation. That they had dared to flog one of his Negroes senseless was almost too much.

Robert Wheeler stood on the far side of the gathering and, from the hard expression on his face, he clearly disapproved of what was taking place on his plantation.

Before the patrol leader—whom he now recognised as Ned Stone, a thoroughly nasty piece of work— could raise his tired, bloodied arm to bring down the lash one more time on to Sam's back, scraps of human flesh stuck to the leather thongs, Christopher rode into the crowd, and it was with a great effort of will that he kept his fury in check, but his face was set hard and grim, a deadly gleam in his dark eyes. Ralph remained on the outer circle while Christopher rode forward, unafraid of the menacing threat posed by the gun-wielding patrol. The atmosphere became tense, and the crowd parted to let him through, his whole manner radiating a strength of purpose. None tried to stop him. The slave catchers all looked at him in amazement, and no one uttered a word as he slid from his horse.

'Cut him down,' he commanded to the nearest of the men.

The tone of his voice and his expression brooked no argument and, taking a knife from his belt, the man hastily did as he was told and severed the rope that bound Sam to the stake. He crumpled to the ground, unconscious. Christopher looked accusingly and with unconcealed loathing at Stone, who had derived such an unholy pleasure in flogging Sam. The others in the patrol closed ranks around their leader, waiting for Christopher to speak.

The face of Stone was lean and cruel, with deep-set pale grey eyes that had narrowed slightly. His features were savage with rage and disappointment at this untimely interruption.

'Well,' he snarled, unperturbed, unlike everyone else, by Christopher's presence, refusing to be intimidated by him. 'If it isn't Mr High and Mighty Cordell himself. Come to see what we do with runaways, have you?'

Christopher felt a shiver of revulsion at the cold cruelty in Stone's eyes. 'I see I wasn't in time to cheat you out of your sport, Stone, but raise that whip once more and I'll give you a taste of it myself.'

Stone's sallow face reddened with rage, and pure madness flamed in his eyes. 'Damn it all, Cordell, this 'ere's a runaway. I was giving him his just deserts—that's all.'

'Just deserts? You call flogging a man to death for running away giving him his just deserts?'

'He isn't a man, he's a Nigra,' he rasped, 'and catchin' runaways is my bizness. They have to be flogged as an example to others who harbour grand ideas in their heads of freedom—and, anyway, how do we know he isn't an insurgent, inciting other slaves to riot? They have to be put down—taught a lesson—and there's only one way to do that. We don't want a rebellion on our hands, now, do we?'

'Sam is not an insurgent and you damn well know it, and *I* say what has to be done with slaves who run away from Tamasee. You have no authority there, and if you set foot on my estate again I'll sure as hell kill you.'

Stone laughed, a ragged sound, and he glared at

Christopher. 'I beg your pardon,' he mocked, 'but he wasn't where he should've been, at Tamasee, and it's right what I've always suspected—what everyone always said of you,' and he thrust his vile face closer to Christopher's, 'that you're a nigger lover.'

'When it comes to filth like you, Stone, I'd as soon love the devil. You're scum, the worst possible kind, and it's not in the too distant past that I retain memories of your handiwork, your sadistic tendencies, where Negroes are concerned. I remember all too well how you hanged those four runaways from the Stanton place in cold blood, and I also remember the tortures, the unimaginable cruelties that were inflicted on them by you. For them death was a merciful release. You are a butcher, Stone, and you should be horsewhipped for this night's work.'

Stone glared at him furiously, but before he could hurl further insults Robert Wheeler had come to stand beside Christopher.

'I don't think there's any further reason for you to be here now, is there, Stone? You've done what you set out to do, so be gone—and take your henchmen with you. I don't want you here any more than Mr Cordell wants you at Tamasee.'

Stone turned and spat into the dust and with a gloating triumph looked down at Sam, who raised his tortured head, allowing Della to place it on her lap.

'You're right, Wheeler,' he said smugly. 'I've done what I set out to do—for now—so I'll go, but you'll come to thank us. This'll cool his appetite for runnin' away, just you see if it don't.' He pointed his whip at Della. 'She was to have been next. All nice an' cosy they were in her little hut. Harbourin' runaways is almos' as serious as runnin' away, but I'll save her for a later date. Anyway, I wouldn't want to outstay my welcome, now, would I?' And with an ugly-sounding laugh he sauntered to where his horse waited.

Everyone was silent and watched as the slave catchers mounted their horses and rode away, the night closing in around them. Christopher knelt beside Sam's body, taking in his pitiable state, and he was stricken to the very soul. He was certain Stone would have killed him had he not come when he had. He got to his feet when Robert spoke, clearly shaken by what had taken place.

'I can't tell you how glad I am to see you, Christopher. I would have done anything to prevent this, but it was impossible. I've been away for most of the day and the flogging was already under way when I got back. He is one of your slaves, isn't he?'

'Yes—he's from Tamasee.'

'Then I'm sorry. You know how much I deplore this kind of punishment. I don't hold with ill-treating slaves. That way you don't get the best out of them. I find they need kindness and understanding. Put terror into their hearts and it incites them to run away.'

'You're right. I abhor flogging. I believe the Negro requires skilful handling. Like you, I've always found they normally respond to kindness. They need firm guidance, but not with whips and chains.'

'Why do you think he came here?' asked Robert.

Christopher sighed and indicated Della, her head bowed, with Sam's head still cradled in her lap. 'There's your reason, Robert—a woman. He came to find her.'

'I see. She's the one I bought at auction a month back. Wasn't she one of yours?' he asked, eyeing Christopher curiously.

'Yes. I don't suppose you'd consider selling her back, would you?'

'Yes. As a matter of fact, I'll be glad to be rid of her.

She's trouble, that one—but then, you'll already know that.'

'No. I've been away in England and only arrived back today, but my overseer thought so. That's why he sold her.'

Robert scratched his head thoughtfully. 'Ah, well— I should've taken note of that when I bought her. It's well known that you never sell any of the slaves from Tamasee unless there's something wrong with them. And you're prepared to take her back?'

'Yes. I value Sam highly, Robert. He's my man-servant and an important part of Tamasee and my life. If it stops him running away I'll have her back.'

'Then she's yours and I'll ask for nothing more than the price I paid for her. Now come into the house. I don't know about you, but after this I feel the need of some strong liquid refreshment.' Seeing Christopher hesitate and cast a concerned glance at Sam, he smiled. 'Don't worry, I'll have Sam tended to. Send a wagon over in the morning for them both.'

CHAPTER TEN

ALONE, Clarissa moved aimlessly to the open window, thinking of Christopher and what it was that could be so important as to keep him from her. She gazed down at the street, letting her thoughts turn with longing to Ashton Park and Richard. In the clarity of her mind's eye she saw it all, the graceful sweep of the park and ancient, noble trees. How she wished she were there, to savour it all, instead of in this new, unfamiliar place. But then, she thought wistfully, if she were back in England then Christopher wouldn't be with her, and suddenly all those girlish dreams of Edward and the bulwark of her security—Ashton Park—began to slip into the past and didn't seem to matter now.

Suddenly, without her noticing, Christopher had become a very important part of her life. He had stood by her, offering her his name, risking his money and his reputation. Letty had been right when she had said that no man would do all these things for a woman he did not care about, and she knew she would rather be here with him than without him at Ashton Park. But what did she feel for him? Did she love him? This she did not know. After Edward she would never trust her judgement again, but when she thought of him, of his darkly handsome face and flashing smile, her body trembled with an unaccustomed desire to have him hold her, to feel his strong arms about her and to rest her head on his broad chest—to have him love her. She was more than ready to become his wife in every sense of the word.

At last her vigil was rewarded when she saw him

come riding down the street towards the hotel accompanied by another man, larger than he was, who she assumed must be his overseer, Ralph Benton. They rode slowly, their bodies slumped in the saddle as if they had ridden far. After a few words they parted company and the other man rode off down the street, taking Christopher's horse with him as he entered the hotel.

With feverish anticipation she turned towards the door, expecting him to come in at any moment. Her heart began to beat quickly and her mouth became dry, the palms of her hands clammy, and then suddenly he was there, standing in the open doorway, his face etched with tired lines, his hair falling untidily over his forehead.

He was pleasantly surprised to find her not in bed and looked at her for a long moment before stepping inside, closing the door softly behind him. All thoughts of Sam and Della vanished as he stared at Clarissa, neither of them speaking, standing just a few feet away from each other. The only sounds Clarissa could hear were the sounds from her own heart, and in that one marvellous moment everything was forgotten but the immense joy they each felt in knowing of their mutual need.

'You needn't have waited up, Clarissa.'

'I wanted to, and, anyway, I wasn't sleepy,' she answered softly.

As he moved towards her she began to feel slightly light-headed, and then he was beside her, reaching out with one hand and letting the tips of his fingers run gently over the filmy lace of her nightdress.

'I remember this,' he said huskily. 'I saw it draped over a chair in your room on our wedding-night.'

Clarissa moved closer to him, her eyes wide and clear, her lips moist and slightly parted. Very slowly she wound her soft arms about his neck, drawing his head down to hers and breaking down any resistance he might have had left.'Let this be our wedding-night,' she murmured, her warm lips against his. 'And I promise you there will be just the two of us, with no room for anyone else.'

Having waited too long for this moment, Christopher took her into his arms and clasped her to him. Like a starving man, he kissed her, feeling the awakening of his desire. It was a kiss that seemed to last forever, that went on and on, until gently he pulled away, gazing into the velvety softness of her eyes.

'I love you, Clarissa. As God is my witness, I love you. From that first moment I saw you at Lady Holland's party I have loved you, my sweet Clarissa— my wife. I have nearly died of wanting you.' At her soft smile he again bent his head, kissing her eyes, her lips, her throat, as though he could never have enough of her. His hands moved over her thin nightdress, realising that beneath it she was as naked as the day she was born.

She didn't stop him when he slipped her nightdress off her shoulders, whereupon it fell in soft folds around her feet. She stepped out of it, and his breath caught in his throat at the splendour of her beauty, her body drenched in the intoxicating sweet scent of roses. His eyes devoured her pale loveliness in the soft light emanating from the lamp and the moon shining in through the window. He reached out and removed the pins from her hair, plunging his hands into the long silken tresses as they tumbled about her shoulders, drawing her close, his lips finding hers yet again.

Clarissa's need for him shook her to the very core. 'Please, Christopher,' she breathed against him.

'Please what, my love? Please make love to you—is that what you want? Oh, my darling, I shall make love to you until you beg me to stop, I promise you,' and with that he swept her up into his arms and carried her to the bed. After divesting himself of his clothes he lay beside her.

It was without shame or shyness that Clarissa wound herself about him, seeking his lips with her own, his hand caressing her with exquisite slowness, stroking the firm swell of her breasts and down over the smooth curve of her belly, bringing her flesh aflame as ecstasy and passion swept through her such as she had never known.

With his lips close to hers he murmured tender, passionate endearments and she closed her eyes, allowing his words to wash over her, experiencing a fierce, primitive hunger that threatened to engulf her completely. With his mouth covering hers she felt his weight crushing her, and she stretched beneath him so that he could feel every inch of her body as joyfully she allowed him to possess her, abandoning her body to his will completely, rejoicing in the delicious sensations of pleasure. In his arms she was filled with an ardent desire that matched his, and as they became one flesh she was plunged into a glorious oblivion.

They made love until towards dawn, when at last they fell into a short but blissful sleep, but before Clarissa closed her eyes, curled within her husband's warm embrace, she knew with a feverish joy, as surely as night followed day, that she loved him. She accepted the truth with a kind of wonder. She loved him with every fibre of her being, he was a part of her, branded on her very soul, and she would never be free again. With this glorious revelation everything she had found so difficult to understand suddenly seemed so simple, so uncomplicated, and now she had only one desire— to stay by his side for always.

* * *

She came awake suddenly when he stirred beside her, and when she opened her eyes he was sitting on the edge of the bed, pulling on his clothes.

'What's the matter?' she murmured sleepily, rolling towards him, and, reaching out, ran the tips of her fingers provocatively down his bare spine.

Christopher shuddered involuntarily, her mere touch sending him dizzy, and, turning, he looked at her as she stretched sensuously among the ravaged bed-clothes, her pale, silken mass of hair spread about her. Unable to resist her, he reached out and tenderly gathered her into his arms, placing his lips in the warm hollow of her throat. 'I have to leave you for a while, my love. There is urgent business to attend to before we can leave for Tamasee.'

She nestled drowsily into his embrace, finding his lips with her own, winding her slender arms like wands about him, bent on conquering him. 'But why must you go?' she murmured. 'Stay here with me—for just a little while longer. Don't you want to?'

'God help me, Clarissa,' he replied hoarsely, placing his firm hands on either side of her face and gazing with longing into her dark, sleepy blue eyes. 'You know I do. You are beautiful—wonderful beyond belief. You are like a witch—a temptress.'

'Then stay with me,' she pleaded.

'No,' he replied, gently but firmly, feeling renewed passion stirring inside him, and, disentangling her clinging arms, he held her away from him. 'There is nothing I want more than to stay here with you and make love to you all day—but unfortunately I cannot. We must leave here before midday. Now,' he said, laughing lightly at the cross frown creasing her brow, 'be good, will you, and go back to sleep?' and, standing up, he continued dressing.

Lying back on the pillows, Clarissa watched him

from beneath half-closed lids, and when he was ready to leave she raised herself on one elbow, the sheet slipping down to reveal one firm white breast. Christopher's breath caught sharply in his throat at her sheer loveliness.

'Won't you kiss me before you go?' she asked.

'No,' he answered, laughing lightly. 'You know damned well what would happen if I so much as touched you. In a moment I would be in that bed beside you and Ralph would be knocking on the door in no time to see what was keeping me.'

Defeated, Clarissa sighed and sank back against the pillows, pulling the covers up to her chin. 'Oh, very well. Go, then. When will you be back?'

'Soon—I promise,' and, laughing softly, blowing her a kiss from the open doorway, he left her alone.

With sunlight streaming in through the window Clarissa no longer felt the desire to sleep and hurriedly climbed out of bed, noticing her nightdress still lying in a crumpled heap on the carpet. Striding over it, she gazed at herself in the dressing-table mirror, seeing her lips slightly swollen from Christopher's kisses and her skin, which seemed to glow from his touch. At the transformation a sense of triumph swept through her, for the face reflected in the mirror was the face of a woman, all trace of innocence having disappeared, and when Betsy tapped on her door and entered, smiling broadly, one look at Clarissa's face and she too noticed the transformation and welcomed it. Never had she seen her look so radiant, so happy.

Later, having dressed and eaten, they were delighted to discover that Christopher had arranged for them to see the town in a very elegant horse-drawn carriage, which had been sent out from Tamasee, driven by an ageing Negro. He had a cheerful face and the broadest smile Clarissa had ever seen, and he delighted in telling them his name was Amos and that he was one of the main coachmen at Tamasee. He sat up front with an air of dignified authority as he prepared to give them a grand tour of Charleston.

Eagerly they climbed inside, travelling along narrow streets, attracting many an admiring glance, especially Clarissa, in her lemon silk day dress. Betsy stared about her, awestruck, treating it all as one huge adventure. The streets swarmed with people and in parts were jammed with carriages and wagons, many loaded with bales of cotton, making for the wharves. Mules and horses alike champed at the bit in sheer frustration as they attempted to force their way through the congestion.

They passed bustling stores, unexpectedly quaint, and bar-rooms, with Amos pointing out places of note, travelling along streets with long rows of dwellings with names like Broad, Queens, Tradd and cobblestoned Chalmers. Blossoms topped garden walls, and houses were of mellowed brick and weathered wood, often two-storeyed open-galleried homes with delicate iron filigree on gateways and railings. There were mansions with long piazzas and elegant white columns looking inward towards shaded courtyards filled with pots of brilliant geraniums, flowering magnolia and azaleas in a variety of colours, their sweet scents filling the air.

Clarissa was enthralled, but she didn't remain that way. The carriage slowed almost to a halt as the jumble of carriages and horses became dense, and curiously she glanced around for a reason. What could it be that had brought so many people to this place? Her eyes were drawn to some posters on the wall of a building in front of them, and she strained her eyes to make out what was written on them, just managing to read the bold print at the top. She read, 'To be Sold'; the writing below was too small for her to read further, but

it didn't matter, she'd read enough. These posters were
advertising the sale of Negroes—this was a slave
auction.

Despite the warmth of the day, a creeping chill stole
over her, and she shuddered instinctively when she
suspected that this might have something to do with
why Christopher had delayed his departure to his
home.

Betsy too had read the large print and understood
only too well what it meant but thought it sensible to
ignore it and drive on. How she wished Clarissa could
have done the same, but when she ordered the carriage
to stop she looked at her in alarm.

'Clarissa, you're not getting out? You mustn't—you
can't—not here.'

'Why not?' she said sharply. 'If I have to live here I
shall have to learn all I can about it, so I consider this
an appropriate place to start. I shall probably learn
more in there during the next few minutes than I shall
in a whole year in Tamasee.'

Seeing that Clarissa was determined to go into the
building, Betsy sighed. 'Very well—then I'd better
come with you. You can't go by yourself,' and, climbing out of the carriage, she followed her inside.

Neither of them noticed the look of abject disapproval on Amos's face at their unseemly behaviour. No
respectable lady would go into that place, but his long
years of servitude had taught him to hold his tongue. It
wasn't his place to tell white folks what to do.

The two of them attracted many a curious glance,
especially from Ralph Benton, who, having recognised
the carriage and Amos, assumed, quite correctly, that
the beautiful young woman disappearing inside the
auction-room must be the new mistress of Tamasee.
What she was doing in this place he had no idea, but

one thing was certain: when Christopher found out he'd be livid.

Clarissa was right. She did learn a lot about slavery in the following minutes and saw it in a light she had never considered before. She watched the scene, transfixed, the moment seeming so unreal, as if she was suspended in some other world, intruding on something positively evil, as slave after slave emerged from the stalls, where they waited before stepping on to a balcony, the auctioneer's voice ringing out above the noise of the crowd.

'Bid up—bid up, gentlemen,' he shouted before proceeding to recount their age, characters and capabilities. They were paraded miserably, their sad, mournful eyes downcast, their whole look being one of despair, but Clarissa wondered at the anger and hatred that must fester in the hearts beneath their black skin for their white masters. Some were scantily clad but most were naked, all human dignity having been stripped from them as planters degraded them, examining their bodies closely to make sure they were healthy.

Owners' initials were branded on their skin, mostly the shoulder of a woman and the chest of a man, and Clarissa could almost feel and smell the brand, as the red-hot iron seared their soft flesh. How many of them would have her husband's brand on them? she wondered, and at this thought bitterness like bile rose in her throat until it almost choked her.

The people shifting restlessly about her regarded everything that was taking place as a perfectly normal practice, talking among themselves, buying and selling these Negroes dispassionately. Wives were separated from husbands, parents, weeping with deep sad sorrow, from children, which, to Clarissa, was against all humanity and reason. They were nothing to these cold southern planters but mere commodities.

A man came out on to the balcony with a woman, and when they were sold separately he cried out at the cruelty and, reaching out, grasped the woman, his wife, to him, tears and sobs and the terrible anguish of broken hearts rending the air. Clarissa watched their piteous pleading with their buyers, wanting to cry out at the injustice.

Unable to watch this spectacle in human misery pass before her eyes any longer, and much to Betsy's relief, she turned and went outside, climbing back into the carriage, her face white and expressionless. This town, which only a short while ago had seemed so warm and exciting, had suddenly taken on a whole new sinister meaning. She no longer had any desire to see through wrought-iron gateways at the beautiful houses and piazzas, whose foundations were the product of the dungeons and slave pens of Africa and the stinking ships that had carried them to America. All this civilised beauty had only been made possible by the oppressive society of South Carolina.

'Drive on,' she called to Amos. 'Take us back to the hotel.' She closed her eyes, breathing deeply as she tried to compose herself, to still the angry beating of her heart and the trembling inside her. 'Dear Lord, Betsy, what have I let myself in for?'

'Are you sorry you went in there?'

'No—no, I'm not. But how can they do it? How shall I be able to endure living with people who treat their fellow human beings with such cruelty, worse than animals, with whips and fetters, their only crime being the colour of their skin?'

'I don't know. It seems to be a state of affairs that's perfectly natural to them. Perhaps when we get to Tamasee things won't be so bad.'

'I hope not. Somehow I find it strange to think of Christopher being involved in anything so evil.'

'I know, but you mustn't forget that he was born a southerner—surrounded by slaves all his life.'

'No—not slaves,' said Clarissa, her lips twisting with irony. 'They prefer them to be called servants or hands. You see, at least I've learnt something. But you know, Betsy, after what we've just seen I know—now more than ever—that, no matter how abominable, how absolutely shocking I consider slavery to be, it's wise to keep my thoughts to myself. I must learn, however hard that might be, not to criticise this way of life, but I shall never be able to accept it. Never. But, like that of the south, my own subsistence depends on it.'

She fell silent as the carriage continued on its way back to the hotel, painfully slowly, but before they reached their destination Betsy suddenly gripped her arm.

'Look,' she said, 'over there—coming out of that store. Isn't that your husband?'

Clarissa directed her gaze to where Betsy indicated and saw that it was indeed Christopher, his arms full of packages, and her heart gave a joyful leap. His name was on her lips in an instant and she was about to call out to him, but she stopped, suddenly thrown off balance, staring at him uncomprehendingly. There was a woman by his side, the most beautiful woman Clarissa had ever seen, with a powerful sensuality. She was quite tall and slender, her long hair, as black as midnight, woven about her head, her skin pale and stretched smoothly over high, angular cheekbones, bringing a slant to her black eyes. The dark green of her silk dress accentuated the hidden charms of her supple, perfect body beneath, and a small matching hat with a dancing plume, set at an angle, was coquettishly perched on her head.

Clarissa watched her walk a little way along the pavement to where an empty carriage waited, noticing that she moved with the grace reminiscent of a cat, while her manner was the image of southern hauteur and arrogance.

Unaware that Clarissa was watching them, Christopher placed the packages inside the carriage before turning again to the woman. They talked for a moment and for some reason the woman was angry, their words heated. But Clarissa watched in horror, turning to rage, as the woman, with her head flung back, slowly slid her gloved hand over his chest, placing it about his neck and pulling his head down to hers, fastening her full red lips on his, kissing him passionately, to which he didn't seem to object in the least. When at last they drew apart, which to Clarissa seemed like a lifetime later, he offered the woman his hand to help her up into the carriage, but she ignored it coldly. Looping the reins through her long fingers and without looking at him again, she urged her horse on, a thin smile on her lips.

Like her carriage, which had conveniently become stuck in yet more congestion, enabling her to witness this touching scene between her husband and a woman she hadn't known existed until now, Clarissa hadn't moved as she struggled with the anger raging inside her, her blood seething. So, this was his urgent business. How dared he? How dared he leave her arms to go to this woman? And to think he had the gall to consort with her in public. Oh, what a stupid, vulnerable fool she'd been, letting him make love to her, believing he loved her, when all the time he must have been thinking of this creature. How he had deceived her and how she had succumbed to his embraces, letting him love her and then toss her aside. No wonder he'd been in such a hurry to get back to Charleston, she thought bitterly. How could she ever forgive him his treachery?

Christopher had disappeared into the crowd and the woman's carriage came close to her own. Glancing casually in Clarissa's direction, instantly she recognised the carriage, and frowned, her pencilled black brows drawing together like wings, her eyes darting to the occupants and fastening on Clarissa, who, stiffened by pride, had managed to dominate her anger and, raising her head, favoured this other woman, whom she saw as a threat to her new-found happiness, with a cool, level stare.

A heavy scent of jasmine wafted across to them from her body as her dark eyes examined Clarissa with curiosity, well aware of who she was and that she must have witnessed the scene. Slowly her eyes narrowed and glittered triumphantly, and she smiled dangerously, her red lips curling scornfully. Clarissa caught a flash of sharp white teeth from between her parted lips, knowing this woman derived a vicious pleasure from the discomfort and anger she knew Clarissa must feel.

Clarissa was convulsed with jealousy, and she had a primitive desire to reach out and strike this creature down. She was relieved that, with a brusque movement of her head, the woman turned away, and with a quick flick of her wrist laid the whip on her horse with such force that it jumped forward at once; then she was gone, leaving Clarissa staring after her, still swamped with anger.

'Well,' gasped Betsy, 'I never. I wonder who she can be?'

'I don't know, Betsy, but I certainly intend finding out.' Breathing deeply, she leaned back on to the soft upholstery as the carriage moved on. 'So, it seems I have another problem. Not only do I have slavery to contend with, but also a faithless husband.'

* * *

However much Clarissa's anger burned inside her, it could not match that of Marie's as she brutally laid the whip on the soft flesh of the horse with such ferocity that it leaped forward. Her beautiful face was convulsed with rage, her heart filled with a fierce hatred, hatred for the woman Christopher had dared to marry and bring back to South Carolina. How dared he deceive her and humiliate her in this way? He belonged to her—she was the one he should have married and taken to be mistress of Tamasee.

Well, this woman, with her insipid looks and simpering English ways, might be his wife, but so much the worse for her, she thought, and a deadly smile distorted her features as her jealous heart hungered for revenge.

Marie was Spanish, born of poor parents in New Orleans, and had dragged herself up from the gutter, making full use of the only assets she possessed—her looks and her body. She had come to Charleston and met Christopher Cordell, one of the wealthiest, most handsome men in South Carolina and, fortunately, unmarried. Determined to entrap him, she had lost no time in luring him into her bed.

Marie had always believed that one day he would marry her, but when the months of waiting had slipped into years she was filled with a growing doubt and impatience. But she had not been prepared for this insult, this humiliation, and, she thought with a sudden savagery, she would teach him a lesson he would never forget for his total rejection of her—casting her aside as if she had meant nothing to him. She might not have the genteel breeding of his cold English wife, but no one treated her like that. No. Not even Christopher Cordell, however rich and powerful he was.

Back at the hotel, Clarissa still seethed as she waited for Christopher. When he strode into the room he didn't at first notice her anger, being too full of his own. His face was set hard, the lines around his mouth tight, and when he stood glowering down at her she asked herself if this was the same man who had left just a few short hours ago, declaring his undying love for her—this angry, impersonal stranger. There was nothing lover-like about him now.

'What did you think you were doing, going to that auction?' he thundered.

For a moment his words distracted Clarissa from her own anger and she flinched, her eyes snapping wide open at his surprise attack. Surely she was the one who should be chiding him? Her heart contracted at his tone, merciless and cutting.

'If I'd known what you intended I would never have arranged for Amos to drive you around Charleston.'

'That isn't fair,' she replied indignantly, her anger restored. 'When I left here I had no intention of going into that place. Anyway, who told you? Amos?'

'No, he didn't have to, and, besides, he wasn't there to forbid what you might do. He knows better.'

'Yes, I'm sure he does,' said Clarissa tersely. 'Then who?'

'Ralph—my overseer,' he answered, preferring to ignore the implication of her remark. 'He recognised Amos and the carriage waiting outside. Clarissa, have you no sense? Can't you see it was the height of folly for a woman of your station to attend a slave auction?' He turned from her, running his fingers through his hair, which had fallen over his forehead, in exasperation.

'No, I can't,' she cried. 'And, whatever you say, it makes no difference. What I saw in that place was inhuman. To rob a man of his freedom is a sin. Black people were bought and sold just like cattle. It was horrible—an experience I shall never forget.'

Christopher rounded on her angrily. 'Please, don't start preaching to me of liberty and the rights of man, Clarissa. How can you argue about something about which you know nothing? Perhaps when you've been at Tamasee for a few weeks you might see things differently.'

His eyes darkened and a hard glitter appeared in them, which should have told Clarissa that his patience was wearing very thin, but her anger was such, brought on by his shameful behaviour with that black-haired woman earlier, that it matched his own, and as she threw back her head her eyes blazed into his defiantly.

'I doubt that.'

'Why?' he growled, his voice low, his face close to hers so that she could feel his warm breath on her face. 'What are you expecting to find? Negroes in shackles? Living in cringing submission of their white masters? Living under the shadow of the whip with the constant dread that they may be sold to more cruel masters, where their situations become even more hopeless? Well, let me tell you that the Negroes at Tamasee have no need to complain of their treatment. They are well fed, well clothed and housed, and the whip is seldom, if ever, used, and once bought they are never resold.' As he said these words his thoughts flew to Della. She had been the first Negro to be sold from Tamasee for a long time, but he believed Ralph had been justified in his reasons.

Beneath his withering gaze Clarissa sighed deeply, suppressing, with effort, the hot, angry words that threatened to burst from her lips. Suddenly everything was going wrong. The last thing she had wanted was this kind of conversation regarding the treatment of slaves. She had never intended becoming involved in an argument about slavery, however unjust she considered it, knowing she must reserve her judgement until she had seen it for herself.

'Christopher, let me explain——'

'There's no time,' he snapped, turning from her abruptly and striding towards the door. 'I want to leave here for Tamasee within the hour, so tell Betsy to get your things together. We'll deal with this matter later.'

His harsh dismissal of her caused Clarissa to summon all her self-control to stop herself bursting out of rage. But it was impossible. 'No,' she said, throwing all caution to the four winds, drawing herself up proudly. 'That is something I'm going to have to deal with in my own way, but what I cannot deal with, what I cannot come to terms with, is your faithlessness.'

Her words arrested him and he turned and looked at her, and for the first time since he had entered the room there was an element of surprise in his eyes, and he stared at her for a long moment before speaking slowly.

'Faithlessness? What on earth are you talking about?'

'You know perfectly well,' she said in a controlled voice, moving slowly towards him, her look as cutting as ice. 'I saw you earlier, Christopher, so don't try denying it. I saw you with a woman in the street.' Desperately she searched his rigid features for some hint of denial—but there was none, and a sudden revulsion filled her, a spasm of pain shooting through her heart. She glared at him with burning resentment.

At her words his face darkened and a look of guilt flashed into his eyes, but it was gone almost as soon as it appeared, and the shadow of a smile crossed his face, softening his expression, which only added fuel to her anger.

'What's the matter?' she fumed, stopping in front of him. 'Don't you remember? Then let me refresh your

memory—black hair, a green silk dress? Why, yes,'
she sneered, 'of course you remember, for you had the
affrontery to kiss her in public.'

To her chagrin, the smile on his lips broadened. It
was the first time he had seen her so angry. It seemed
he had married quite a little spitfire, and in that
moment, with the flush of fury on her soft cheeks and
her magnificent eyes blazing, to him she had never
looked more lovely. 'As I remember it, I wasn't the
one doing the kissing.'

She found his teasing intolerable. 'I do not find it
amusing, Christopher. Your behaviour was highly
reprehensible, to say the least. No wonder you were so
eager to leave my bed—after all, she is very beautiful.'

'Yes, she is,' he agreed infuriatingly.

'And was her bed warmer than mine?'

He sighed. 'Marie and I are old friends, Clarissa.'

'Ah, Marie—so that's her name. And do you deny
that you are lovers?'

'Yes, I do deny it. We were—a long time ago—but
not any more. The charms of Marie's bed long since
ceased to hold any attractions for me.'

'Why didn't you marry her?'

He shrugged nonchalantly. 'Quite simple, really. I
didn't love her.'

Clarissa's lips twisted with angry contempt. 'Don't
take me for a fool, Christopher. I saw you with my
own eyes. Have you any idea how I felt? The humiliation I felt?'

At her persistence a hard, disquieting line settled
between Christopher's black brows and a spark of
anger flamed in his eyes. The teasing note in his voice
disappeared as he reached out and gripped her
shoulders, pulling her towards him so that his face was
close to her own, his fingers biting into her soft flesh.

'Yes, I do know how you felt,' he hissed with brutal

sarcasm, 'and I don't want to bring up old grudges, Clarissa, but wasn't I in the same position once? Do you remember that, or can it be that you have forgotten so soon how I might have felt, finding my wife with another man in his bedroom? God forbid—do you think I lived the life of a monk before I met you?'

'No,' she flared, 'I most certainly do not, but if you think for one minute that you are going to keep me on your plantation with the servile obedience of one of your slaves while you continue one of your unsavoury affairs here in Charleston then you are very much mistaken. I have too much self-respect for that.'

'Damnation, Clarissa,' he thundered, his fingers tightening their hold on her shoulders. 'Marie is not my mistress. What more can I say?'

'Then tell me what you were doing with her,' she cried, hot, angry tears threatening to engulf her at any minute, 'letting her kiss you like that.'

'After I had finished my business with Ralph at the auction we ran into one another quite by chance.'

'And you expect me to believe that?'

'Believe what you like, but you are making a mountain out of a molehill. She means nothing to me. She is of no consequence. Can't you see?' he said, his face full of both fury and desire as he tried to make her understand. 'Are you so blind, you stupid little fool, as not to see that it is you I love? Since I first set eyes on you there has been no room in my heart for any other woman. What Marie and I had was finished before I ever laid eyes on you.'

Clarissa stared at him, tears starting to her eyes as her nerve finally broke and her anger began to drain away. He sounded so convincing, and how she wanted to believe him, to know for certain that that woman meant nothing to him any more, but his words could not repair the hurt that seeing them together had inflicted on her. Her image was still there. It still stood between them. Tears ran from her eyes. 'Is it true?' she whispered.

His fingers relaxed their painful grip on her shoulders, but instead of letting her go he pulled her closer still, his breath fanning her cheeks, his dark face suffused with passion as his eyes fastened on her soft trembling lips.

'Idiot,' he murmured. 'But I'm sorry, and you have a perfect right to be angry. The last thing I want is to hurt you. But do you think I could want any woman but you after last night? You are a part of me now, my love, branded upon my heart forever, and I shall never be free of you.' Unable to resist her any longer, he bent his head, covering her mouth with his own, tasting the salt of her tears and feeling her lips quivering beneath his own as he kissed her tenderly. 'Now come,' he said, his lips leaving hers. 'We must prepare to leave Charleston. I want to show you Tamasee—our home— before dark. I want your first glimpse of it to be one you'll always remember.'

CHAPTER ELEVEN

TAMASEE lay some three hours west of Charleston. Leaving the coastal swamps behind for a while, they followed the Cooper river, travelling further inland. The carriage bore them along the dusty road, driven by Amos, and a wagon sent out from Tamasee followed with the three field hands bought at auction. Having gone to the Wheeler plantation for Sam and Della, Ralph would not be arriving at Tamasee until much later.

They travelled through forests with hardwoods such as oak and hickory, the shade of their foliage and huge branches offering them welcome relief from the warm sun. Behind gateways were the stately houses of plantations, which owed something in both their design and the leisured, sophisticated lives of their owners to the gentry of eighteenth-century England. Spring in all its glory was spread before them, the woods clothed with varicoloured blossoms, white dogwood, yellow jasmine and wild azalea, the ground carpeted with purple violets and the sweet scent of honeysuckle carried on the soft warm breeze.

The carriage passed through a huge stone gateway, without the heraldic bearings of those at Ashton Park, but no less grand. They travelled slowly up a hill, the drive lined on either side by giant twisted oaks, dripping with moss, offering a cool, gentle shadiness, but before they topped the rise Christopher ordered Amos to stop the carriage. He climbed down, holding his hand out to Clarissa.

'Come—I'll show you Tamasee.'

Holding her hand, he led her to the top of the rise, the carriage waiting behind, Amos's face split in a broad smile. Without realising she was doing so, Clarissa held her breath when she gazed in wonder at what she thought must be a dream, an illusion, at the gentle sweep of the valley unfolding before her eyes. Acres of fields stretched almost as far as the eye could see, with straight furrows of well ploughed earth waiting for the spring planting of the cotton. Everything looked fresh and green, with pastures full of horses and cattle.

Clarissa gazed with wide-eyed enchantment at Tamasee, her husband's domain, and when her eyes at last rested on the house, white but glowing rose-pink in the red glow of the late-afternoon sun, she gasped in awe. It rose like a jewel out of the cool, dark shade of tall, moss-draped cypress and oak, surpassing anything she had seen so far in South Carolina. It stood stately and supreme, surrounded by lawns like green velvet and orchards of peach blossoms covering the country-side like a delicate pink cloud. The house had tall, gleaming windows with shutters to close out the sun. In front the roof rose to a point above tall Doric columns, with a wide, spacious veranda, reached up a flight of impressive marble steps. Beyond the house were the outbuildings and neat rows of slave cabins.

Watching her reaction, Christopher smiled slowly. 'I'm glad to see you're not disappointed.'

'Disappointed? How could I be?' she sighed. 'Oh, Christopher—I never imagined Tamasee being as beautiful as this.'

'Yes—I think so,' he replied with pride. 'Are you happy?'

She nodded without taking her eyes off Tamasee, which held them like a magnet.

'No regrets?'

'No, not one. But tell me—what does Tamasee mean? It's such a strange name.'

'Yes, it is. It's Cherokee and means "the place of the sunlight of God".'

'Yes,' she whispered, 'and I can see why.'

'It was my great-grandfather, Jonathan Cordell, who founded Tamasee. It wasn't easy for him in the beginning, having come from England, the regions being uncivilised with constant battles with the Indians, who, as more and more whites came, found themselves being pushed further and further back. Feeling a natural resentment, they fought to retain their homelands and hunting grounds. And yet,' he said quietly, gazing far into the distance, 'it is an Indian, a Cherokee chief, we have to thank for Tamasee.'

Clarissa looked at him curiously, waiting for him to go on, wondering why she had never asked him about his home before.

'During a storm my great-grandfather saved the Cherokee's daughter from drowning. In return for her life and knowing he was looking for a place to settle, the Indian chief rewarded him by bringing him to this place, and it was here that he put down his roots, feeling that he had come home.'

'What a lovely story,' said Clarissa.

Christopher grinned down at her. 'You might think so now, but then it was hard. It was only after many trials and adversities that he at last achieved success and created a rich estate, the one you now see. One to be handed down with pride to his descendants—and one, my love,' he said, 'that you and I shall one day hand down to our children. All this is yours now and I want you to feel for it as I do.'

She smiled up at him. 'I don't think that will be too difficult.'

'Come,' he said, turning and slowly escorting her

back to the carriage. 'We'd better get back before
Betsy comes to see what's keeping us. I'm glad you
brought her with you, Clarissa, that you haven't aban-
doned everything from your home in England. If you're
wondering about a maid, don't, because I think I have
just the girl. Her name's Della, and before she came to
Tamasee she'd been on a sugar plantation in Louisiana
and, I regret to say, was mistreated. Before I left for
England she was helping Agatha in the house, but by
all accounts they didn't get on and she wouldn't settle
down. Because of this Ralph felt it necessary to sell
her. For reasons I shall go in to later, I have since
bought the girl back, although what Agatha will have
to say when she finds out I shudder to think.'

'But—but I thought Agatha was a—a——'

'A slave?' and he grinned. 'Wait till you meet her.
She's a formidable lady, is Agatha, and feels she owns
the Cordells body and soul. She was born at Tamasee
and presides over the house and other Negroes like
some kind of matriarch, and her code of conduct is
such that it would match any of your matrons back in
England. Believe me, Agatha is a force to be reckoned
with.'

Clarissa frowned. 'How will she take to me? It could
be that she is unwilling to hand over the position that
has been hers for a good many years. Will she not feel
threatened and resent me—a total stranger?'

Christopher laughed lightly at the worried look on
her face. 'Of course not, and don't worry. She told me
long since to find myself a wife to ease her burden.
She'll love you—just as I do. She may not show it—
but she'll love you just the same.'

Although Christopher had told her all about Agatha,
his housekeeper and one-time nurse, Clarissa was quite
unprepared for the woman who came out on to the
veranda to welcome them home with an air of dignified

authority. She was quite tall and extremely thin, and her skin, stretched tight over her bones, was as black as ebony, but in stark contrast her grizzled hair was as white as driven snow, pulled with a severity from her face and squeezed into a large bun at the back of her head from which no rebellious strands dared to escape. Her features were fine, and as she saw Christopher her thin lips broke into a welcoming smile, transforming her stern expression to one of loving tenderness.

He strode forward to embrace her, wrapping his strong arms about her, and Clarissa thought that if he was not careful his housekeeper would snap in two.

'Ah, Agatha,' he sighed. 'You've no idea how good it is to be home again. I sure missed you and your cooking, but come—I have someone I want you to meet.' Turning, he brought Agatha to where Clarissa stood with Betsy a little way behind. 'Agatha—I would like to present my wife. Clarissa, this is Agatha.'

The two women were of the same height and their eyes met, blue ones meeting black ones. Agatha stared at Clarissa quite openly, although there was nothing insolent about her stare. It was as if she was trying to read there the answer to a question she had been asking herself ever since Christopher's letter had arrived from England, informing her of his marriage. Would this woman make him a good wife and would she prove to be a suitable mistress for Tamasee? It was important that she would, on both counts.

She was not disappointed and, having made up her mind, smiled slowly. Her black eyes held a gentle kindness and were now full of complete admiration for this fair-skinned, beautiful young woman from England, with the cool self-assurance of someone who had suffered and come through. Yes—she would be glad to have her shoulder some of the load at Tamasee.

'Welcome to Tamasee,' she murmured with a smile

of real pleasure, her voice as deep and rich as velvet. 'This sure is a happy day.'

Clarissa smiled, sighing with relief, some of the apprehension and tension she had been feeling over her meeting with Agatha disappearing. She wasn't nearly as formidable as she'd expected and, unlike that of all the other Negroes she had come into contact with since arriving in South Carolina, Agatha's mode of speech had been affected by her long years of servitude to the whites so that she had come to talk like them with the deep southern drawl.

'Thank you, Agatha, and I can't tell you what a pleasure it is to meet you at last. Christopher has told me so much about you.' She turned slightly and, grasping Betsy's hand, drew her forward. 'This is Betsy. Betsy is my companion.'

Still smiling, Agatha bowed her head slightly to the smaller, dark-haired woman. 'The welcome extends to you too, Miss Betsy. I hope you'll be happy at Tamasee.'

'Would you show Clarissa and Betsy to their rooms, Agatha?' asked Christopher. 'I'm sure they'd welcome a bath and a change of clothes after the journey.'

'Yes, Massa Chris, and I have refreshments ready and waiting.'

What seemed like dozens of black servants suddenly appeared and began unloading the baggage from the wagon while the two women followed Agatha's straight back in silence, looking dazedly about them, their feet sliding easily over the marble floor of the flower-decked hall, large and light and surprisingly cool. Doors led off to other rooms and, as Clarissa was to find out later, all were tastefully furnished with pieces from England and France. In general the colour of the hall was white with gilt-edged scroll-work on the ceiling, from which hung a single, magnificent crystal chandelier. They mounted a staircase, which rose grandly, its carpet a deep blue with a gold pattern. Clarissa was overwhelmed by it all. The interior at Tamasee was no less grand than the exterior.

A servant appeared to show Betsy to her room, close to the master bedroom which Clarissa was to share with Christopher. This room was no less startling than what she had already seen. But here, instead of the stark white, this room was decorated in softer, more restful shades of beige, the walls hung with ornate baroque mirrors and pictures, with a huge four-poster bed occupying the centre of the room.

Agatha stood to one side, showing pleasure at Clarissa's obvious delight.

'This is a lovely room, Agatha, and look,' she exclaimed, moving towards the slightly open french windows leading on to a balcony with curtains like gossamer blowing gently in the soft breeze. She opened them wide, stepping out on to the balcony, letting her eyes travel over the lawns to the fields beyond. 'What a lovely view.' For a moment she let her gaze rest contentedly on the rich acres of Tamasee before, sighing and turning, she went back inside, where servants were beginning to carry in her trunks.

'I'm glad you like it,' smiled Agatha. 'Massa Chris wrote and told me from England how he wanted it.'

'Then he chose well. Has this always been my husband's room?'

'No, miss. His was further down the landing. This was Miss Rosalind's room—his mother's—until she died.'

Clarissa noticed how her voice trembled when she mentioned Christopher's mother, and she detected a hint of sadness. 'Were you very fond of her?'

She nodded. 'Oh, yes. She was like an angel—a

remarkable lady and, like you, she came from England.'

Clarissa looked at her, intrigued, her curiosity about her predecessor increasing all the time. 'Did she find it easy to adjust to life here, Agatha?'

'Oh, yes—but then, she and the massa were so much in love. It did take her a while to settle down, but as soon as she learnt how to run a household as big as this she was just fine.'

'What was Christopher's father like? Did he look like him?'

'No. Massa Chris is like his mother,' and she shook her head slowly, her black eyes clouding over as her memory slipped back over the years. 'It sure was a terrible day when his daddy and young Massa Andrew died on the river boat during a storm—one of the wust storms I remember. Do you know about that?'

'Yes—he told me.'

'Massa Andrew was such a handsome young man— just like his daddy. Miss Rosalind was so distraught that I thought she would surely die of a broken heart. Mebbe she would have if Massa Chris hadn't come from England so quickly. He took charge of everythin' right away—even though his heart wasn't in it—and him bein' so young. I could see what he was goin' through but, you see, he had to take over, forgettin' everythin' else. It was either that or sell Tamasee, and to him that was unthinkable. If he'd done that the soul of Jonathan Cordell and all the others who came after him would have risen up and condemned him.' She moved to where Clarissa stood, giving her a sudden keen look, a serious expression in her wise old eyes. She nodded slowly. 'I think Tamasee is in for better days. You'll make Massa Chris a good wife—I know, I feel it here,' she said, placing her clenched fist firmly over her heart. 'But it will not be easy for you. A woman's lot is never easy at Tamasee.'

'I know it won't, Agatha, but I am more than willing to learn. I only hope you will teach me—and be patient, I am afraid there are many things about this land that I am going to have to get used to.'

Agatha nodded but remained silent, understanding by her quiet words that by this she was referring to slavery, something she herself had been forced to accept at a very early age. But then, she had not had a choice, and hadn't Miss Rosalind said the very same thing to her when she too had come to Tamasee as a young bride? Although Rosalind Cordell had never breathed a word to her husband or Agatha, the old woman knew the young miss never had come to terms with this evil that was necessary to keep the south alive. But not a word of this would she utter to this new miss. Like Miss Rosalind, she would have to bow to the inevitable—to cope with the realities of slavery in her own way.

Clarissa saw nothing of Christopher until dinner. He was waiting for her in the dining-room, having washed and changed, looking strikingly handsome in his calf-coloured pantaloons and a black jacket, which was stretched smoothly over his broad shoulders.

Despite Christopher's attempts during dinner to make everything appear normal, there was an unease and tension about him, an alert, waiting look. Instinctively Clarissa knew he was worrying because Ralph hadn't arrived from Charleston.

When dinner was over Betsy tactfully retired to her room. Christopher took Clarissa out on to the veranda, the draught from the open doors causing the candle flames to waver. He moved towards the balustrade, staring silently up the drive, which in the silvery moonlight was like a long white ribbon disappearing into the night, a rosy tint on the horizon. Strange noises of insects that had come with the night could be heard along with the soft chant of the Negroes from where they rested in their cabins after their long day of toiling in the fields.

Clarissa looked up at the grim profile of her husband, noticing how tense the muscles were in his face. 'What's worrying you, Christopher?'

He turned suddenly and smiled down at the concern filling her deep blue eyes and, bending slightly, placed a kiss gently on her soft lips. 'Now why should anything be worrying me when I consider myself to be one of the most fortunate men in South Carolina?'

'Because I think I know you well enough to know when something's bothering you. Can't you tell me what it is?'

He sighed, no longer trying to hide his anxiety. 'Yes, there is something, but it shouldn't concern you.'

'Christopher, I am your wife now,' she said sharply, 'and if I am to be mistress here, how do you expect me to learn if you constantly keep things from me? It's Ralph, isn't it? Are you worried because he isn't back yet?'

He nodded. 'Yes. I had expected him before now.'

'Where did he go when he left Charleston this afternoon?'

'To collect two Negroes from a plantation just north of the town.'

'Are they two you bought?'

'No. One is the girl I told you about—Della's her name—the one Ralph saw fit to sell while I was in England because of her disruptive influence on the others.'

'Then why did you buy her back? And what makes

you think she'll make a suitable maid for me if she's so disruptive?'

'Because that's what she was trained to be in Louisiana—a lady's maid—and, besides, I liked her. Because there was no lady at Tamasee she was put to work in the kitchen, which she no doubt considered beneath her and which led to conflict between her and Agatha. She was also immersed in witchcraft, which unsettled the other Negroes.'

Clarissa stared at him, feeling a quick stab of super-stitious horror. 'Witchcraft?'

'Yes. Devil worship and things like that. When the Africans were brought to America they brought with them their own traditional beliefs, a dark knowledge of obscure, insidious things that, unfortunately, are no longer confined to the Caribbean islands and Louisiana. Coming from there, Della practised those strange rites, which aren't recognised as much here in South Carolina, but nevertheless it unnerves the other slaves. Negroes are a strange lot, Clarissa, as you will soon learn for yourself, and they have a way of communicating with each other that we whites will never be able to fathom. I suppose that's something in their African background. Those who live and work in the house consider them-selves to be way above field hands, and no doubt Della thought herself way above any of them—her position, next to Agatha's, of course, being higher than any of theirs. Maybe this time she'll be able to settle down when she finds she has a lady to work for. But I bought her back because the other Negro Ralph has gone to collect, who is called Sam, ran away from here a few days ago to try and find her.'

'I see,' said Clarissa quietly. 'Was she his wife?'

'No.'

'Couldn't anyone have stopped him running away?'

'No. His feelings were such that he couldn't live without her. She meant everything to him.'

'Then I can understand why he ran away,' she said softly. 'You must think highly of him to risk buying back the girl.'

'Yes, I do. Sam is a fine man, Clarissa. We grew up together. He's my valet, my friend—call him what you like. But he's as much a part of Tamasee as I am.' He was silent for a few moments and when he next spoke his voice was low, and he had great difficulty in keeping it from quivering with anger as he remembered how he had found Sam at the Wheeler place. He looked straight ahead, avoiding Clarissa's eyes. 'There's only one thing. The slave patrol—who can only be described as a sadistic, murderous rabble who spend their time tracking down runaway slaves—somehow got wind that Sam had run away.' He swallowed hard, a vivid picture of Sam hanging from the stake, his life's blood dripping to the ground, flashing before his eyes, and he was unable to keep his voice from shaking with anger when he next spoke. His fingers were white, gripping the balustrade. 'Unfortunately, they got to him before I did.'

Clarissa felt a cold hand clasp her heart. 'What did they do?'

'Flogged him. But they'd have damned near killed him if Ralph and I hadn't turned up when we did—Della, as well, for harbouring him.'

Clarissa stared at him, aghast. 'But—but she's a woman. Surely they——?'

'That doesn't make any difference,' he rasped, turning his angry, pain-filled eyes to her. 'And for precisely that reason they would have subjected her to all the indecent indignities it is possible for a woman to suffer before flogging her half to death.'

At his words Clarissa's throat constricted and she

stared at him in horror. 'Dear Lord—that's dreadful,' she whispered.

'Yes. I'm afraid it will take Sam a long time to get over this. I will not countenance cruelty towards any of the slaves at Tamasee, Clarissa, please believe that, and I don't know how the others are going to react to this. The slave catchers proclaim they are doing a service, hunting down runaways with their dogs, and I am ashamed to say that there are those planters who employ them and support their filthy work, those who consider their slaves to be lower than animals. I can well imagine how smug they will feel over this. When a slave has reason to run away it does nothing to suggest contentment. Like the patrol, they have long awaited an opportunity like this—for an excuse to flog one of the slaves from Tamasee—especially one with a high standing like Sam. I'm not sure if they flogged Sam to punish him or as a way of getting at me because I have different ideas from theirs concerning the treatment of slaves.'

Hearing the grinding wheels of a wagon accompanied by the hoof beats of a horse on the gravel, they fell silent. Their eyes discerned that it was being driven slowly by Ralph so as to cause Sam as little discomfort as possible. They watched it come to a halt at the bottom of the steps. As though she had been waiting for this moment, Agatha came to stand beside them on the veranda, her face expressionless. Christopher moved away from Clarissa and she made as if to follow, but he turned to her sharply.

'Can't I come with you?' she asked.

'I'd prefer it if you didn't. Not for anything do I want you to witness what they've done to Sam.'

For a moment she hesitated, on the point of doing what she was told and stepping back, but she noticed Agatha watching her carefully, curious as to how she would deal with this situation, her eyes seeming to bore right through into Clarissa's innermost heart, holding a challenge, daring her to defy her husband on this matter, and as Clarissa battled with her decision those eyes never faltered in their gaze. Suddenly Clarissa saw with dreadful clarity what her life would be like at Tamasee if she did obey her husband and stand aside while others did the work. It would be something everyone would expect her to do whenever an unpleasant situation arose and that was not the way she wanted it. If she was to take on the responsibilities of this house and earn the respect and trust of everyone in it then she intended knowing everything that went on under its roof, and if that included nursing slaves who had been flogged mercilessly she would do that too, but she would not stand back while others did the unpleasant tasks in whispers lest they offend her.

Gently but firmly she stepped towards him, meeting his gaze squarely. 'No, Christopher,' she said with a suggestion of pride and defiance, 'and will you please stop trying to spare my feelings? Perhaps I can be of help to Agatha.'

The ghost of a smile appeared fleetingly on Agatha's lips and she nodded ever so slightly, obviously pleased with the way Clarissa had asserted herself.

Seeing the determined set of her jaw, Christopher did not contradict her. He nodded slowly, a brief flash of admiration entering his eyes. 'Very well. I'm sure Agatha will be glad of all the assistance she can get but, I promise you, the slave catchers' handiwork is not for the squeamish.'

'No. I didn't expect it would be.'

Christopher turned to Ralph, who was climbing into the back of the wagon in order to lift Sam out.

'Sorry I'm late,' he said, 'but I couldn't hurry. Every rut was agony for Sam. Luckily he passed out an hour or so after leaving the Wheeler place, which made it easier. Let's get him inside.'

The dark silhouette of a girl was bending over Sam as he lay on the boards of the wagon and Clarissa's eyes were drawn to her, realising that this must be Della. No sound passed her lips as she climbed out of the wagon and stood aside as the strong arms of Christopher and Ralph and two footmen lifted him out and carried him carefully up the steps and into the house. They bore him to a room in the servants' quarters, which Clarissa presumed must be his own. They placed him on the bed, and everyone stood around uneasily until Agatha came in, taking charge immediately.

'Water—get some water and bandages,' she ordered. The footmen left to do her bidding and she looked at Christopher and Ralph. 'You can leave us. We'll see to him now.'

Left in the room with Sam were just the three women—Clarissa, Agatha and Della, her still, silent presence oppressive. After glaring at her with a deep, profound hatred, which did not go unnoticed by Clarissa, Agatha now ignored the girl completely, not at all happy at her reappearance at Tamasee. She alone was the one she blamed for Sam's running away and being caught by the patrol; no one else.

Unintentionally Clarissa found herself studying Della, admiring her lithe, slender form. Seeing her close to, she found her strikingly beautiful, having a strange, savage kind of beauty, her Negroid ancestry showing in her large nose and full ripe lips, her skin black and flawless. The only emotion Clarissa could discern in her was the unconcealed love and anguish in her misty, sloe-like eyes, almost beyond any woman's endurance, as they rested on Sam lying unconscious and face down on the bed as Agatha began cutting away at the shirt stuck to his back, stained with crimson patches of fresh blood.

Clarissa tore her eyes off Della and began to assist Agatha as she cut away at the thin fabric. But, however determined she had been when she had insisted on helping her, when the fleshy pulp that had once been Sam's back and buttocks lay exposed she had to turn away as nausea threatened to engulf her. Only Agatha's hand placed firmly over her own stopped her from running out of that room, and it was on seeing this that Della moved soundlessly towards the bed, falling to her knees and beginning to help Agatha.

After taking several deep, gulping breaths Clarissa pulled herself together and turned back to the bed, meeting Della's challenging stare, but also something else—a flicker of understanding.

For Sam, slipping in and out of consciousness, the pain was excruciating. Each time he opened his eyes and tried lifting his head he groaned wearily. The source of his pain was indiscernible. It had invaded and seemed to occupy every inch, every nerve in his battered, punished body.

Horror and revulsion brought a bitter taste of bile to Clarissa's mouth, and she tried not to let her eyes dwell on the places where white, glistening bone shone through the deep welts cleaved into his back. Conflicting emotions about this new land and its people ran riot inside her head and she wondered what sort of men could inflict such torture on their fellow humans. In her anger she prayed that the wrath of God would strike them down, for surely this was the devil's own handiwork.

It was almost two hours later when she emerged from that room and went in search of her husband. She found him alone in the library, just staring out of the window. When she entered he turned and, seeing the strain etched on her lovely face, he stretched out his arms; like a child seeking succour, she walked straight into them, letting him wrap his arms around her while she laid her tired head thankfully on his broad chest, breathing a deep sigh.

'I think he'll be all right,' she whispered.

'Thank God,' said Christopher, his lips against her hair.

'He's lost an awful lot of blood and he'll be horrendously scarred, but I believe he'll come through. We've done what we can, and Della will stay with him tonight. She must be worn out, but she won't leave him.'

'Is he still unconscious?'

'No. He's in terrible pain, but Agatha's going to give him something for that.'

'What did you think of Della?'

'She's a strange girl.'

'How do you feel about her being your maid?'

'I don't know. Honestly, Christopher, I don't. I can't help remembering what you told me earlier. I find it disquieting and do not understand. Call it what you like, but I find witchcraft and magic alien, something I cannot begin to comprehend. It scares me. But not only that—she seems to have so much bitterness inside her, so much resentment.'

'You can't blame her. Be patient with her, Clarissa. She's had a tough time and has no cause to love the whites, having suffered only cruelty at their hands. I can't send her to work in the fields, nor can I ask Agatha to take her back in the kitchen, and for Sam's sake I can't sell her.'

Clarissa raised her head sharply and looked at him. 'No, you can't do that.' She sighed resignedly. 'So that leaves just me. All right, Christopher—she can be my maid—at least for now. We'll see how it works out. And,' she said, placing her head back on his chest and closing her eyes, 'can we talk about this in the morning?'

'Of course,' he murmured, placing a kiss on the top of her head. 'And I promise that as soon as Sam's well enough I'll get him to have a word with her about those strange practices of hers—that they cannot be allowed to continue if she wants to remain at Tamasee. You must be tired; I'm sorry.'

'What for?' she asked, a wave of tiredness sweeping over her.

'This was hardly the kind of welcome I'd intended. I doubt you'll forget your first day at Tamasee in a hurry.'

'I shall never forget,' she whispered. 'Ever.'

His arms tightened about her. 'Is there anything you want before we go to bed?'

'No—all I want is to go to bed and for you to hold me.' She sighed deeply and, raising her head, half opened her eyes; lifting her arms, she brought his head down to hers, placing her lips lightly on his, recognising the passions she had aroused in him in his dark eyes. Her mouth against his, she whispered, 'Please, take me to bed.'

This he did, and they made love while all Tamasee slept. All, that was, except Della, keeping a sad, silent vigil over Sam.

CHAPTER TWELVE

THE days after Clarissa's arrival at Tamasee were full and long and far from easy, beginning at sunrise, when the gangs of Negroes, with their drivers and white overseers, went out into the fields. Under Agatha's tuition Clarissa learnt surprisingly quickly how to supervise the slaves and how the household was run, which wasn't much different from Ashton Park; but, whereas at Ashton Park she would merely discuss with the housekeeper what had to be done, here she did many of the tasks herself. There was always so much to do, and with five hundred slaves at Tamasee their food rations and clothing had to be organised and sick Negroes had to be tended.

Sam's recovery was slow, and Della refused to leave his side. As the days passed an understanding grew between Clarissa and her new maid, and the quiet, contemptuous attitude and hostility Della seemed to have for everyone at Tamasee began to crumble. At last she started to realise that the courtesy and kindness of her new mistress was genuine and that the land she came from was so much different from this, where people were not kept in bondage, and she even began to understand how difficult these early days at Tamasee were for her too.

Clarissa missed Ashton Park, but in spite of this she was happy, and the times she treasured most were the nights when she and Christopher would close their bedroom door on the outside, and the busy, hectic world that went to make up Tamasee was forgotten and she would become a woman of pleasure. She would lie in his arms and experience bliss, swcct, sweet bliss as his lips burned her skin, his fingers searching, caressing her gently, urgently, until senses soared and sweet dark oblivion claimed them both.

His lovemaking took her to such heights of pleasure she had never even dreamed of. He was a potently sensual male and he showed Clarissa a side to her nature she had never known existed. Their need for each other was desperate, a torment, crying out for release, and Clarissa would tremble with sweet anticipation, a warmth glowing and spreading in the pit of her stomach as her body arched to meet his.

They loved, they slept, then loved again, and when they awoke with sunlight invading their privacy, their legs entwined, their skin warm and moist, Christopher would lean over and kiss her, her eyes opening momentarily, and she would smile before sleepily closing them again, and then he would leave her and she would turn and nestle into his warm, vacant place, the aroma of his body mingling with the sweet scent of jasmine on the sheets.

Before she had come to South Carolina she had known how much he loved his home, but it was only now that she understood just how much. On many of their rides he didn't bother changing out of the clothes he wore for his work in the fields, and Clarissa saw a side to him she was not used to seeing, casually dressed in calf-coloured breeches tucked into his black leather boots, and loose white shirt, open to reveal his strong, muscular chest, his hair falling untidily over his forehead, but it was a Christopher she found extremely appealing.

On one occasion they paused to watch the Negroes planting cotton. Clarissa returned to the subject of slavery and her words caused a knot to form in

Christopher's stomach but his expression did not change.

'I suppose,' she said, 'that the more cotton that is grown and the bigger the plantation then the demand for slaves increases.'

'Yes. Negroes are necessary for the plantation system to survive.'

'But surely that will become difficult now that slaves can no longer be imported?'

He nodded. 'Yes, and as a result the prices have gone sky-high.' He avoided telling her that because of this, Virginia and Maryland had found it more profitable to become slave-breeding states, to raise not cotton but Negroes, as one would mules or horses, a system he found abhorrent.

'Don't any of them read or write?' she asked. 'Don't they have any kind of education?'

He looked at her sharply. 'Of course not. Negroes are like children, with the same unpredictability.'

'They're like children because they're not permitted to be anything else,' she quipped.

'That's not exactly true.'

'Isn't it? Well, how can they be anything else when they've never been given the opportunity? Teach them and they will be able to read and write as well as you and I.'

Christopher found her questioning disconcerting, and frowned. 'That may be so, but there are many here in the south who believe the more the Negroes learn, the more aware they become and the greater the likelihood of revolt.'

She turned and looked at him, her lovely blue eyes open wide. 'Why should they do that if, as you say, they are treated with kindness? Why should they want to revolt and run away?' She asked this calmly, fixing him with a level gaze, with no sign of accusation in her voice, only a deep need to understand a system she was going to have to live with for the rest of her life, but when Christopher replied she sensed a note of anger.

'I've never tried to fool myself about slavery, Clarissa, or justify it, and there are those who believe that keeping them in ignorance will keep them down. I know only too well how some planters employ brutal methods to exact the most from their Negroes. Some have different ideas about keeping order among slaves, but ultimately even the paternalist and the patriarch, however sincere, will have to be capable of asserting their authority from the barrel of a gun, forcing them to respect and fear their white masters. They instil into them the notion that they are inferior, and even some ministers of the church preach to them that it is right and proper for them to be slaves, that if they are neglectful of their duties towards their white masters in this life then they will suffer hell and damnation in the next.'

Clarissa stared at him in horror. 'But that's dreadful.'

'Yes. It would be ridiculous of me to say most are content with their lot, but we have been lucky at Tamasee. We haven't had the insurrections that occur on other plantations, but,' he sighed, 'it does make me wonder, especially when I hear how some blacks prefer horrendous punishment and even death to subjection. Already I am criticised for treating the Negroes at Tamasee with humanity—and you have seen for yourself,' he said, referring to Sam, 'what they are capable of when I put a foot out of line. Can you possibly imagine what would happen if I began teaching them to read and write? There are exceptions, of course, especially when slaves are constantly in close contact with the whites. Sam can read and write, elementary stuff, I know, and so can a few others at Tamasee, but usually they are taught the basic physical tasks and no more.'

'Please forgive me, Christopher. I didn't mean to sound critical. It's just that I am trying my best to understand your ways and you must realise that this way of life is so different for me.'

'I do, and must confess that I've always felt uncomfortable about owning slaves. I've learned from my visits to the north and abroad, where there is no slavery, that the system must be questioned and changed. It won't always be like this. America is making such rapid technical advances, especially in the north, that there will come a time when there is no justification for it. Perhaps it will take a war to bring about nationwide emancipation—who knows? What I do know is that it won't happen yet, but when it does I hope I can be a part of it.'

Christopher's reference to war brought another thought to Clarissa's mind, of this other war everyone talked about and seemed even more imminent as the days passed, a war she thought of with cold dread.

'What about this war that is being talked of between England and America?' she asked quietly. 'Will—will you go and fight if it does come?'

Christopher glanced across at her, at the troubled frown on her brow as she looked straight ahead, and he smiled to himself, drawing his horse to a halt beneath the trees. Dismounting quickly, he strode towards her horse, holding out his arms, which she slid into with ease.

'I cannot bear to think that you'll have to go—to leave me so soon.'

'If war comes then I must.'

'But why? You're not a soldier.'

'Maybe not in the sense you mean, but I have long served in the militia, and if South Carolina goes then I must go with her.' He sank on to the grass, pulling her down beside him, trying to dispel her fears. Reaching out, he removed her hat, tossing it on the ground beside him. 'Now, no more talk of slavery or war, Clarissa, it's too nice a day. Instead let us talk about us and your introduction into society.'

She sighed, lying back on the soft, sweet-smelling grass, in the wide circle of his arms, the shadows spread about them, hearing the lazy hum of insects. 'Do we have to? I'm quite happy as we are.'

'So am I, my love, but people are beginning to talk and I have kept you to myself for far too long. The neighbourhood is agog with curiosity—all are impatient for me to introduce you. You cannot say you are not aware of the invitations to social functions that have been pouring in since your arrival at Tamasee.'

She gazed up at him in wide-eyed amazement, a slow, teasing smile curving her lips. 'You mean they don't come all the time?'

He laughed softly. 'You know they don't, you minx,' and, rolling over on to his stomach, he rested his weight on his arms, looking down into her lovely face, her pale blonde hair spread about her on the grass like a giant halo. 'Oh, my love, there is nothing I want more than to keep you here at Tamasee all to myself, forever. But I cannot. That would be too selfish.'

She reached up and placed her hand lovingly on the side of his face. 'I know, but I'm so nervous about meeting everyone.'

'There's absolutely nothing for you to worry about,' he said, turning his head slightly and kissing the palm of her hand. 'They'll adore you.'

Clarissa gazed up at him, at the sun filtering through the trees, feeling its balmy warmth, and she revelled in the luxury, stretching contentedly, squinting up at him through half-closed lids, tiny flecks of light and shade dancing on his hair. He leaned down and planted his lips in the warm, pulsating hollow of her throat and she sensed the desire stirring within him. Feeling his warm lips on her flesh, she laid her hand on his thick unruly hair, feeling the familiar, urgent ache for him in the pit of her stomach, an ache he never failed to arouse in her. She tried to resist the warm, tingling sensations, but it was useless.

Lifting his head, he looked down at her with undisguised passion, his eyes dark and pleading. 'I want to make love to you,' he breathed, 'here and now.'

She laughed softly, shakily, trying to still her wildly beating heart. 'Later,' she sighed. 'It would not be seemly if someone saw.'

'Why not?' he murmured. 'They'd only envy me.' He looked deeply into her eyes, his own filled with the intensity of his love. 'Ah, Clarissa, when I first saw you you were the most beautiful, most captivating woman I had ever seen.'

'And now?'

'Now you are even more so because you are my wife, and I love you so much that I cannot bear the thought of another man touching you. I swear I shall kill any man who does. I have said this before, but never did I mean it as much as I do now.'

He spoke with much intensity, and Clarissa was aware of an underlying seriousness, knowing instinctively that he was remembering Edward. It would be a long time, if ever, that he would be able to put him from his thoughts.

'Don't worry,' she said softly. 'No one shall.'

'Whatever happens, Clarissa, whatever is to come, know that I love you.'

She gazed at him with something like awe and she knew he loved her, really loved her in the true sense of the word, as she loved him, and she was overwhelmed by it.

'And I love you,' she whispered, knowing as she said these words that it was not the first time she had admitted it to herself, let alone said it to Christopher— and it would not be the last. With each day that dawned all the chains that had bound her to the past began to fall away.

And so began the endless round of social events as Clarissa was swept along as if on a tidal wave. She never failed to look stunning, and Christopher proudly escorted her to all the parties and balls, introducing her to all the people who were someone in South Carolina. She was undoubtedly the biggest attraction at any event she attended and was received warmly. Never had she believed she could be so happy.

The lives of the people in this new society in which Clarissa mixed were varied and full. Most of them managed their estates and slaves, visited their neighbours, hunted, danced and gambled, making frequent visits to the race-track, and many of these privileged landowners also engaged in politics, dominating society and local government. Christopher was no exception, although he was not as deeply committed as some. There was no reason why he couldn't be both planter and politician but he chose not to, knowing that eventually the political side of his nature would take over, and, no matter how much this appealed to him, his decision to be a planter, making a success of it, had been made when his father had died.

Among his friends Christopher was a man respected for the way he had taken over and wrestled with the responsibilities of a large plantation after the tragic deaths of his father and older brother, but he was also a man respected for his integrity and intellectual clarity.

He was conscientious and hard working and amply endowed with common sense. He had also developed a keen knowledge of military science during his long service with the militia and had gained influence and popularity, and as the talk of war with Britain gathered momentum he could not remain uncommitted. His more frequent attendances at political meetings were both noted and welcomed.

Anti-British feeling in America was strong. Tempers were inflamed because of Britain's continued harassment of and interference with American ships and America's right as a neutral nation to trade with legitimate markets in Europe and the West Indies. This, along with the matter of impressment, the seizing and detaining of vessels, touched a raw nerve of the people of this new, independent nation.

In England itself the economy was crumbling, with widespread unemployment, and British exports had fallen considerably. Britain realised that quarrelling with the United States was not in her best interests, this country being her best customer, and peace with her was cheaper and less troublesome than war. But, however many complaints America had, Britain considered she had her grievances too. Under her neutral flag, America was supplying France—with whom Britain was still in a state of war—with goods that Britain needed badly, and this alone made Britain more hostile and resentful towards the gathering strength of America as an independent nation.

But the central issue was impressment, and Britain asked why America should complain if the Royal Navy asked for its own men back, men the Americans had encouraged to desert to American ships, so what matter if some Americans were mistakenly taken? Surely it was fair exchange? Britain was not unduly worried by America's complaints and most British people did not see her as a threat, considering her utterly incapable of offensive warfare. But they had not reckoned on President Madison and his newly elected members of Congress, the so-called 'War Hawks', led by Henry Clay of Kentucky and John C Calhoun of South Carolina, just two of the new rising generation of politicians. They retaliated against Britain, making military threats, stating that unless she altered her navigation laws then the most valuable of all her colonies, Canada, would be torn from her grasp.

America continued to be patient, endlessly negotiating with Britain, asking her to change her policies, hoping that common sense would prevail in the end, but their patience was growing thin. They were doing everything they decently could to avoid war, although provocations continued to be endless and unreasonable. Britain treated America as if she were still part of her colonial system. The choice facing President Madison was either war or submission. America either had to fight or undo one of the main fundamental achievements of the revolution by accepting total submission in international affairs to England.

War was unnecessary but from America's point of view inescapable. No alternative was left but war or the abandonment of their right as an independent nation.

It was in June '12 that Britain at last agreed to cancel restrictions on American trade, and it finally did so in July '12—but it did not dispose of the impressment of British soldiers from American ships. Unfortunately, by the time they'd made up their mind it was too late. By mid-June, in ignorance of Britain's relaxation, President Madison finally gave up in response of a Congressional vote and declared war on Great Britain.

* * *

Clarissa's idyll was shattered when Christopher told her he was to leave Tamasee on a business trip to the north to consult some of the factory owners with whom he did business and to find others, hoping they would take more of his cotton while he was unable to ship it to Europe because of the war. Unable to bear the thought of being without him, Clarissa asked if she could go with him, but he steadfastly refused. With all this talk of war he considered she would be safer at Tamasee.

But then he told her that she couldn't go with him because, along with more of his friends who had seen long service with the militia, he was also going north to enlist, where recruiting and preparations were being made for the invasion of Canada. Clarissa was stunned. There was absolutely nothing she could say. Regardless of his views, stating that war with Britain would ruin them all, he felt duty bound to go and, however hard it was to even contemplate being without him, she was determined to make his few remaining days at Tamasee happy ones.

She had just changed for dinner and was in her room, sitting at her dressing-table brushing her hair, when Della brought her the letter from Letty, the second she'd received while she'd been at Tamasee. Excitedly she placed the brush down and opened it, knowing Letty would give her a long account of Richard's marriage to Laura. She avidly read Letty's writing, which flowed over the page, and yes, the wedding had gone well, but her presence had been missed. It had been a quiet affair at Ashton Park, rather like her own wedding. She gave a detailed account of the whole day and ended by saying that bride and groom were immensely happy.

Clarissa paused in her reading, trying to visualise what it must have been like, and she felt an ache in her

heart at the thought of Ashton Park having a new
mistress, but she was happy it was Laura.

She read on. Most of what Letty wrote was gossip
about what was happening in London, but unlike in
her first letter, when she had made no mention of
Edward, knowing how much both Clarissa and
Christopher must want to forget him and that terrible
day, in this one she felt it was in their best interests
that they know what he was about.

As Clarissa read a coldness crept through her and
her expression became a hard mask. It appeared
Edward's father had died and, as he was the oldest
son, the estate had passed on to him. He had resigned
his commission in the Dragoons and spent little time in
London. Letty went on to say that since the duel and
the time when Clarissa had left England for America
Edward had become a changed character. As far as she
was aware, he had stopped drinking and gambling and
he hadn't been seen with a woman since. Some said it
was because he was taking his new responsibilities
seriously—but Letty felt differently.

Since that terrible incident she had only come face
to face with him once and she hoped she would never
have the misfortune of doing so again. He was cold and
unyielding—it was an Edward she hadn't recognised—
and by his attitude he had made it quite plain that he
would neither forget nor forgive Christopher's making
a fool of him. Seething with hatred and resentment, he
was a man with a burning desire for vengeance but, she
went on,

> I believe he's fallen in love with you, Clarissa, and
> he is consumed by his own obsession to get you
> back. Nothing will persuade him that you love your
> husband. He is convinced you married him for no
> other reason than to secure Ashton Park.

Shortly afterwards Letty had heard news that had
alarmed her, that Edward had left England, for how
long no one seemed to know, not even his brother,
whom he had left in charge of the estate, but it was
almost certain that he'd taken a ship bound for
America.

The very words struck terror into Clarissa's heart,
which seemed to have stopped beating. She felt weak,
and the fear she hadn't felt since the night, that terrible
night, when he had tried to rape her returned.

'It cannot be true,' she whispered. 'It cannot possibly
be true.'

Della paused in what she was doing and looked
across at her mistress, at the deathly pallor on her face,
and swiftly and silently she crossed the room to her
side, where she hovered without speaking, but she
might just as well have been invisible, for Clarissa was
oblivious to everything but the pounding inside her
head. She continued to stare at the letter. Surely
Edward wouldn't come all this way to America to settle
an old score? But would he? Surely she knew, now
more than ever, that he was capable of anything, and
yes, a voice screamed inside her head, yes, he would,
but what did he hope to achieve? Nothing but revenge
for his own hurt pride, and surely that wasn't worth
coming all this way for?

Grasping at straws, she asked herself if Letty could
have been mistaken. He could have gone anywhere,
and she knew he had friends in the West Indies. But,
she thought wryly, what was the use of fooling herself?
Of course he was coming to find them, to exact his
revenge. However, one thing she was certain of—she
couldn't tell Christopher about this, not now, not when
he was about to leave for the north. He had enough to
worry about without this. Like everyone else in the
south, he was worried as to where he was going to sell

his cotton now the European markets were closed to
him—and he was leaving her to fight for his country.
She couldn't let him go knowing Edward was at liberty
in America.

Gazing into the mirror, thinking of this, she didn't
hear someone come into the room or Della go out until
suddenly a voice broke into her thoughts, making her
start. It was Christopher. He placed his hands on her
shoulders and, bending his head, met her eyes in the
mirror.

'Thinking of me?' he asked fondly.

She smiled nervously, hoping he hadn't noticed the
alarm in her eyes. 'How did you know?' she said,
hurriedly folding the letter, trying to still her shaking
fingers as she opened a drawer and placed it inside.

'What has Letty to say?' he asked, bending his head
and gently nuzzling her neck with his warm lips.

'Oh—mainly gossip,' she laughed, trying to sound
normal. 'You know Letty. And she wrote about the
wedding.'

He looked up, once again meeting her gaze, sensing
her unease, mistakenly believing it was because of the
wedding and that she might be feeling homesick. His
fingers tightened on her shoulders. 'So, Ashton Park
has a new mistress. Does it worry you very much?'

She shook her head. 'No. How could it? It was
always my home and perhaps you, more than anyone
else, know what it meant to me, how much I loved it,
but I could never be mistress of Ashton Park—at least
not in the sense Laura can be as Richard's wife. God
certainly did me a favour, providing me with you and
Laura. I might miss Ashton Park but I don't have to
worry about it any more. This is my home now, here,
with you, and—I love you so very much.' There was a
catch in her voice as she struggled not to think of the

implications of the words Letty had written, and gently Christopher turned her round to face him.

'Convince me,' and, pulling her to him, he kissed her long and deep. She melted into his arms.

When they finally drew apart she stood up, seeing the desire in his dark eyes, his lips parted ready to kiss her again. Playfully she pushed him away.

'Come along, Christopher. Don't start something we haven't the time to finish, and don't forget Ralph and Betsy will be waiting to start dinner. They'll be wondering where we've got to.'

'Damn dinner,' he murmured, ignoring her pleas and pulling her towards him once more. 'And, besides, I doubt they'll miss us—in fact, I think they'd be more than happy to be without us for once.'

Clarissa smiled, knowing he was probably right. Anyone would have to be blind not to see what was happening between his overseer and Betsy. 'I'm sure you're right, Christopher, but nevertheless I'm hungry. First we'll eat and then,' she said, kissing him lightly and extricating herself from his arms, 'we'll continue this later.'

CHAPTER THIRTEEN

As THEY went down the stairs neither of them saw Della silently watching from the shadows, her sharp instinct telling her that her mistress was more anxious than she wanted her husband to know. She went back into the room, making straight for the drawer containing the letter. She opened it and, taking out the white paper, unfolded it. Without any qualms whatsoever she began reading Letty's bold handwriting.

Della was fortunate, having learnt how to read and write when she'd been a lady's maid in Louisiana, sitting through lessons with the mistress's two daughters in case one of the young misses should need anything fetching. Secretly she had taken the opportunity to learn her letters, absorbing almost everything their tutor taught them, so determined had she been to rise above the other slaves. She'd never met any other who could read and write—not, that was, until she'd met Sam.

Della was a slave. She was born a slave and no doubt would die a slave, and the only thing she wanted in his life, apart from her freedom, was Sam. Sam—so strong and yet so gentle, the only person during her brutal and miserable existence, apart from her new mistress, who had shown her any kindness. Sam who, on hearing she was to be sold, had fiercely promised that he would find her. When she had pleaded with him not to, reminding him he would be hunted down and shot, he had simply said, 'What does it matter? I have only my life to lose.' She had been sold and he had run away, and he had found her and almost died for it. But they

203

were together now and in return for what he'd done she gave him all her love and would do all in her power to see that no further harm came to him.

Quickly her sharp eyes scanned the pages in an attempt to find out what could have upset her mistress, but it wasn't until she came almost to the end of the letter that she began to understand what it was. She read on to the end before calmly replacing the letter inside the drawer, knowing as she did so that this man, this Edward Montgomery, was someone her mistress did not like. He was coming to find her mistress, to take her away, back to her own country, and if she went then Agatha would see to it that she, Della, was sold away once again from Tamasee and Sam.

Della had seen and recognised the fear in her mistress's eyes of this man—the same kind of fear she herself had felt of her master in Louisiana whenever he had looked her way, and if this was so then she was determined to see that he would not harm her. Miss Clarissa was the only truly good person she had ever known; in fact, she hadn't known such people existed, and by keeping her from harm she would be protecting her own and Sam's existence at Tamasee.

She had promised Sam she would no longer practise her African rituals but when the need arose, to protect her own, she would not hesitate in turning to it and her absolute belief in the power of the fetish. White people might laugh, treating them as harmless African superstitions, saying that the fetish objects they used were nothing more than scarecrows and toys, but, living in Louisiana on plantations alive with superstition and distrust and lurid acts of cruelty, she had borne witness to all the violent results.

Clarissa tried not to think of Edward at this crucial time, having convinced herself that he couldn't possibly be in America anyway now that war had been declared. She was busy making preparations for Christopher's departure, trying hard not to think of what it would be like to be without him. He spent hours with Ralph, going over what had to be done in his absence, until the moment she had been dreading, when he had to leave, finally came, and their painful farewell was said in the privacy of their room before going downstairs, where everyone would be gathered on the steps.

Clarissa felt his arms holding her tightly and she was determined not to cry. He cupped her face lovingly in his hands and kissed her lips, cherishing them with his own.

'Goodbye, Clarissa, and, as I've said a thousand times before, know that I love you.'

'Yes,' she gulped, 'and I love you. But it isn't goodbye—never goodbye. You will come back—I know you will. I couldn't bear it if anything happened to you. Take care, my darling.'

'I shall, and of course I'm coming back,' he said, folding her once more in his arms as if he was trying to make them one person. 'We shall be together again, my love. It's only a matter of time,' and after one last kiss, into which he infused all the passion of his love, they went downstairs.

Clarissa watched him go, having absolutely no idea when she would see him again.

As the days turned into weeks the suspicion that had been growing inside Clarissa that she might be with child turned into reality. She was deliriously happy, but how she wished she could tell Christopher. She wrote to him, but it wasn't the same. Agatha was overjoyed at the prospect of having a baby in the house again and immediately began turning out the nursery, which hadn't been used since Christopher was a child.

She also suggested that Clarissa take a trip to
Charleston to do some shopping for the baby while she
was able, taking Betsy with her and, of course, Della.
Anything to get the girl out of her way for a while. But
she had to admit that she wasn't as difficult as she had
been that first time she'd come to Tamasee, and she
reckoned she had the mistress to thank for that. She
certainly seemed to have a way of handling the slaves,
who adored her.

Considering Agatha's suggestion a good idea, and
that it was best they go now before the start of the
cotton picking at the beginning of August, which could
last for anything up to three months, Clarissa, with
Betsy and Della, left for Charleston. Besides, the
summer was so hot at Tamasee that it would be a
welcome relief to feel the cool breezes blowing in from
the Atlantic.

Rooms had been reserved for them at the Planters'
Hotel, the one she had stayed at when Christopher had
first brought her to South Carolina. It felt good to be
away from Tamasee, if just for a little while, to feel the
cool breezes of Charleston, the energetic restlessness
of this fine coastal city, proudly conscious of its importance as the capital city of South Carolina.

It was the day after their arrival, after a morning's
successful shopping, when they were in the carriage
returning to the hotel for lunch that Clarissa glanced
casually in the direction of the people on the pavement,
her eye drawn to one man in particular. He was quite
tall and tastefully dressed in a dark blue suit, his thick
fair hair gleaming like spun gold in the sun. His
handsome face was familiar, becoming even more so,
and then, suddenly, she recognised him and was overcome with terror.

He glanced idly in her direction, and when he

recognised her his eyebrows arched and his lips curled
in a thin, cynical smile that made Clarissa's blood
freeze in her veins. She stared at him with incredulous
horror but apart from the pallor on her face her
expression did not change, although at this one cruel
blow she saw the beautiful life she had built for herself
shattering into tiny pieces at her feet—for this man was
indeed Edward Montgomery, the man she had thought
never to see again.

The carriage passed on. Betsy had been too preoccupied to notice anything amiss, exclaiming rapturously
over some articles she had just bought, but Della,
sitting beside her, hadn't. She noticed her mistress's
sudden pallor and, following her gaze, her keen eyes
had observed the stranger staring openly at her, and
his smile was not so much insolent as knowing. She
knew immediately that this was the man in the letter,
the man who had come to take her mistress back to
England.

As the carriage moved away the man looked directly
at the beautiful slave girl sitting ramrod-straight beside
Clarissa, her black eyes narrowed with open dislike as
she stared at him, without the humility usually found
in a slave, but something in her look took the smile
from Edward's handsome face. If he could have seen
the first of the small, crude wooden effigies she made
when alone in her room later, her gaze transfixed, her
expression intense, relentless as she watched it burn,
he would have fled from Charleston, taking the first
available route back to England.

Back at the hotel, Clarissa pleaded a headache,
wanting desperately to be alone so that she could think
properly. Surely she must have been mistaken? It must
have been an illusion. It could not possibly have been
Edward she had seen, but she knew, the instant one of
the bell boys came to tell her there was a gentleman

waiting to speak to her in Reception, that she had not been mistaken and that as she made her way mechanically down the stairs, seeing him waiting with ease by the desk, it was indeed no illusion. As she moved towards him her reaction was not one of surprise but of indifference and revulsion—that he had dared come all this way to try to ruin what happiness she had found.

Her proud eyes met his without flinching. Letty had said how changed he was. Physically he looked the same except that there was a maturity about him that hadn't been there before but, she thought wryly, she suspected that beneath all this he was still the same arrogant, conceited Edward, with no thought for anyone save himself. After all she had suffered at his hands, she felt surprisingly calm. The unspecified terrors she had experienced since Letty's letter disappeared now she was face to face with him, and she realised she had reached a state of mind in which she no longer had any reason to fear him. The harm had been done and she had only one desire, which was to get this meeting over and done with as quickly as possible.

She moved towards him, cool and serene, the steadiness of her gaze unflinching. He smiled crookedly and bowed slightly, his eyes never leaving hers for a second, as if trying to unnerve her, but it must have been disconcerting for him to receive nothing but a stare of profound boredom.

'Well, Edward,' she said, her voice as cool as ice. 'What do you want?'

'Want? Why, I merely wished to pay my respects. Why should I want anything?'

'Don't play games with me. What do you hope to achieve by coming all this way? I would have thought, after our last encounter, that we had nothing left to say

to each other—that I'd made it quite plain I never
wanted to see you again.'

Edward stopped smiling and wore an expression
Clarissa had never seen before, unmarred by arrogance
or pride—which was totally out of character and did
nothing to allay her suspicion that it was merely a ruse
to soften her, to throw her off guard—but it did
nothing to dispel the hardness in her eyes.

'You're wrong, Clarissa,' he said, glancing about
him, suddenly conscious that they were attracting
attention to themselves. 'Please, can't we sit down and
talk a little? I think we're attracting too much
attention.'

Clarissa saw he was right. People were beginning to
look curiously their way. Although since coming to
Charleston she had caused many a head to turn and
look at her, merely because she was married to
Christopher Cordell. 'Very well, but say what you have
to say and then be gone. Although whatever it is that
is so important as to prompt you to cross the Atlantic—
especially now, when we are at war with England—I
wish you'd written.'

Edward raised his eyebrows in surprise. 'We? You
surprise me, Clarissa. Surely your loyalties should lie
with England at a time like this—not this barbarous
nation.'

'This "barbarous nation", as you call it, is my home
now, and my loyalties are with my husband. Anyway,
if you feel that way you can always leave,' she said
tartly.

They seated themselves in a room off the foyer
where several people were taking tea, although Clarissa
paid slight attention to them. Settling back on the
cushions, one booted leg lazily crossed over the other,
Edward let his eyes linger appreciatively on Clarissa's
lovely face, noticing, as if for the first time, the long

slender column of her neck and the soft swell of her breasts beneath her lemon dress, and his breath caught in his throat. She was certainly lovely and he cursed himself for not having taken notice before. What a fool he'd been to let her slip away. But, he thought, he was here to get her back and he was determined he would. Whatever methods he had to use to get her away from that pompous Cordell, he would use them. He would make him regret not killing him when he had the chance.

'Would you care for some tea?' he asked suddenly.

Clarissa stared at him in stupefied amazement. 'Tea? This is not a drawing-room in England, Edward. You have the effrontery to ask me to have tea with you after all you have done? That you have the audacity to approach me at all astounds me.'

He smiled, but it did not reach those cold grey eyes. 'Why not? You were to have been my wife. You cannot have forgotten.'

'I'm hardly likely to do that,' she replied coldly. 'I am indeed fortunate to have been saved from such a fate. When I first saw you, in my innocence and naïveté I thought I loved you. I trusted you. I believed in you. For me you could do no wrong,' and she laughed harshly at the memory, studying his face dispassionately. 'How stupid and childish I must have seemed. What a pity I couldn't see you for what you really were.'

A look of irritation crossed Edward's face. 'I can only suppose you have listened too much to Letty.'

'No. My mistake was in not listening to her enough. If I had I would never have become betrothed to you in the first place. And can it be possible that you have forgotten the circumstances of our last meeting? How you almost destroyed me? How you tried to rape me— showing me just the kind of animal you are?'

'Would you believe me if I said I wish to apologise? That I deeply regret what happened? I realise my conduct that night was inexcusable—certainly not the conduct of a gentleman. My only excuse is that I was shocked to find you'd married someone else.'

'Especially when you discovered that the man I'd married was Christopher Cordell, a man who'd already crossed you. And no, I would not believe you,' she scorned, not taken in by his unusually contrite manner, 'and you're right. Your behaviour most certainly was not that of a gentleman. But tell me, was the shock you felt over losing me or—more to the point—over the damage done to your arrogant male pride?'

'Whatever it was, I deeply regret it.'

'That is your misfortune,' she said coldly. 'Now, say what you have to say. I have no wish to prolong this meeting.'

He nodded slowly, a steely glint entering his eyes, a hard note to his voice when he spoke. 'Very well. It's quite simple really. I want you to return with me to England.'

She stared at him in shocked amazement for a long moment before speaking. 'You are incredible. Have you forgotten that I am married to Christopher—the man you would happily have killed?'

'No, but I am willing to overlook the fact. You will be able to divorce him easily enough. Come back to England with me, Clarissa. My father is dead—the estate is mine. You can have anything you want.'

'Anything money can buy,' she scoffed.

He looked at her hard. 'If that's what it takes to get you back, then yes. After all, you allowed yourself to be bought once. Remember?'

Clarissa looked at him with complete loathing. She felt herself trembling inwardly with anger and it was with great effort that she controlled herself and managed to speak. 'How callous you are. I would as soon associate with the devil as you. But tell me, why this sudden change in you? Why should you want me to go back with you? Can it be that you've discovered you love me after all?' she asked with sarcasm.

'Yes,' he replied, matter-of-factly, 'I think I do. Since you left I've found myself thinking of you constantly. I haven't been able to get you out of my mind. I've known many women, I admit that, but none have affected me like you. So, if that is love, then yes, I do.'

'Love? You don't know the meaning of the word, and why is it that I have the feeling you are not sincere? Besides, is it really me you want, or am I part of some squalid, hideous scheme you've hatched to get even with Christopher? When will you realise that I cannot stand the sight of you?'

Edward nodded slowly, his eyes becoming like ice, his face taut. Clarissa could sense his anger mounting but he managed to remain infuriatingly calm, looking at her with a faint deprecatory smile on his lips.

'Be that as it may, I have no intention of leaving without you. I would as soon see you dead than for you to remain married to him.'

Nothing could have blatantly underlined his determination to get her back as those words, but she refused to let him intimidate her. 'I could make things very difficult for you—you do realise that?' she said.

'Really? In what way?' he asked, unperturbed.

'How many people here in Charleston know who you are?'

He shrugged. 'I really don't have the faintest idea. I presume everyone thinks I'm here from the north. But what does it matter, anyway?'

'Don't be a fool, Edward. This is America and you are an Englishman—out of uniform. What do you think would happen to you if you were found out?

You'd be thrown in gaol or—even worse—executed as a spy.'

He laughed mirthlessly. 'Me—a spy? Don't be ridiculous, Clarissa. There are hundreds of English over here, caught up one way or another in the war. So you would denounce me.'

'Yes, if I have to. I think the authorities would take my word against yours, don't you?'

'Maybe, but that would do more harm than good.'

'Really? How?'

'Why, your husband's standing in the community, my dear. I might just have a tasty little story or two of my own to mention before they. . .execute me,' he mocked. 'What matter if I elaborate a little here and there? Think of the scandal.'

'I am,' she said. 'And I'm thinking how it would make Christopher laugh. But do your worst, Edward. Nothing you can say or do frightens me any more.'

'Nevertheless, know this,' he hissed, suddenly sitting forward, the anger and emotion he had kept in check beginning to show itself, 'when I'm finished with him he'll have nothing. He'll be a pauper—yes, I'll strip him of everything: wealth, power, position, even you. I am going to destroy him. I shall burn his southern palace to the ground—he will have nothing left but ashes—and when I am finished you will come crawling back to me.'

When he'd finished speaking he waited for her to say something, but she remained coolly silent, which was far more effective than any words could have been, and a look of pure madness flamed in his eyes. She rose abruptly, about to leave him, but his next words held her attention.

'Your husband's in the north, isn't he?'

She looked at him sharply. 'How do you know that?'

'I've made it my business to know. He'll be gone for

quite some time, I believe—a long time for you to be alone. Why, anything might happen.'

'Nothing is going to happen. Why can't you accept that I despise you and go back to England? You have no place here. If Christopher should return he would not spare your life a third time.'

He ignored her threat and sighed deeply. 'I like Charleston. I have a mind to spend a little time here before I move on.'

As Clarissa was about to move away he caught her wrist, his fingers closing round it like a vice, forcing her to turn and look at him again. Their eyes met and held.

'But be sure that when I do, Clarissa, you will come with me.'

'No. To me you are dead. You died in Spain and shall remain dead.' Snatching her hand from his grasp, she strode out of the room, unaware as she did so of the woman sitting alone at a table in the corner of the room, whose beautiful sharp black eyes had watched the whole episode with a great deal of interest.

Marie watched as Clarissa walked out of the room, poised and elegant, every other woman's eye turning to her in envy, and Marie's black eyes narrowed dangerously. How she loathed that golden-haired woman with her charming ways and typically English manner, hating her with such vicious savagery that she wanted nothing more than to see her dead.

She glanced across at the man still sitting where Clarissa had left him, and a malicious smile curved her lips at the evil thought that had been growing while they had talked. Christopher was in the north. Could it be that his precious, darling wife was carrying on an intrigue while he was away fighting for his country? Could it be that the mistress of Tamasee had a lover? Although there had been nothing lover-like in their behaviour. As far as she knew, Christopher's wife had never accompanied him on his trips to Charleston. Strange she should wait until he'd gone away to come here.

Suddenly her heart lurched with an exultant sense of triumph that at last the moment had come when she might get her own back, to repay Christopher for all the mocking, jeering smiles and comments, the slights and insults she had had to endure, which had touched a raw nerve, when he had brought his English bride to Charleston.

She looked at the man with the thick blond hair with renewed interest. A mite too fancy for her liking, she thought, noticing the elaborate waistcoat and neck-cloth, but handsome just the same—arrogant, too—which appealed to her baser instincts. Yes, she might just make it her business to get to know this fine gentleman, and she was certain that what she might discover would be of interest to Christopher.

She rose and moved across the room towards him, triumph shining in her eyes, in every line of her beautiful body, and exultation that at last she could pay the mighty Christopher Cordell of Tamasee back for rejecting her. She stood looking down at the stranger, her eyes hard and shining, like a cat poised to spring.

When Edward looked up his expression was one of hauteur, and then he smiled in frank appreciation of her dark beauty. His features were perfect in every detail, his smile engaging, but Marie was not deceived, for when she looked into the depths of those cold grey eyes she recognised that which was in herself—that they were two of a kind and, however dubious his friendship might be, she realised he would make a mighty dangerous enemy.

* * *

Edward wasn't too perturbed when he learned that Clarissa had hastily departed for Tamasee. He waited and listened and bided his time, learning as much as he could concerning Christopher Cordell. The hatred he felt for this man festered in his mind so that he could think of nothing else, and the fact that he was highly respected, one of the leading citizens of Charleston, wealthy and all-powerful, was all the better, for, the more he possessed and the higher his standing in the community, the further he would have to fall—and the greater would be Edward's own satisfaction when he'd succeeded. He would then take Clarissa back with him to England—he would stop at nothing to achieve this.

His greatest asset at this time was Marie, and it didn't take either of them long to make their minds up about the other—that they were too much alike to be friends. They were full of vindictive malice as they plotted and schemed to bring about the downfall of their most hatest enemies, each making full use of the other to gain their own evil ends. But, thought Edward smugly, Marie could plot and scheme all she liked to find a way of disposing of Clarissa and he would help her, but he knew that, even if she succeeded, Cordell would not take her back. It didn't enter his head for a moment that the same could be applied to himself where Clarissa was concerned, so convinced was he that she would come back to him in the end.

They needed someone to help them put their devious plot into operation, someone who could watch Tamasee without attracting too much attention. Marie immediately suggested Ned Stone, the leader of the slave patrol; he was a thoroughly unsavoury character, but she had a feeling he was just the man they were looking for.

Edward found Ned Stone in one of the seedy bars he frequented near the docks, discovering to his immense satisfaction that Marie was right, that Ned Stone's hatred of Cordell was something akin to his own, having many an old score to settle. He was only too eager to offer his services—for a price. Although Edward knew he was just the man he needed, he neither liked nor trusted him and would be relieved when the job was done and he was shot of him.

Feeling the throbbing ache from the wound in his shoulder, a result of the ill fated duel, only added fuel to his desire for revenge, and inwardly he felt a warm glow of satisfaction and certainty that at last the time had come to bring about Cordell's downfall.

CHAPTER FOURTEEN

BY AUTUMN Tamasee was like an island in a sea of white cotton. After the long weeks of cultivation cotton picking began in earnest. Beyond Tamasee, hundreds of miles to the north, was the war and Chistopher. Clarissa counted the days they were apart, trying not to worry, trying not to think he might be lying wounded somewhere—or, even worse, that he might be dead. This was too awful to contemplate, but in her heart of hearts she knew he was alive. So imbedded was he in her heart and mind that if he had ceased to live then in some way she would be aware of it.

In spite of the shock of seeing Edward, she refused to let her mind dwell on him and the fact that he was still at liberty in Charleston, or his threat to burn Tamasee to the ground, but it hung over her like an ugly black cloud. She knew from Ralph, who made frequent visits to Charleston, that he hadn't left and that he'd become more than friendly with Marie Pendleton.

What Ralph didn't tell Clarissa, however, because he did not wish to worry her unduly, was that this Edward Montgomery had also been keeping the company of the odious Ned Stone, the slave catcher, who had been seen on and around Tamasee more often of late—searching for runaways, he said, but Ralph had a gut feeling that he had some other motive, that there was something going on between him and that Montgomery fellow, and he would do well to keep his eyes and ears open.

Clarissa had neither seen nor heard of Ned Stone, so

when he rode up to the house with half a dozen men and a pack of yapping, snarling dogs she was facing a complete stranger.

Her eyes settled on the man in front of the rest as he halted his horse and looked up at her. She knew at once that she didn't like him. He was rough-looking, dirty and grizzled, chewing on a wad of tobacco, his small, deep-set eyes squinting in the glare from the sun, travelling over her body with a bold insolence, lingering on the swell of her pregnancy beneath her loose-fitting cotton dress, knowing perfectly well who she was but treating her with utter disregard to her station.

Della had come to stand close behind Clarissa, and at the sharp intake of her breath she turned and looked at her.

'What is it, Della?'

'Dis man is Ned Stone, Miss Clarissa, de man dat beat Sam. He evil, dat one. Evil.'

A rush of memories of the night when she had witnessed the mindless cruelties inflicted on a slave by the patrol, of Sam's wretched condition, flashed into Clarissa's mind, and she was incensed by an anger so strong that she shook, feeling sick inside. She fixed Ned Stone with an ice-cold stare, freezing him in the saddle as he was about to dismount.

'What can we do for you?' her voice rang out.

'My name's Ned Stone——'

'I don't care what your name is. I know perfectly well who you are. What do you want here?'

Stone slouched forward in his saddle and pushed his hat further back on his head, revealing more of his lank hair. He shifted the wad of tobacco to the other side of his mouth and studied Clarissa, this proud mistress of Tamasee he'd heard so much about, finding her as high and mighty as that husband of hers—

beautiful, too, and he could see why Montgomery wanted her so bad, although she was a mite too uppity for his liking.

'Well, now, I reckon you might just have a runaway we're lookin' for hidin' here. He was last seen headin' this way, so, if it's all the same to you, I'd like to take a look around.'

'No, it is not all the same to me,' Clarissa replied in a voice with cutting contempt. 'And the only Negroes at Tamasee are the ones who belong here. Now—please go.'

'It's my job to find runaways, Mrs Cordell. Got to make an example of 'em. Show 'em what 'appens when they take the law into their own hands.'

'I've already seen one of your examples and I would be obliged if you would leave this property.'

'Still like to take a look around.'

'Do you doubt my word, Mr Stone?'

'Why, no, ma'am, only——'

'Good. Then, seeing as there is no reason for you to remain, will you please go?'

At that moment, and much to Clarissa's relief, Ralph came riding round the corner of the house. Working in the fields, he'd seen the patrol heading in this direction and came as quickly as he could.

'What Mrs Cordell says is the truth, Stone. There are no runaways at Tamasee—as I've already told you. Hell, man, what more do I have to say to convince you? Now get off this property before I throw you off. You've no business here.'

'Now, Mr Benton,' said Stone in an irritating, wheedling voice, 'no cause takin' that attitude. Catchin' runaways is our bizness, as well you know, and I've reason to believe some of your Nigras might be har-bourin' one of 'em.' His eyes narrowed as they came to rest on Della, whom he'd already recognised, and

his thin lips twisted in an evil smile as he pointed a
steady finger at her. 'Ask that there nigger wench. She
knows—and she knows I still 'aven't forgot that she's
to be punished for harbourin' slaves. No, suh—I ain't
forgot.'

Infuriated by the threat, Ralph moved close to Stone
and his hand lashed out, gripping the man's arm tightly,
glaring into his cold eyes. 'Feel you're safe, don't you,
making threats and riding around here while Mr
Cordell's away at the war? Well, let me tell you
something: if you dare touch her or any of the Negroes
at Tamasee, Stone, then I'll kill you myself. Now do as
Mrs Cordell says and get off this property.'

Stone glared at him and nodded slowly. 'For now,
mebbe—for now. But I'll be back. Mark my words—
I'll be back,' and with a last meaningful look at Della
he turned and, surrounded by his companions and
yapping dogs, rode off up the gravel drive.

Ralph looked at Clarissa with concern. Like everyone else at Tamasee, his liking and admiration for her
had grown immensely over the months and it hadn't
taken him long to admit that Christopher had made a
perfect choice. Those early days hadn't been easy for
her, but he'd liked the way she'd squared her
shoulders, determined to take her part in the running
of Tamasee. 'You all right, Clarissa?'

She sighed with relief. 'Yes—yes, I'm all right,
Ralph. Thank you for coming when you did, although
I can't say I like Mr Stone much.'

Ralph grinned. 'Don't worry about him. No one does.'

Clarissa turned to Della, who hadn't moved, and put
a comforting hand on her arm. 'Don't worry, Della.
We won't let him harm you.'

'Yo' don' know him, miss. Dat man evil—an' yo'
see, he do as he says.'

* * *

The cotton picking was over and the sheds beyond the
slave cabins stacked high. An invitation came for
Clarissa to attend an engagement party over at
Fairlawns, the Whitaker plantation, their closest
neighbours.

On their arrival a smiling Mrs Whitaker met Clarissa
and Betsy on the veranda, taking them under her wing
with a friendly warmth, ushering them inside to introduce them to the other guests. At first Clarissa was
slightly ill at ease, knowing just a few neighbours, the
rest of the gathering, more than she had anticipated,
having come from Charleston, but she soon began to
relax in the easy, friendly atmosphere and was glad
she'd taken Agatha's advice to get away from Tamasee
for a while.

Footmen circulated with trays of food and champagne while people chatted, exchanging news and
views about the war. Guests continued to arrive as the
afternoon wore on, the atmosphere warm and vibrant,
noisy laughter ringing out as more champagne was
drunk.

Feeling tired and needing to relax somewhere quiet,
Clarissa excused herself and wandered out into the
gardens, the party receding into the distance. She
turned a corner, hoping to find a quiet, secluded spot,
but suddenly she stopped, and, despite the warmth of
the day, she went cold all over, feeling the colour drain
from her cheeks, for there, sitting on a bench, was
Marie Pendleton, as stunning as she had been that day
in Charleston.

She showed no surprise at Clarissa's sudden appearance and stood up, a hard glint in her black eyes,
looking exquisite in a gown of black lace, a sharp
contrast to Clarissa, who wore a flowing ivory silk
dress, although it did not conceal her pregnancy; she
noticed a faint look of surprise cross Marie's face, but

it was gone in an instant, replaced by something else, which Clarissa recognised as jealousy.

Immediately Clarissa turned to go back to the house, the mere thought of confronting this woman, Christopher's one-time mistress, making her feel physically sick. But before she could do so Marie's voice rang out coolly, halting her in her steps.

'I do hope you're not leaving on my account?'

Clarissa turned and faced her. 'Of course not,' she replied calmly. 'I simply did not wish to disturb your privacy.'

'How considerate of you,' said Marie with false casualness, slowly sauntering towards her, her dislike obvious and the thin smile on her crimson lips insincere. Her black eyes shone ruthlessly like those of a cat, her claws coming out to play. 'But don't you think you and I should talk?'

Clarissa returned her stare, intending to remain calm, refusing to be intimidated. 'I don't think we have anything to say to each other. Now, if you will excuse me, I really would like to go back to the house,' she said with a quiet dignity, about to turn away.

'No, wait,' said Marie, halting her yet again.

Clarissa sighed. 'What do you want? Why did you come here today?'

'Because, like you, I was invited. I am a friend of William Markham, Amanda Whitaker's fiancé. What other reason could there be?'

'What indeed?' said Clarissa drily. 'However, I doubt you would have come to Fairlawns had it not been so close to Tamasee. You knew I'd be here, didn't you?'

Marie laughed harshly. 'Don't flatter yourself—of course I didn't. How could I?' She looked at her steadily. 'But—so you know who I am?'

'Yes—and who you were.'

'Who I was and who I still am,' purred Marie, malice

glittering in her eyes. 'Surely you must know Christopher and I never stopped seeing each other—that he's still in love with me?'

'If it suits you to think so, then do,' said Clarissa coldly. 'But what do you hope to achieve by telling me this?'

'Achieve? Why, nothing. I am merely putting you in the picture—that is all. I always think it is so mean of men not to tell their wives the truth about what they get up to when they're away from them, don't you?'

'What are you saying?' asked Clarissa stiffly.

'Why, that, whatever you may think, Christopher does still love me—he'll always love me, and he never stopped seeing me. Whenever he came to Charleston on business he made a point of seeing me. All those nights he wasn't with you he was with me.'

'I do not believe you—they are just wicked, jealous lies. If he'd loved you he would have married you and, whatever you say, I have never had reason to doubt my husband's fidelity to me.'

'Why, even in his letters he says——'

Clarissa looked at her sharply, her face turning white. 'Letters? He writes to you?'

A fierce surge of pleasure shot through Marie, knowing one of her arrows had hit its mark, that this was the reason she had come here today, to humiliate and shatter this woman's most sensitive feelings, to make her cringe and feel how she had felt when she'd discovered Christopher had spurned her. There was a note of triumph in her voice when she spoke.

'Of course he writes to me—all the time.'

Clarissa shook her head, still refusing to believe her. 'No—I still don't believe you.'

'Only because you don't want to,' and Marie twisted her mouth in an ugly sneer, bringing her face close to Clarissa's, staring into her eyes so that Clarissa had an overwhelming urge to strike the impudent twisted features, but she shook her head slowly, trying to remain calm, which only infuriated Marie further. 'Don't deceive yourself,' she snarled. 'He doesn't love you. He never has.'

'You're mad to think that,' said Clarissa quietly. 'Quite mad, and I pity you.'

'Pity? Ha—don't pity me, madam. It is you who is to be pitied. It is you who will be lying in soon, and when you are remember this. If Christopher is home and decides to visit Charleston—think of us then. Think of him in my arms—in my bed. He never was a patient man, so don't imagine for one minute that he'll be waiting by your bed for you to get well again so he can share it, because he won't.'

Clarissa stared at her with a coolness that astounded Marie.

'How coarse you are. There's not one shred of decency in you. I can understand now why Christopher didn't marry you. When he stopped seeing you you got just what you deserved, and whatever lies you attempt to fill my head with you will not destroy my faith in him.'

All of a sudden Marie laughed, somewhat hysterically. 'Oh, you're so smug,' she said, and her voice dropped, low and intense. Her eyes narrowed, glittering as she thrust her face forward. 'So high and mighty. But then, I suppose you can afford to be—being mistress of Tamasee.' Her lips curled cruelly. 'How I despise you, and you were right: I did come here today knowing I'd see you. I came to tell you something, not only that Christopher still loves me—and, however much you refuse to believe it, it's true—but also that I'll get him in the end, you see if I don't. I've been patient but you'll pay a hundred times over for stealing him from me. I swear it.' Pure cold madness flamed in her eyes and her chest heaved beneath her black lace dress with angry emotion as she glared at her rival— two women in love with the same man.

Clarissa looked at her in amazement. 'You are mad,' she breathed. 'Anyone who behaves as you do has to be.'

At that moment a shadow fell between them and it somehow came as no surprise to see Edward emerge from the trees and pause beside Marie, but it was Clarissa who held all his attention.

'So,' said Clarissa, gazing from one to the other with cold contempt. 'I might have known you'd be here. After all, what is it they say about birds of a feather?'

Edward ignored her sarcasm and, bowing his head slightly, smiled, but when his eyes took in her condition he froze. His mouth tightened and his eyes narrowed dangerously, glaring at her, his fists clenched tight as he struggled to control his impotent rage.

'So,' he said, a scornful curl to his lips, his voice like steel, 'you are to have his child.'

Clarissa met his gaze squarely, defiantly. No longer had he the power to frighten her. 'How observant of you, Edward. Perhaps now you will realise the futility of your revenge, that there is no sense in remaining here any longer, and go back to England.'

His eyes darkened, his nostrils pinched. 'Don't waste your breath and don't think you're getting rid of me that easily, for, in spite of this and the revulsion I feel at your coupling with him, I shall learn to overcome it. As far as I am concerned, nothing has changed—only that he has one more thing to lose that will make my revenge sweeter.'

Clarissa stared at him, horror-struck, trying to understand why he should want to continue treating her like this. 'Why? Why do you hate me, Edward?' she asked in a last attempt to reason with him, reaching out her hand in supplication. 'What have I done that makes you want to treat me this way, apart from marrying Christopher, believing you were dead? And, besides, you didn't love me, so why should you object?'

Edward moved to stand directly in front of her, looking like a man possessed of the devil, his face twisted out of all recognition. Clarissa shrank back, for the man before her was a stranger and the eyes that bored into hers were those of a madman, and she knew, with a sinking heart, that this was indeed what he was, for only a madman would behave this way.

'I told you, I don't hate you—in fact, quite the contrary. But he has made a fool of me, shamed me, dishonoured my name, and for that he will pay. My purpose is strong, Clarissa. I shall kill him.'

'You are out of your mind, Edward. You have lost your senses. Go back to England before you regret your actions.'

'Regret?' and he laughed insanely. 'I shall regret nothing I do where he is concerned.'

Clarissa swallowed hard, looking from one to the other. 'Then there is nothing more to be said to either of you. You have descended into the very realms of evil, so you know nothing else.'

Clarissa and Betsy passed Ned Stone and his companions on the road back to Tamasee, but Clarissa paid him no heed, having too much on her mind, and it was with immense relief that she climbed out of the carriage at Tamasee and turned to Betsy.

'I must find Ralph. It's important that he knows what's happened.'

'No,' said Betsy firmly. 'I'll go and find him and send him to you. Go along into the house. You look tired.'

Clarissa smiled gratefully. 'Yes, I am. I don't know if it's the heat, the party or the ordeal of meeting

Edward. When I've had a word with Ralph I'll go and lie down for a while.'

As she climbed the steps she noticed one of the grooms leading a horse that was lathered, having been ridden hard, towards the stables, and she wondered curiously whose it could be. Agatha appeared on the veranda just as she reached the top of the steps, her black face wreathed in smiles. Clarissa looked at her in surprise.

'Why, Agatha, what is it?'

'He's home, Miss Clarissa. Massa Chris is home.'

Clarissa stared at her with incredulity, a rush of joy pervading her whole being, and Edward, his threats and Marie were all swept away in the glorious realisation that her husband was home. 'What?' she whispered. 'Christopher? Home? Oh, Agatha. . .' and the next instant she picked up her skirts with both hands and went flying into the house, her weariness forgotten, tears wetting her cheeks, calling his name incoherently as she sped through the hall and into the library and then, with a cry of joy that was almost a sob, she was in his arms, locked in his embrace, clinging to him without speaking.

She hung there until at last she was able to lift her head and look at him, observing joyously that he hadn't changed. His eyes were heavy with fatigue, his face strained and more clearly defined and his clothes travel-stained, but he was still the same, and she reached out her hand, her fingers as light as air as they touched his face as if to reassure herself he was real. She smiled softly, her eyes bright with tears.

'Oh, Christopher,' she whispered. 'I've missed you so much.'

His hands cupped her face and he looked wonderingly down at her, almost overwhelmed by her beauty. Seeing the quiet joy in her eyes, he thought that nothing and no one in the whole world was as lovely as she and, bending his head, he covered her mouth with his own, devouring her lips like a starving man, making up for all the weeks and months they had been apart, when he had dreamed of this moment, and something like terror moved in the region of his heart when he remembered the moment Marie's letter had reached him, when she had written how Clarissa was keeping the company of one Edward Montgomery. But Christopher was no fool, all too aware of what she hoped to achieve with her malicious lies, and the very depth of his and Clarissa's love for each other was enough to crush any jealous words Marie might try to instil into his heart.

But the letter had made him mad with impotent fury and alarmed, knowing only too well that the very fact that Montgomery was in Charleston, of the torment he might subject Clarissa to, posed a threat not only to her but also to their unborn child; when he had imagined the terror Clarissa must be feeling he had immediately arranged for leave and come home as quickly as he could, pausing only long enough in Charleston to seek out Montgomery, but he was not there.

Now he studied Clarissa's face closely for some sign that he had harmed her but, thank God, there was none. 'How are you, Clarissa?'

'I'm well. How long can you stay?'

'A few days at the most.'

Disappointment clouded her eyes, but she nodded in acceptance. 'Then we shall have to make the most of what little time we have. What's it like where you are, Christopher? We hear so little about the war here in the south that it might just as well be on another planet.'

'It's like all wars, I suppose. Marching; trudging through forests and swamps, all potentially hostile and unmapped, unbridged territory; never enough to eat because supplies don't get through—but enough of war, Clarissa. Tell me about you and our child. I cannot begin to describe the joy I felt when you wrote me.'

'Yes—it is wonderful, isn't it? And he's just fine,' she laughed, placing her hand on the swell of her stomach. 'At least he's energetic enough.'

Christopher raised his eyebrows in mock surprise. 'He? What makes you so certain it will be a boy?'

'Because I know it, and he's going to look just like you.' But then she frowned at more serious thoughts. 'Why have you come home, Christopher? Is there a reason?'

His face suddenly became grave. 'Yes; I know about Edward—that he's here in South Carolina. It was fortunate I was able to obtain leave so quickly. May God help him if he's harmed you.'

'Harmed me? No. But who told you he was here? Ralph?'

He shook his head. 'Marie.'

Clarissa stared at him in silence. 'So,' she said at last, 'she was right. You have seen her.'

'No. She wrote me a letter, full of malicious intent, saying it was in my best interests that I should know what was going on between my wife and a certain Edward Montgomery. Of course, I dismissed it as the ravings of a jealous woman, but,' he frowned, eyeing her curiously, 'it appears you've seen her.'

'Yes, just this afternoon over at the Whitakers'. It was their daughter Amanda's engagement party. If I'd known Marie was to be there I would never have gone.'

'What did she say to you?'

'That you were still seeing each other, that you were sending her letters and that it's her you love and not me.'

'That's ridiculous. You didn't believe her?'

'No, of course not, and however hard she tried to destroy my faith in you she did not succeed, but she'll never forgive you for marrying me. If, as you say, you had stopped seeing her before you knew me, then it's unimportant. But at least,' she said, her cheeks dimpling as she tried to suppress a smile, 'it shows she has good taste.'

He smiled. 'I suppose you're right. Marie is so steeped in a morass of lies that she probably believes them herself; my only regret is that she might have hurt you.'

'No. I think I know you well enough now. I don't see her as a threat and I know you wouldn't try to deceive me—for two reasons. First, because you, my wonderful husband, have a true sense of honour and would never indulge in anything so low as deceit, and the second is that I would not let you, and when this son of yours has been born,' she said, indicating the swell of the child, 'I shall convince you that you will have no need for other women.'

Christopher stared at her for several moments and then laughed lightly, pulling her into his arms. 'You are wonderful, do you know that? I do not deserve you, and to me you have never looked more lovely. But,' he said, a serious note entering his voice, 'I must ask you about Edward. You have seen him? It is true he's here—in South Carolina?'

She nodded, swallowing hard, her lovely eyes clouding over. 'Yes—yes, it is true. I saw him in Charleston and then again today. He was with Marie. They seem to have formed quite an attachment, those two. Perhaps it's because they have much in common.'

'Tell me what's happened, Clarissa. I want to know everything.'

They sat close together while Clarissa haltingly told her story, of how she had met Edward in Charleston, and, when she spoke of his terrible threats and how he had repeated them earlier when they had met at the Whitakers' place, tears smarted and blurred her eyes.

Christopher's questions were gentle and he listened to her calmly, to cause her the minimum distress, but as she spoke, her soft voice faltering now and then, his face grew darker. 'So,' he said bitterly, 'again he shows his hand. Again he has dared threaten our happiness,' and what was in his heart was rage and murder against Montgomery that he had the gall to come to America, to his home, and cause Clarissa such distress that it might have resulted in her losing the child.

Clarissa stared at him with fear-filled eyes. 'He's changed, Christopher. There was something unrecognisable about him this afternoon—almost satanic—and I really do believe that his consuming obsession for revenge has caused him to go clean out of his mind. I don't know what he intends to do—but he means to ruin us. He'll kill you if he can—I'm sure of it.'

Christopher put his arm around her, calming her, bringing some measure of comfort to her trembling body. 'Not if I can help it and, besides, I do have the advantage of surprise over him. He'll have no idea I'm home.' But his eyes were hard as he thought over what Clarissa had told him, the hideous recollections of the events of the day he had married her and the duel all too vivid, the memory still fresh and painful inside his mind—for it would not go away—and he knew, with a certainty, that while ever Edward Montgomery was alive he would be a constant threat to everything he held most dear—Clarissa and Tamasee—so it was up to him now to make an end to it. 'How I wish I'd driven my sword into his fiendish heart and finished him for good,' he said fiercely. 'But one thing I am sure of—I will not be cheated out of the pleasure of killing him this time.'

'What will you do?' asked Clarissa in a small voice.

'Find him. Was he still at the Whitakers' when you left?'

'Yes.'

'Then I'll start there.'

'Please—please take care.'

'I will. But you do understand what I have to do?' he said, looking at her steadily. 'That I cannot let this pass?'

CHAPTER FIFTEEN

DUSK was gathering and the wind had risen to a frenzy when half an hour later, clad in clean clothes, Christopher, along with Ralph, rode off up the gravel drive. Clarissa watched him go and, much as she wanted to call him back, she couldn't, for in the back of her mind was a deep sense of futility, for the moment when he would meet Edward could no longer be avoided, and what would happen when the two men came face to face she didn't want to imagine.

Only when they were out of sight did she turn to Betsy and Agatha, suddenly feeling so very tired and weary. The events of the day were beginning to take their toll, but even now she had a terrible feeling of oppression, of impending doom, that the day was far from over.

Sighing deeply, she placed her hand in the small of her aching back, the child suddenly feeling so heavy. 'I think I'll go to my room for a while and have Della prepare me a bath. I think a good soak might make me feel better.'

Agatha suddenly frowned at the mention of Della. 'Della? Why, I don't think she's back yet. With all the excitement I'd clean forgot about her.'

Clarissa looked at her sharply. 'Why? Where did she go?'

'Over to Ralph's house with some clean laundry. I was going to send one of the others with it until she offered, having nothing much to do.'

'How long has she been gone?'

'About an hour.'

234

Clarissa felt herself going very cold, and a sickening fear gripped her heart. Her tiredness was suddenly forgotten. To get to Ralph's house she would have to go past the slave cabins, follow the path alongside the river and past the cotton sheds before reaching the house. 'But—but it should only have taken her half an hour at the most,' and she stared at Agatha, her mouth going very dry as the hint of a suspicion took root in her breast and became larger with every second until it became a terrible certainty. 'Oh, dear God,' she whispered. 'Ned Stone. I should have known he was up to no good. We passed him—do you remember, Betsy?—on the road back to Tamasee. Agatha—you don't think—— Oh, dear, merciful God,' she said, her trembling hand gripping her throat.

Alarmed by Clarissa's stricken face, Betsy took her arm and propelled her into the drawing-room. 'Don't worry, Clarissa. She's more than likely gossiping somewhere.'

'No. Della isn't one for gossiping—you know that.'

'But what reason could Ned Stone have for harming Della? She's done nothing wrong,' said Agatha.

'We might not think so, but he does. When she was at the Wheeler place he accused her of harbouring Sam when he ran away to find her. When he came here not long ago he saw Della and recognised her. He made it quite plain then that he hadn't forgotten what she'd done and that she still had to be punished for her crime.'

At Clarissa's words Agatha's face tightened and she knew they had cause for concern. Lord knew, she had no liking for the girl, but she had no desire to see her brought back to the house in the same condition as Sam after he'd run away. But it would be worse for Della because she was a woman. Undoubtedly she would be raped before being flogged—and God help her if she resisted.

It wasn't long before their worst fears were realised when one of the field hands, breathless, his black, terror-filled eyes darting from one to the other of the three women, was ushered into the drawing-room to tell them that the slave catchers had got Della.

Clarissa stood up from the couch, her face ashen. 'Where is she?'

'Out near de cotton sheds, Miss Clarissa. De patrol er mighty drunk an' de's goin' ter flog 'er.'

'Then we must stop them.' She turned to Agatha. 'They'll kill her if we don't. Is there anyone we can send?'

'No. No one will dare interfere with the patrol. They're too terrified for their own skins.'

'Then I'll go myself. They must be stopped and made to realise that they cannot come on to other people's property and take the law into their own hands in this way.'

Betsy gasped, horrified. 'You can't go. You can't possibly go out and face them in your condition and, besides, you heard what the boy said. They're drunk. There's no telling what might happen.'

'Just try stopping me. I'm going, Betsy. I'm the only one here with any authority.'

'Please wait for Christopher and Ralph to get back,' she pleaded.

'There's no time. Della could be dead by then.'

Seeing that Clarissa was determined, Betsy relented. 'All right. But I'm coming with you,' she insisted. 'Just wait until I fetch our cloaks. It's enough to freeze you to death out there, and it's blowing a gale.'

Darker and darker grew the sky as the two women made their way past the neat rows of slave cabins, the

doors tightly shut as the trembling Negroes hid behind
them in stark terror of the slave hunters. The very
name instilled fear into them, as tales had come to
Tamasee of atrocities and persecution on others less
fortunate. Although none had suffered at their hands
at Tamasee, nothing would induce them to come out
of their cabins until they'd gone.

They hurried along a narrow path that ran beside the
river towards the cotton sheds, the wind bitterly cold,
bending trees almost double, making their bare
branches creak. It was an ugly, menacing wind and
Clarissa hated it as it pulled relentlessly at their cloaks,
whipping their hair about their faces, stirring up dead
leaves at their feet and also a memory of another
night—for wasn't it on a night such as this that she'd
gone in search of Edward at the Black Boar? She
quickly thrust the memory from her mind. They heard
the first rumble of thunder followed by a vivid flash of
lightning, and Clarissa shivered, clutching her cloak
tightly about her.

The journey from the house seemed interminable as
they battled on, fraught with worry, their nerves raw
as they thought of nothing except reaching Della in
time. They saw the dark, ghostly shapes of the cotton
sheds ahead and the faint glow of burning torches amid
the darkness of the trees becoming brighter the closer
they got, the noise of drunken voices carried to them
on the wind growing stronger with ever-increasing
force.

Their eyes became riveted on the scene before them,
which seemed unreal, and Clarissa felt a nervous
quivering in the pit of her stomach, wishing
Christopher and Ralph were here to deal with this.
Bravely she moved towards the cluster of rough-looking individuals squatting and sprawling on the ground,
kegs of cheap liquor passing among them, some already

drunk out of their minds, with slack mouths and glazed
eyes. She saw the unmistakable figure of Ned Stone
slouched against a tree and she suspected he was not
as drunk as the rest, but it was on a figure not far from
him that her eyes rested.

In the flickering torch-light she could see it was
Della, a piteous sight, but although her clothes had
been brutally torn, and her proud young breasts
exposed, despite her attempts to cover them with her
arms, while shivering from the bitter cold, she
appeared unharmed; however, several eyes rested on
her greedily, eyes that she met with admirable defiance.
There was something strange about the whole scene,
and Clarissa thought it odd that no one had touched
Della. It was almost as if they were waiting for something or someone.

As the two women stepped into the circle of light the
dogs suddenly bounded forward, yapping and snarling
ferociously, their fangs bared and eyes gleaming.
Clarissa paled but tried not to show fear as she looked
directly at Ned Stone. Fear had to be set aside if she
was to help Della.

'Call them off,' she commanded.

He looked up, showing no surprise at her appearance. It was almost as if she was expected. He let out a
low whistle. 'Stay,' he ordered, at which the dogs
reluctantly ceased their snarling but continued to growl
as they sat back on their haunches, still alert, still
threatening, waiting for instructions. He looked up at
Clarissa, his gaze indifferent, as if he was bored by the
whole incident and, turning his head, he spat on the
ground before again fixing her with a bold stare. 'Well,'
he drawled, 'come to watch the entertainment?'

'Release her,' said Clarissa icily. 'She's done nothing
wrong.'

He merely shrugged, unperturbed by her anger.

'Taint no use mixin' in our bizness, miss. We've a right to punish niggers what done wrong—no 'ceptions. You don' understand our ways, so it's best not ter interfere.'

A sudden fury seized Clarissa. 'Then what are you waiting for? Why haven't you flogged her? Or is it your way to prolong the agony?'

'Nope. Only waitin' for someone, that's all.'

Clarissa was about to ask who when at that moment a figure emerged from the trees, but he was too far beyond the light for her to discern who it was. She watched him come closer, purposefully taking his time. A trickle of cold sweat ran down Clarissa's back, and as the man stepped into the light, a shock of blond hair falling casually over his forehead, a sardonic twist to his firm lips, she felt the blood drain out of her face, but she refused to give way to fear as she faced Edward.

'So,' she said, 'it is you,' and with sudden clarity she knew the situation had been set up by him. Her eyes settled on him with complete hatred. 'It was you who sent the man to the house, wasn't it? Knowing Ralph, our overseer, was away?'

His cold grey eyes widened in mock surprise. 'How perceptive of you, my dear, and yes—it was me. I've waited a long time for a chance such as this, but,' he said, looking with distaste at Della, 'little did I know that she would be the bait. I have Ned Stone to thank for that, having an old score to settle with her himself. I had no doubt that you would come to the aid of your own personal slave, having learnt, of course, that no one, unless they are white, would dare interfere with the slave patrol and their work—although even then they have to be careful lest they be accused of being nigger lovers.'

'You learn quickly, Edward,' scoffed Clarissa. 'And are you also to stay and witness the flogging of an innocent girl?'

'I think not. Their methods of dealing with servants are really quite barbarous, don't you think? They lack the finesse, the refinement of us in England. Don't know how you put up with it—whole damn south is teeming with niggers. Don't mind if I never see one again, I can tell you.'

Hot words in defence of the Negroes rose to Clarissa's lips, but she restrained herself. 'Why are you here at Tamasee, Edward? What do you want?'

'You,' he said without hesitation. 'I have a carriage waiting to take us to Charleston. Tomorrow we will leave for the Indies and from there go on to England.'

Clarissa stared at him incredulously, and if the moment hadn't been so serious she would have laughed. 'And Christopher? Do you think he won't come after me?'

'I'm sure he will, but he is in the north. It will be a long time before he will be able to come after you. And when he does I shall be ready for him.'

'You make it sound so easy, Edward. But after all your plotting and scheming to kidnap me you have overlooked one important fact—that Christopher is here, at Tamasee. He arrived earlier today and at this very minute he is with Ralph—looking for you.'

Edward stared at her in disbelief and then his face twisted with sudden fury. 'You lie,' he spat.

'No, I do not lie, and it is Marie you have to thank. She is the one who wrote to him, telling him of your presence in Charleston.'

'The bitch,' he snarled. 'Well—no matter. We shall leave now.'

As he was about to grasp her wrist Ned Stone rose and stood between them. 'Not so fast, Mr Montgomery. There is a matter of unfinished bizness.'

Edward looked at him sharply. 'What do you mean?'

Ned Stone glanced meaningfully down at Della, and Edward, aware of his intent, glared at him furiously.

'There's no time now. We'll have to let her go.'

'Ye've a lot to learn 'bout our ways. We never let niggers go and, besides,' he grinned, a lop-sided evil grin as he indicated Clarissa, 'ye'll never git her back to Charleston without us. Minute you lay a finger on 'er she'll start kickin' an' hollerin' like a hell cat. Nope— way I see it, ye'll just 'ave ter wait 'till we're done.'

'But there isn't time,' persisted Edward.

Ned Stone ignored him and urged his men to their feet. 'Do your work,' he commanded, the wind snatching the words from his lips. He pointed towards the nearest of the cotton sheds. 'Take 'er in there and string 'er to one of the beams.'

Two men staggered forward and seized Della, hoisting her roughly to her feet, dragging her towards the already open door. Clarissa was about to run forward, but Betsy held her back.

'Clarissa,' she shouted, 'you mustn't. There's nothing you can do.'

They watched helplessly as Della struggled frantically, and when the remnants of her torn bodice was ripped from her she raked her nails down the face of one of her captors, at which he gave a yelp of pain and dealt her a mighty blow that sent her sprawling to the ground, senseless. The men bent over her as a gust of wind sucked at a burning torch and Clarissa and Betsy watched, horror-struck, as a spark, borne on the wind, was blown towards the cotton shed and through the open door.

At first it was only a spark that, if near enough, anyone could have extinguished, but, drunk as Ned Stone's men were, it was nigh impossible. The wind caught the living spark, becoming a living tongue, licking and feasting greedily on the dry bales of closely packed cotton. The wind caught the flame and the fire took hold, leaping and dancing, penetrating higher into the night sky.

Ned Stone's men stared at the fire, their mouths agape and eyes half crazed before turning and fleeing into the woods. Clarissa turned to Betsy, her body functioning automatically.

'Quick, Betsy. Go to the slave quarters and fetch as many as you can with buckets. They can get the water from the river. We have to stop the fire from spreading to the other sheds.'

Betsy didn't need to be told twice and fled back along the path. Turning her attention to the shed, Clarissa could still see Della lying on the ground and would have run towards her, but Edward barred her way. At the sight of him she vented all her pent-up fury on him.

'There,' she cried accusingly. 'Are you satisfied? This is what you wanted, wasn't it?'

'If you hadn't been so foolish none of this would have happened in the first place. If only you had waited for me,' he shouted over the noise of the wind and fire.

'Foolish? I, foolish? No, Edward, not me. It was through your foolishness that you lost me and I must thank you, for because of it I met and married Christopher and it freed me from you. I love him in a way you could never understand, and if you intend to dispose of his life then you will also be disposing of mine, for I would rather die than go back with you to England.'

At that moment two men came riding out of the trees, drawn by the blaze, and Clarissa gave a cry of relief when she saw it was Christopher and Ralph. She ran to them just as Negroes began appearing from the direction of the slave quarters. Dismounting quickly, Christopher turned to Clarissa, but at the same time he saw Edward, and his face darkened with a murderous fury.

'You,' he spat. 'I might have known. This is your work. You can be sure I'll deal with you when I've brought the fire under control.'

He turned away, taking command immediately, shouting above the roar of the fire and wind, which, mercifully, was blowing away from the other sheds, although it could change direction at any minute. Ralph and Betsy organised the Negroes, who formed a human chain to the river, passing buckets from one to the other, drenching the other sheds for fear of rogue sparks blowing their way, There was nothing that could be done for the burning shed but contain it.

Christopher turned back to Clarissa and, taking her hand, pulled her away. 'Go back to the house,' he ordered. 'This is no place for you.'

'But—I——'

'Go, Clarissa. I've enough to do here without having you to worry about.'

'Wait—please,' she cried, grasping his arm, and the intensity in her eyes made him pause.

'What is it?'

'Della's by the shed. We must get her away. It's because of her that I'm here. The patrol came and took her. They were going to flog her.'

'Good God.' Immediately he ordered one of the Negroes closest to him to pour a bucket of water over him before plunging through the wall of smoke.

The night was suddenly torn asunder as lightning ripped across the sky, and the noise from the fire was like the angry roar of an enraged animal. A hideous red glow filled the sky into which belched a pall of black smoke, and the crash of falling timbers could be heard from inside, sending up fountains of sparks as

mercifully, at long last, providence came to their rescue
and they felt the first drops of rain.

It seemed an eternity but couldn't have been more
than seconds before Christopher emerged with the now
semi-conscious Della, coughing and choking from the
effects of the smoke, in his arms, but as he stepped
through the doorway one of the scorched beams came
crashing down, pinning one of his legs to the ground.
He managed to throw Della clear. Ralph immediately
ran to his aid and tried raising the heavy beam,
uncaring that it blistered and burned his hands, but it
was too heavy to lift alone. Frantically he called for
help.

Clarissa watched it all, her mind blank with terror as
the shed became a blazing inferno, but, seeing
Christopher pinned helplessly to the ground, a wall of
burning bales likely to come crashing down on top of
him at any second, she came alive. Smoke smarted her
eyes and burned her nostrils and she could feel the
intense, searing heat, the smoke choking her, filling
her lungs so she could hardly breathe. She flung herself
forward with a strangled cry, calling his name, tears
flooding her cheeks mingling with the rain. But suddenly hands gripped her shoulders, pulling her back. It
was Edward and she struggled wildly against him.

'No,' she screamed. 'I must go to him. Let me go.'

'You little fool,' he spat. 'You can't.'

'Why?' she cried, staring at him, her eyes wide, filled
with madness. 'Why can't I? Whatever you intend
tonight, Edward, if Christopher dies then as surely as
if you had thrust the knife into his heart you will have
killed him. Are you prepared to burden your heart
with his murder—and mine? Because I will not go on
living without him. You will have my death on your
conscience too.'

For the first time since she had known him his face

expressed no mockery, no anger, only a complete and utter wretchedness, but after all he had done to harm her she could not feel sorry for him.

'No,' he said, so softly that she only just caught the words. 'I'm sorry, Clarissa. That I do not want.'

Clarissa laughed triumphantly, a half-crazed sound, full of a cruel sweetness at finding she could hurt him at last. 'Let me go,' she cried, trying to shake off his hands. 'I must go to him.'

'No—stay here. I'll go.'

As he left her Clarissa felt nausea rising inside her, and her head began to swim as darkness closed in. Her vision was obscured by a grey mist and she was conscious of a feeling of weightlessness as slowly she slumped to the ground. It was into a deep, merciful oblivion that she sank, merciful because she did not see Edward lift the beam with Ralph, who managed to pull Christopher free, or the wall of blazing bales which chose that moment to come tumbling down on Edward. Nor did she see Della's satisfied smile.

The blessed rain at last came lashing down, sizzling fiercely as it met the searing heat, and a cry of abject relief went up from the Negroes at this welcome help from heaven—but too late to help Edward, whose charred and blackened body was pulled from the ashes the following day.

For Christopher the war was over; for America it had two more years to run, though it was obscured throughout by the continuing conflict in Europe. An American attempt to invade Canada failed dismally, but neither were the United States successfully invaded. British expeditions were checked on the Great Lakes at Baltimore, but they managed to capture Washington, burning its public buildings, including the House of Representatives and the President's home, sorely injuring American pride. This was restored by General Andrew Jackson, the great American hero of the war, as the British invasion moved south in the hope of taking New Orleans. That offensive was blocked by Jackson, who repelled the attack, inflicting such heavy losses that the British were forced to abandon their attempt on New Orleans.

This was America's most decisive victory of the war, which had covered three years of scattered, indecisive battles, both on land and sea, with many lives lost. Only then were the leaders of both countries persuaded that it was preferable to compromise than to fight, though the peace treaty was little more than an agreement to stop fighting, for neither side would make concessions. Had that been possible, the war need never have been fought at all. Yet out of this peculiar conflict America obtained a new confidence, a self-awareness, and Britain at last learned, after all her bullying and inflexibility, that war with the United States was not worthwhile and had to admit a reluctant respect for her former colony.

After sending someone for the doctor, Ralph picked Clarissa up and quickly carried her back to the house with Betsy hurrying beside him. Christopher was transported on a crude litter and the pain he suffered from his shattered leg was sheer torture, intensified with each jarring step and, adding to his agony, he could scarcely breathe, his lungs were so full of smoke. He prayed he would lose consciousness to escape the crippling pain and mercifully his prayers were answered before he reached the house, where he was put to bed in his old room.

Clarissa was attended to by Agatha and Betsy, anxiously waiting for the doctor to come and examine her, fearful that because of her ordeal she would lose the child.

When she opened her eyes she didn't know how much later it was. Perhaps hours, days, weeks, when it was, in fact, just two hours and the doctor had left her to attend Christopher. The first person she saw was Betsy, her eyes full of loving concern, who smiled with tears of relief glistening on her lashes when she saw she was awake.

'Christopher—how's Christopher?' Clarissa asked with difficulty.

'Unconscious but alive. The doctor's with him now.'

'Thank God,' she whispered. 'And—and my baby?'

'Your baby's just fine, Clarissa.'

She smiled softly and then sank into a deep sleep.

The doctor, having been a military surgeon, was accustomed to broken limbs, and with Sam's help he worked for hours straightening Christopher's shattered leg, which was badly broken in several places, the bones having pierced the scorched flesh. Later, with Christopher's leg splinted and swathed in bandages, the doctor left, promising to be back the following morning, but after having a word with Agatha he left her in no doubt that even without infection setting in, which was always a danger in these cases, his recovery would be slow. It would be weeks before he would be able to leave his bed and months before he could attempt to walk. And when he did he would always have a limp.

When Agatha told Clarissa this when she awoke the following day she was sad but realised it could have been far worse, that a few seconds longer, pinned beneath that beam, and he would not be here at all. The wall of bales would have fallen on him instead of Edward, which was something she couldn't bear to think about. But when she thought of Edward and what he had tried to do she could feel only anger. In time she would write to his brother, telling him what had happened—he had a right to know that—but not just yet. At the moment she didn't want to think of Edward or what had prompted him to rush forward and save Christopher's life. Whatever his reasons, she didn't want to know.

The doctor was right: Christopher's recovery was slow and painful, which wasn't surprising, considering the severity of his injuries, and he would have gone clean out of his mind with sheer frustration at being tied to a sick-bed had it not been for Clarissa and Ralph, who kept him informed on matters concerning the plantation and the war.

He became reconciled to the fact that he would not go back to his regiment, and as his broken bones knit together he concentrated on regaining his strength, determined that when he was back on his feet, limp or no limp, there was much to do. He was looking forward to taking an active part in the politics of South Carolina, and who knew where it would take him once the war was over? He remembered the conversation he had had with his uncle, Lord Buckley, at his club in London, the day after he'd first seen Clarissa, when he'd told him of the great opportunities America had to offer and how he wanted his children to have a part in the building of their country. Then he had not considered that the opportunities were there for him too, having made up his mind to be a planter until the day he died. But not any more, and he became consumed with a driving ambition, a sense of elation and expectation, for at long last he accepted what his friends had been telling him for years, ever since the death of his father, that there was no reason why he couldn't be both master of Tamasee and politician.

He would be able to pursue the subject that was

uppermost in his mind—the question of slavery. As a politician he would be in a prominent position to help bring about a movement for abolition by moral and political action. He had inherited a labour system he was no longer able to live with and ever since he had returned from England ideas had been forming in his mind. To appease his conscience he would begin by freeing the slaves at Tamasee, and by paying them a wage he hoped they would remain and work for him. But he did not delude himself. The path he had set would be a hard, ceaseless struggle. This private act of manumission would most certainly be frowned upon as irresponsible by his neighbours, but if he was to make abolition his central issue he had no choice.

What the consequence of his action would be he could not foresee, but he had no doubt that what he was doing was right. But he wasn't doing it just for himself. It would be for his children and Clarissa, too, for, however hard she might try, she would never be able to accept slavery as a fact of life. Whatever he decided, he knew she would support him wholeheartedly and be with him every step of the way. She would even be able to put into effect her idea for educating the children. That would please her.

Clarissa was sitting on Christopher's bed when Ralph left them, having just returned from Charleston bringing them eagerly awaited news about Ned Stone. Knowing he was to be accused of starting the fire at Tamasee in which a man had died, he had fled the state. No one had set eyes on him since. The other news he brought was that Marie had also gone—back to New Orleans.

The relief Clarissa felt when he told them this was overwhelming. It was like having a heavy load lifted from her mind. All the old fears that had tormented her for so long began to fade into the past and the future stretched before her, bright with joy. A future she had once been too afraid to contemplate.

'So,' said Christopher, 'Ned Stone has evaded justice. Ah, well, it doesn't surprise me, but one day you can be sure he'll get what he deserves. And Marie—so she's gone too,' and he smiled. 'It seems all our enemies have deserted us.'

Clarissa nodded. 'Yes, thank goodness. But, you know, I'm not sorry Edward's dead, Christopher. Do you think it's terrible of me to say that?'

'After what he put you through? No.'

'You were only injured,' she said softly, 'when you could so easily have been killed. Edward paid for what he did with his life. But what I shall never understand is why he saved you. When you were pinned beneath that beam everyone could see the bales were about to fall.' She sighed, shaking her head slowly. 'I don't suppose I shall ever know why he did it.'

Christopher reached out and placed his fingers beneath her chin, lifting her face to his own, gazing steadily into her eyes, those beautiful blue eyes, which had so entrapped him from the start. Then they had been devoid of love—but not any more. 'Don't you? I think I do. Perhaps he remembered what might have been had he treated you differently. He set a trap for you but fell into it himself. When you became unattainable, in his own peculiar way and as much as Edward was capable of feeling love for any woman, I believe he fell in love with you.' He swept her into his arms, the very force of their love causing the child to stir within her. 'But he could never love you as I do, Clarissa. God, how I love you.'

The very tenderness on his face brought tears to her eyes. 'It's over now, isn't it, Christopher? Edward, Marie—neither of them can harm us ever again.'

'No, my love. You needn't be afraid any more. Everything is going to be all right,' and as he said this he knew the time had come for him to tell her of his plans for the future.

'I never believed I could be so happy,' she murmured through her tears, resting her head on his shoulder. 'I'm so happy I feel I could die of it.'

He laughed lightly. 'You'll soon get used to it— you'll see.'

It was the greatest day Tamasee had known for several decades when the master's son was born, beginning a round of festivities suited to such a happy occasion. Happiness reigned over the great plantation. All were celebrating at once the freedom of the slaves and the new heir.

Christopher sat on the bed with his arm around Clarissa, who was gazing down at the child sleeping soundlessly in her arms. He thought how changed she was. Happiness suited her. With the birth of their son her beauty bloomed with a new contentment and maturity as never before.

'What are you thinking?' he asked.

She sighed. 'About everything. About us and how happy you've made me.'

'Don't you think you deserve it after all you've been through?'

'Not only me—you deserve it, too. Oh, Christopher, this really is a time for celebration. I'm so proud of you. Just listen,' she said, looking towards the open window, through which drifted the sound of laughter and singing coming from the ex-slaves' quarters. The moon had risen and the celebrations would go on well into the night. 'They sound so happy. I hope many more plantation owners follow your example and free their slaves.'

'I doubt it, somehow. We've a long way to go before we see the end of slavery in the south, Clarissa. It may not be in our lifetime, but,' he said, gazing proudly at his son, 'God willing, it will be in his. The tide will turn one day.'

'Can Tamasee survive without it? Will it prove too difficult for us to live here?' She felt his arm tighten about her shoulders, and his voice took on a fierce determination when he answered.

'Yes, Tamasee can survive, and not only Tamasee but we also will survive—the Cordells as a family, with our pride and honour and our love. Whatever hardships are thrust at us, we will face the future together. Giving the slaves their freedom is only the beginning, but we'll win through in the end. You'll see.'

FAIR GAME
Sheila Bishop

Miss Olivia Fenimore was happy to spend the summer
months with her relatives in Parmouth, Devon, though
she was disturbed to find the family in an uncomfortable
situation. Mr Tom Brooke had apparently led her young
cousin Hetty somewhat astray, something not easy to
hide in a small community. It was Olivia's misfortune
that she also found Mr Brooke deeply attractive, but a
man who appeared to consider women fair game was
not for her. . .

Look out for the two intriguing

Romances coming next month

THE FALCON AND THE DOVE
Paula Marshall

In the Tuscany of 1430, the impoverished Lord of San Giorgio was lazy and a slattern, who kept his sister Bianca on short rations and worse clothing. So when the beautiful and renowned condottiero, Piero de' Manfredini, asked for her in marriage, Bianca was astounded *and* furious when her brother threatened her with a convent if she refused! Intelligent and ambitious, Piero was playing a deep game, but as the game progressed, the plain and astringent Bianca confounded him, and the game's end was not at all what he expected. . .

THE CAPTAIN'S ANGEL
Marie-Louise Hall

Despite the bitter Russian winter and Napoleon's threat to Moscow, Angèle's problem was closer to home. She knew it was only a matter of time before her cousin André forced his will on her. She must escape to England!

But taking shelter from the snowstorm brought her face to face with Captain Tristan Beaumaris, one of Napoleon's Chasseurs, wounded and feverish, but intent on reaching his men. Now that they were forced to travel together, their attraction grew—but what hope was there, when they were on opposing sides?

Available in November

An irresistible offer for you

Here at Reader Service we would love you to become a regular reader of Masquerade. And to welcome you, we'd like you to have 2 books, a cuddly teddy and a mystery gift - ABSOLUTELY FREE and without obligation.

Then, every 2 months you could look forward to receiving 4 more brand-new Masquerade historical romances for just £2.25 each, delivered to your door, postage and packing free. Plus our free Newsletter featuring special offers, author news, competitions with some great prizes, and lots more!

This invitation comes with no strings attached. You may cancel or suspend your subscription at any time, and still keep your free books and gifts.

It's so easy. Send no money now. Simply fill in the coupon below at once and post it to - Reader Service, FREEPOST, PO Box 236, Croydon, Surrey CR9 9EL.

- - - - - - - - **NO STAMP REQUIRED** - - - - - - - -

Yes! Please rush me 2 FREE Masquerade romances and 2 FREE gifts! Please also reserve me a Reader Service subscription. If I decide to subscribe, I can look forward to receiving 4 brand new Masquerade romances every 2 months for just £9.00, delivered direct to my door, postage and packing free. If I choose not to subscribe I shall write to you within 10 days - I can keep the books and gifts whatever I decide. I may cancel or suspend my subscription at any time. I am over 18 years of age.

EP30M

Mrs/Miss/Ms/Mr _____

Address _____

_____

Postcode _____ Signature _____

mps
MAILING
PREFERENCE
SERVICE